Murder

of a

Silent Man

Phillip Strang

D0557318

BOOKS BY PHILLIP STRANG

DCI Isaac Cook Series
MURDER IS A TRICKY BUSINESS
MURDER HOUSE
MURDER IS ONLY A NUMBER
MURDER IN LITTLE VENICE
MURDER IS THE ONLY OPTION
MURDER IN NOTTING HILL
MURDER IN ROOM 346
MURDER OF A SILENT MAN
MURDER WITHOUT REASON

DI Keith Tremayne Series
DEATH UNHOLY
DEATH AND THE ASSASSIN'S BLADE
DEATH AND THE LUCKY MAN
DEATH AT COOMBE FARM
DEATH BY A DEAD MAN'S HAND

Steve Case Series
HOSTAGE OF ISLAM
THE HABERMAN VIRUS
PRELUDE TO WAR

Standalone Books
MALIKA'S REVENGE

Copyright Page

Dedication

For Elli and Tais who both had the perseverance to make me sit down and write.

Chapter 1

No one gave much credence to the man when he was alive. In fact, most people never knew who he was, although those who had lived in the area for many years recognised the tired-looking and shabbily dressed man as he shuffled along, regular as clockwork on a Thursday at seven in the evening, to the local off-licence. It was always the same: a bottle of whisky, premium brand, and a packet of cigarettes. He paid his money over the counter, took hold of the plastic bag containing his purchases, and then walked back down the road with the same rhythmic shuffle. He said not one word to anyone on the street or in the shop.

Apart from the three-storey mansion where he lived, one of the best residences on one of the best streets in London, with its windows permanently shuttered, no one would have regarded him as anything other than homeless and destitute. Just a harmless eccentric, until the morning when he was found dead in his front garden.

'Never spoken to him, and that's the honest truth,' Jim Porter said. He was a lean man with a pronounced chin, and a strong Cockney accent. 'I've been delivering letters down this street for the last twelve years. Seeing him lying there was the first time I'd ever seen him. Down at the sorting office we called him Ebenezer, no chance of a tip at Christmas, not so much as a thank you. No doubt we shouldn't have, but he's lived in that place for over thirty years, and not one word to my predecessor or me. Weird, if you ask me.'

Detective Chief Inspector Isaac Cook looked at the postman. 'You found the body?' he said. Tall, the son of Jamaican immigrants, and the first in his family to go to university, the first to join the police force, Isaac Cook was an impressive man, as well as a good police officer. Others had told him so, but he was not a man susceptible to flattery, even if he had to admit there was a modicum of truth.

'More by chance. I could see the letterbox was full, the letters no longer going through the slot, and I couldn't take them back with me,' Porter said.

'What do you do when that happens?'

'I can't remember it happening before. Mind you, not many people get letters these days, only bills. I knew about the man inside, so I thought I'd look around, see if I could find a stick or something to push the letters through. Otherwise, he could have been lying there for God knows how long.'

'The lawns are mowed regularly,' Larry Hill, Isaac's detective inspector, said.

'You're right, but it's winter. Once a month would be sufficient. Strange, isn't it?'

'What do you mean?'

'The neglected house, the garden neat and tidy.'

'Is it neglected?'

'I'd say so. I was here once, and I looked through a crack in one of the shutters. There was a single light in the ceiling and some old furniture, decay everywhere. It gave me a cold shiver, almost like one of those horror movies that you see on the television.'

Isaac Cook was not sure about the man. He looked over at the letterbox, noticed that the slot was clear. If the man had found a body, why would he have cleared the letterbox? Isaac decided to say nothing. Once back at Challis Street Police Station, he'd ask Bridget Halloran to check out Jim Porter, the postman, as well as the mansion's owner, Gilbert Lawrence.

***

'Never a word, not Mr Lawrence,' Molly Dempster said. She was a small woman with a slight stoop.

Isaac Cook and Larry Hill were standing in the hallway of her house. The only information they had about the dead man had been a note to Molly, and an invoice in her name with her address as well.

'That's how Mr Lawrence liked it. I'd come in twice a week, iron and press, not that there was much to do. I'd tidy around the few rooms at the back, make him food for the next few days and put it in the fridge.'

'He never spoke?' Isaac asked.

'The last time I heard him speak was over twenty years ago, and then it was only for a couple of minutes.'

'What did he want?'

'A toothache. The man was in agony, and he wanted me to find him a dentist.'

'And you did?'

'I did. But he was generous, at least to me. And you can't understand how good it was to have an employer who never complained, always paid on time.'

'It's still unusual,' Larry Hill said.

'You must have formed an opinion of the man,' Isaac said.

'I've been cleaning for Mr Lawrence for over fifty years. Back when I started, his wife was still here, a lovely woman, although she plastered on the make-up, but always beautifully dressed. Quite the picture she was.'

'She's dead?'

'There were some, gossip mongers, who said he killed her, buried her in the garden, but I don't believe that. I'd seen them together, always loving, never a cross word.'

'Was there an inquiry?'

'One day she disappeared, all her clothes left in the house. Mr Lawrence, he was frantic, and the police dredged the river, organised search parties, put up posters, but nothing.'

'Did they eventually find her?'

'Never. She was a delicate woman, subject to going a little crazy sometimes, but don't we all. Well, not as crazy as her. Two weeks confined to her room, and then she'd be fine. In time, Mr Lawrence came to accept that she had come to some harm due to her craziness, and that was that. And such beautiful children, two of them, although I've not seen them in a long time.'

'We'll check the records,' Isaac said. 'It's before our time.'

'What about the bolted door in the house?' Larry said.

'You've seen how he lives?' Molly Dempster said.

'We've seen it.'

'After Mr Lawrence's wife vanished, he started to become morose. Can't blame him, but before that he had been sociable, and always generous at Christmas. I had a room out the back of the house, above the garage.'

'You were permanent?'

'They needed someone full time.'

'After his wife disappeared?' Isaac said.

'He changed. As though he could never get over it, that close they were. I started to see him less and less, and when I was in one room, he would be in another.'

'Did he go out?'

'Rarely. And then one day…'

'What happened?'

'It was five, maybe six months after Mrs Lawrence had gone. There were men in the house, builders.'

'Doing what?'

'They were installing the bolted door and converting the dining room into a bedroom. There was already a toilet and a small bathroom off to one side of the kitchen. The men were there for five days, and then they left. That was the last time I went past the bolted door.'

'But you still work there.'

'There was a letter on the kitchen sink when I arrived one day. I opened it.'

'What did it say?'

'It was from Mr Lawrence. He thanked me for all that I had done for the family, but he no longer needed a full-time housekeeper, although he needed someone twice a week to clean and tidy up, and to prepare meals for him.'

'Your reaction?'

'Stunned. But what could I say? The man had always been generous to me, and his family were my

5

family. He gave me the address of his solicitor and a time to visit him.'

'You went?'

'Mr Dundas, a stern man, I never liked him. Well, he was polite, asked me to sit down, and made sure I had a cup of tea. Earl Grey, not my favourite.'

It was clear to Isaac and Larry that the woman was glad of the company and wanted to talk. They had a body waiting to be transported to Pathology and a crime scene team at Lawrence's mansion. They wanted to be elsewhere.

'What did Mr Dundas have to say?'

'He was acting under the instructions of Mr Lawrence. I was to be given a house to live in for perpetuity. It was to be furnished to my satisfaction, and I would not be required to pay for anything. Also, I would continue to receive my salary.'

'You accepted?'

'What else could I do? It was all a little strange, but Mr Dundas explained that Mr Lawrence wanted a life of solitude and that he wished to retire from the world. From that day on, I've never paid anything for my house, my salary has been paid weekly, and I've only ever communicated with Mr Lawrence by messages on the kitchen sink.'

'He used to go to the off-licence. You could have seen him there.'

'I never attempted to talk to him, and if I saw him outside the house, I walked the other way.'

'Did anyone visit him?'

'Mr Dundas would come, but it was sporadic. He was in the house three weeks ago.'

***

Back at Gilbert Lawrence's house, the crime scene investigators were still busy. Isaac and Larry arrived back to see the body of the dead man being removed.

'Not much to tell you,' Gordon Windsor, the crime scene examiner, said.

Isaac knew that Windsor would tell him as much as the pathologist, but without the detailed report.

'It's murder, but I suppose that's obvious with a knife protruding from his back.'

'Fatal?' Larry said.

'Not immediately, but the dead man was in his eighties, not in great health. The cold ground would have finished him off.'

'He was reclusive. We've just spoken to the housekeeper.'

'We're checking where he lived. Functional, but not very agreeable. Beautiful building,' Windsor said, looking up from where he was stooped over a broken pot in the garden.

Isaac and Larry had to agree. It was unique for the area in that the mansion was detached and it had a substantial garden.

'There's a couple of cars in the garage, although neither has moved for a long time.'

'What type of cars?'

'Expensive. We've opened the door that was bolted inside the house. Be careful of the dust and the cobwebs when you go in.'

'According to the housekeeper, it's been unused for thirty years,' Isaac said.

'All that money, and mad as a hatter,' Windsor said.

'Was he?'

'What else could he have been. How did he make his money, any idea?'

'We're off to see his solicitor, no doubt he had an accountant. We'll find out, but it appears to be property speculation.'

'We found a filing cabinet inside.'

'We'll need to check it out.'

'We'll leave it where it is for now. Apart from that, the main part of the building hasn't been used, although Lawrence had been in there.'

'Proof?'

'Upstairs, you'd better have a look before you leave.'

Chapter 2

There were not many sights that Isaac and Larry could not deal with, but a dead body propped up in bed, as though it was watching the old television in the corner, was definitely one of the most bizarre.

'My God,' Isaac exclaimed as he entered the room.

Grant Meston, Windsor's number 2, stood to one side. 'Mrs Lawrence, we're assuming,' he said.

'How long?'

'If he bolted the door over thirty years ago, then I'd say she's been here that long.'

'But she's just a skeleton,' Larry said.

'That's what happens to the human body. The hair is still there, so are the teeth, but not a lot of skin. There are relatives, I assume.'

'A son and a daughter. We're contacting them now.'

'How do you tell them that their father has been keeping the dead body of their mother in the house?'

'We've dealt with worse.'

Isaac walked around the bed. There appeared to have been no attempt to clean the body or the bed, not even the room. A lone flower in a vase by the side of the bed was the only sign of any attempt at sanctifying the area, and it had been placed there years before.

'It's a first,' Meston said.

'For all of us. That clarifies whether Gilbert Lawrence was mentally unstable or not.'

'He's been in here,' Meston said. 'Probably not in the room for several months. But outside on the landing, we found his footprints.'

'You'll remove her body?'

'Eventually. The body outside is more important. Mrs Lawrence, what's her history?'

'We're still checking. What we know from the housekeeper is that Mrs Lawrence just upped and vanished one day. Apparently, she had issues. After that, the husband slowly retreated from the world.'

'Makes you wonder, doesn't it?' Meston said.

'Wonder about what?'

'Whether all this money's worth having. Did you see the cars?'

'No. Windsor said they were special.'

'Two vintage Rolls Royces.'

'They're not really important, are they?'

'No. The two bodies are.'

'Then I suggest you concentrate on them,' Isaac said.

'Point taken, DCI.'

'The rest of the house?'

'There has been movement throughout the house, but not much.'

'Gilbert Lawrence?'

'It appears to be only the one person. Any suspects for his death?'

'Not yet.'

***

'My father and mother were very close. Sometimes my brother and I felt left out, not that we were ever badly treated, on the contrary,' Caroline Dickson, née Lawrence, said. Isaac could see that compared to her father's mansion where she lived was smaller, but it was immaculate. The interior walls of the house in Chelsea were lined with paintings, and most of the furniture looked antique.

'It would be better if you took a seat,' Larry said.

A confident and strong-willed woman, Caroline Dickson remained standing. 'I've already been told about my father,' she said.

'Who told you?'

'Molly phoned, the first time in many years.'

'How long since you've seen him?'

'We saw him for a few weeks after our mother disappeared, but then he would walk away from us and lock himself in another room. After that, we haven't seen him since, my brother and I.'

'Not even when he was walking to the off-licence?'

'Once or twice, but it was difficult. I never spoke to him, and I don't think Ralph, my brother, did.'

'Why?'

'Our father was such a dynamic man. You know what he achieved?'

'Property speculation?'

'Speculation is when you played the game, took a chance. With our father, there was no risk-taking. He bought property, fixed it up, and rarely sold it. He was not a man to show off, though.'

'Apart from the mansion and the cars in the garage.'

'He didn't hide his wealth, although he preferred not to talk about it. He had grown up poor, a slum somewhere up north. The mansion was for him and for us. The cars were a childhood passion, not that he ever used them, but they were always polished and ready to go. After so long, no doubt they're not looking so good.'

'We still need you to sit down,' Larry said.

'My father's been murdered. What else is there?'

'Who would want to kill your father?'

'No one that I would know of. Ralph and I will probably inherit, not that it means much to me.'

'Why?'

'Desmond, my husband, is a fine arts dealer, very successful. We have enough money, although I wouldn't mind one of the cars.'

'Why?'

'Desmond's got a thing about vintage cars.'

'Your brother?'

'Ralph's not had it so good. A few failed marriages, a son off the rails, and a couple of businesses that went belly-up.'

'Anything else about him?'

'You'd better ask him. We talk once or twice a year, but Desmond can't stand him. Ralph, unfortunately, is his own worst enemy.'

'Could he have killed your father?'

'He could do with the money, but not Ralph.'

'Sisterly love?'

'The last time we spoke, Ralph was in Spain.'

'He could have flown here.'

'He's in jail.'

'What have you done about it?'

'Nothing. It's not the first time, won't be the last. And each time, he promises to pay us back, but he never does.'

Isaac looked around the room where the three of them were. He could see the affluence, although an art dealer could have the antiques and the paintings on loan.

An appearance of wealth did not mean that there was wealth.

It was clear that Caroline Dickson was not going to sit down. Instead, Isaac sat down. 'We've found your mother,' he said.

That was enough to make the woman sit and place her hand across her mouth. 'Where?'

'When was the last time you went inside your father's house?'

'Over thirty years.'

'Your mother is upstairs in the main bedroom. She's been there, we believe, for all that time.'

'We thought she had disappeared, had an accident.'

'Your mother is propped up in her bed.'

'Dead? I suppose that's a silly question.'

'It's not, but yes, she's dead.'

'How?'

'We don't know yet. Pathology will probably give us the answers.'

'Did our father…?'

'Kill your mother? We don't know either. Tell us about the day she disappeared.'

'I want to see her first.'

'It's a crime scene, and your mother has lain in that bed for a very long time.'

'I still have a right to see her.'

'It's highly irregular,' Isaac said.

'Check my records. I'm a qualified doctor. Death holds no fear for me.'

'She's your mother.'

'Will you deny me?'

Isaac called Gordon Windsor at the mansion. 'We've removed her father. If, as you say, she's a doctor, then under the circumstances, we can make an exception,' Windsor said. 'She could have killed her father, you know that.'

'I do.'

At the conclusion of the call, Isaac turned to Caroline Dickson. 'If you're sure?'

'I am.'

***

Nobody said a word on the drive back to Gilbert and Dorothy Lawrence's house. Isaac was in the driver's seat, Larry beside him. In the back of the car, Caroline Dickson with her husband, Desmond. He was holding her hand. Caroline looked impassively forward, her eyes closed. Both of the police officers were unsure about the wisdom of allowing the woman to see the skeletal remains of her mother.

Outside the neglected mansion, Caroline looked up at its foreboding frontage. 'I've not been here for a long time,' she said.

'It's not necessary to do this,' her husband said.

'It is. She's my mother. I always hoped that one day she would walk in the door.'

'You always knew she was dead.'

'Is that true?' Isaac said. He was standing to one side of the woman. In his hands he had coveralls for her to put on, as well as nitrile gloves, overshoes, and a mask.

'What else could I think? She disappears, our father is beside himself, and I'm out there looking for her.'

'Were you still living here then?'

'I was married to Desmond.'

'The house is big enough for you both to have lived here.'

'We weren't, neither was Ralph. I used to come over several times a week, although Ralph never did.'

'Why?'

'My father had little time for him. Ralph had already been married and divorced by then, and he was always after money.'

'Did your father help him?'

'You never knew our father, or you'd not ask that question.'

'What do you mean?'

'We had the best education, and all that was needed to succeed in life. After that, we were on our own. Our father did not believe in children sponging off the parents, no matter how much money they had. He was all into character building, finding your own way in the world.'

'And you?'

'I went to university, studied medicine. I met Desmond while I was studying and we were married. I still practise, three days a week. You can check. You'll find what I've told you to be true.'

'If he believed in his children finding their way, then why will you and your brother inherit?'

'Our mother believed that we should, but our father was circumspect. But he was a great believer in the family, and there's nowhere else he could leave it to. Don't get me wrong. He was a firm but fair father, and I loved him.'

'Your mother?'

'Not as much as my father, but now...'

'We've no proof of death. The room is almost as if it's a shrine to her.'

15

'Mrs Dickson and one other,' Grant Meston said as he came around the corner.

'I'll go,' Isaac said.

'Very well. Mrs Dickson, you cannot touch the body, is that clear?'

'I've seen dead bodies before.'

'Not like this.'

'Are you sure it's her?'

'Not totally, but the body is in your parents' room. She's dressed in one of her nightdresses.'

Larry stood back, as did Desmond Dickson. 'I could do with a cigarette. This place gives me the creeps,' Dickson said.

'I'll join you. Have you been here before?'

'Once. Gilbert was pleasant. I remember that well enough.'

'His wife?'

'Dorothy, Caroline's mother, was exceedingly gracious. An attractive woman, beautifully dressed. Caroline's not so keen on dressing up to the nines, but her mother was.'

'Ralph Lawrence?'

'Gilbert had no time for him, neither did I. We've not seen him for a few years, and last time, he wasn't looking so good.'

'What do you mean?'

'He'd put on weight, and, as usual, he was only one step ahead of the debt collectors. No money, but it didn't stop him driving a late-model Mercedes, a woman on his arm.'

'What sort of woman?'

'The sort who are impressed by money. Attractive in a tarty way, no doubt a lot of fun.'

Before entering the house, Caroline Dickson was required to sign some forms. After that, a lecture on the procedure to be followed at a crime scene. She nodded her head, said yes and no as appropriate.

The three entered through the back door of the house and moved through the kitchen. 'I'm not so sure now,' Caroline said.

'It's not too late,' Isaac said.

'I want to see her, whatever happens.'

One of the CSEs was standing to one side of the main entrance. An elaborate and vast staircase was on the other side. 'We used to slide down the bannister when we were young.'

'Dangerous?'

'Ralph fell off once and broke his leg. After that, we weren't allowed. Ralph was mischievous. No doubt why we got on so well.'

'Was your father a humorous man?'

'Not father. He thrived on his work ethic. We rarely saw him relax, and he wasn't the sort of parent who'd come and read us a bedtime story.'

'Your mother?'

'She would.'

'Are you sure about this, Mrs Dickson?' Meston said. 'Most relatives have a bad enough time when we conduct a formal identification, but there we've had a chance to make it more congenial.'

'Don't worry, I'll be fine,' Caroline said.

'Is it familiar?'

'Apart from the decay.'

Upstairs, another of the CSEs had strung crime scene tape across the entrance to the door of the main bedroom.

'Anything?' Meston asked the young woman.

'No sign of cause of death.'

Caroline Dickson stood transfixed as she looked into the room. She remembered it when it had been bright and smelt of her mother's perfume. Now it was dark and musty after decades of neglect. 'What about the putrefaction, the pungent smell, the rotting carpet, the sign of insect infestation?' she said.

Isaac looked; the woman was right.

'Your mother was only put there after the process had completed,' Meston said.

'Then where was she?'

'We're checking the cellar now.'

'I want to see.'

'It may help your investigation,' Isaac said to Meston.

'As part of my time at university, I spent a month with a pathologist,' Caroline said. 'There was one murder, an old man who had been shot. I was friendly with the crime scene team. They allowed me to go along.'

'A family member is not the same as an old man you never knew.'

'I know, and I'm sick to my stomach. What went on here? What had my father done? And what about my mother? It's as if my whole belief system has been destroyed.'

'It's not confirmed as murder yet.'

'My father is, though. Why kill him?'

'Because of your mother?'

'But who knew? We never did.'

***

'My father's wine cellar. Also, the boiler for the hot water used to be down here,' Caroline said.

A wooden staircase led down – it creaked. At the bottom, the crime scene team had set up a floodlight, which gave an eerie glow throughout the cavernous area. On either side, a row of wine racks. 'Some of the wines are worth a lot of money,' Caroline said. 'My brother and I used to sneak down here and help ourselves to a bottle occasionally.'

'Your father?'

'He knew, but he never said anything, as long as we didn't take the vintage wines.'

From one end of the basement, 'Over here,' one of the CSIs said.

The three visitors walked over to where the man was standing. 'What is it?' Meston said.

'The soil's been disturbed here. A long time ago, but we believe this is where the body was.'

'That doesn't make sense,' Caroline said. 'We searched the house for days afterwards.'

'Did you?' Isaac said.

'We weren't professionals.'

'It depends what happened. It's possible your mother died elsewhere. Would you suspect your father of killing your mother?'

'No. They were devoted.'

'We'll follow through,' Meston said. 'It's a cold case at the present time. Your father is more immediate.'

'It will be nice to give our mother a proper burial. I can never believe that my father acted other than honourably towards my mother.'

'It's best that way,' Isaac said. If, as appeared to be the case, Gilbert Lawrence had been the only person in the closed-off part of the house since the door was bolted, it did not bode well for the man.

Chapter 3

Emma Lawrence arrived at Challis Street Police Station two days after her brother, Gilbert, had died. It was early morning, and it was raining heavily. 'I demand to see someone,' she said.

'Miss Lawrence, finally,' Isaac said as he met her at reception.

'Why wasn't I informed?'

'We had no idea where you were.'

'I am in the phone book. And besides, you're the police. You should have been able to find me.'

'We had three addresses for you from Caroline Dickson, plus a couple of phone numbers. We checked them all.'

Isaac knew the woman to be seventy-nine, and not close to her brother. She had also remained elusive for some years, not that anyone had gone looking for her. She was colourfully dressed, not like her brother who had adopted drab and dreary as his fashion statement. Lawrence's body was with Pathology, and so far, there was nothing more than the usual. A knife wound in the back, heart failure coupled with blood loss, exposure to the cold weather.

Emma Lawrence, an articulate woman, even if her repetitions about why she hadn't been contacted were annoying, was someone that Homicide had wanted to meet. She was of the same generation as Gilbert and Dorothy Lawrence, and her knowledge of the pair could well be more useful.

Wendy Gladstone, Isaac Cook's sergeant, and in her fifties, could sympathise with the old woman who walked with the aid of a stick, the effects of arthritis. Wendy instinctively liked a woman who still maintained a resilience about her, a woman who did not allow age or infirmity to impede her any more than necessary. It was Wendy who put her close to a heater and gave her a hot mug of tea.

Once Emma Lawrence was settled, Isaac and Wendy questioned her about her brother and his wife.

'I'm sad that he's dead, even though we have not seen each other for many years,' Miss Lawrence said.

'Is there any reason why not?' Isaac asked.

'As children, Gilbert was always intense, always wanting more, not wanting to share.'

'And you?'

'I was easier going, more like my mother. That's why I embraced the hippy movement, an original flower child, even if I was older than most.'

'Free love,' Wendy said.

'Plenty of that back then. Alas, nowadays nothing is free, and as for love, that's a faded memory.'

'You're still active for your age.'

'That's as maybe, but life has a finality. Soon, I'll be reunited with Gilbert and his wife. Then we can get back to what we did best.'

'And what's that?'

'Arguing.'

'Is that why you hadn't seen him for so long?'

'A stupid dispute over our father's inheritance.'

'Did your father have money?'

'Not as much as Gilbert, but we were wealthy. Our father owned an engineering firm, and we lived well.

When he died, the money was to be divided between the two of us.'

'And there was a dispute?'

'Isn't there always?'

'Not always, but money often causes conflict.'

'Our father divided his assets between Gilbert and me, fifty-fifty. Our mother had passed away by then. Gilbert reneged on the agreement, only paid me a quarter.'

'Any reason why?'

'I was irresponsible. He was right, of course. I was always falling in love, always falling out. I had racked up an appreciable debt by then, and Gilbert had always bailed me out.'

'Why not your father?'

'We weren't talking when he died. I was close to Gilbert, even if we quarrelled, and he'd complain, but he always helped.'

'I take it that it changed,' Isaac said.

'He changed when he took control of our father's money. Up until then, Gilbert had been buying properties, renovating them and then selling. He was doing well, but once he had the cash injection from our father, he became a different man. Always arguing the cost of everything, checking that nothing was wasted. No throwing out a pot of jam or honey unless it was licked clean.'

'Licked?'

'You know what I mean. The man became a skinflint.'

'Dorothy, your sister-in-law?'

'It was remarkable. Gilbert met her two years after our father died. She was working in an estate agent's office. For whatever reason, my father fell for her, she for him. They were married within months, and then Ralph and Caroline came along.'

'Did you go to the wedding?'

'I did, not that I could forgive Gilbert.'

'Did you need money from him?'

'Not any more. At that time, I had embraced minimalism, and I was living in a commune. Gilbert didn't approve, and he knew even if he helped, that I'd give it to them.'

'Was he right?'

'Yes. It was silly really, and now I live on my own in a modest flat. Don't get me wrong, I'm not complaining. I have all I need, and I don't need any of Gilbert's money.'

'No reason to wish him dead?'

'What for?'

'Tell us about Dorothy,' Wendy said.

'They worshipped each other and the children. With them, Gilbert was generous and made sure they had everything they wanted. You've seen the house, met Caroline.'

'How do you know we've met her?'

'I read about Gilbert in the newspaper. I phoned her.'

'You've had no contact with your brother for nearly thirty years, yet you knew how to contact Caroline.'

'Why not? And besides, I always met with Dorothy once a year on my birthday. It was our little secret. She was devoted to Gilbert, but she never told him about us.'

'Why was that?'

'I'm not sure. The reasons that separated Gilbert and me were never spoken about. I suppose we just drifted apart. Caroline contacted me a few years ago, and we'd meet occasionally. A lovely woman, similar to Dorothy, although Ralph hasn't turned out too well.'

'How much do you know about your brother's death?'

'I know about Dorothy upstairs in the house. Did Gilbert kill her?'

'Why? Should he have?'

'I'm not talking murder, but Dorothy, she would have these periods where she'd go a little crazy.'

'What can you tell us?'

'Manic-depressive. Not that it happened often, and very few knew outside of the house. Gilbert gave her the best medical treatment that money could buy, and after a few weeks, she'd be fine again. I know she never left the house during those times. That's why there were shutters on every window, to keep her isolated from the influences outside, to keep people from peering.'

'A virtual prisoner?' Wendy said.

'In her own home? I don't think so. If she had been in a hospital, it would have been a straitjacket and isolation.'

'She could be violent?'

'Very. Whenever it happened, Ralph and Caroline would go and stay with friends. They may have known, but probably not the full story.'

'But you did?'

'Dorothy told me everything. The darkness she felt, the despair, the need to lash out or to sit and cry for hours. We became very close.'

'Yet you never spoke to your brother.'

'Never. I don't know if he knew that Dorothy was meeting me, although he may have. Regardless, he never interfered. She could have flung herself down the stairs, broken her neck.'

'Do you know this is what happened?'

'I don't know what killed her. The only certainty is that my brother is not responsible.'

'Let us go back to when Dorothy disappeared,' Wendy said. 'What do you remember?'

'I remember trying to contact Gilbert, but he wouldn't talk to me. I spoke to the housekeeper.'

'Molly Dempster?'

'That was it. She said that Gilbert did not want to have any contact with me.'

'Were you surprised by his reaction?'

'Not really. Gilbert was always a private man, and if Dorothy had disappeared, then he would deal with it himself.'

'She could have been kidnapped, murdered.'

'Molly said she hadn't and my brother was convinced she had had one of her turns and would not be coming back.'

'How could he be so sure?'

'It's too late to ask him now.'

'Are you sad that he's died?'

'I would like to have become friends with him again. To have sat down and reminisced. We had a shared history, a devotion to Dorothy.'

'Are you surprised that he kept her upstairs in the bedroom?'

'He would not have wanted to be parted from her. He was a decent man, even though he had treated me poorly over the years. I had seen him walking out in the street once or twice, but he seemed a broken man. I suppose having his dead wife upstairs in that house for all those years must have driven him crazy.'

'He never spoke one word to anyone, apart from his solicitor.'

'Leonard Dundas. He'll know more than me.'

***

Detective Chief Superintendent Richard Goddard, never far from Homicide when there was a murder, sat in Isaac's office. 'Tough one, the corpse upstairs,' he said. He was a good man, even a friend, but he always seemed to come when Isaac was rushing out of the door.

'We're going back to the house,' Isaac said, more by way of a hint than anything else. Although he had to admit that having Goddard back in charge was preferable to when Superintendent Caddick had been in Goddard's office, and causing trouble with his incessant demand for reports, and his constant incompetent interfering. The man was now consigned out of London, far enough to no longer be a nuisance.

'Macabre.'

'It's out of the ordinary, although Gilbert Lawrence is our priority.'

'It could be related.'

'Only if someone else knew what was upstairs, and if the husband had killed her.'

'Speculation, but it's worth considering. Any suspects?'

Isaac had expected the inevitable question. The chief superintendent was always looking for a quick arrest, but so far there were no clues that led to a killer of Gilbert, no indication that anyone else had been involved with preserving the body of a long-dead woman.

Once free of the superintendent, Isaac and Larry Hill drove over to the Lawrence house. On arrival they walked over to where Gordon Windsor was standing.

This time, the man was on the footpath outside the home, coveralls were not required.

'We're convinced that Gilbert Lawrence buried his wife in the cellar for a few years. Once she had decomposed, he cleaned the bones and any loose skin with dermestid beetles,' Windsor said.

'What are they?'

'Skin beetles. Taxidermists, museums, hunters, use them to clean the flesh off a body. They'll only eat dead flesh. It takes time, and he would have had to buy them. We found a tank that he had used.'

'By why clean the bones? The woman's dead. Surely he'd want to see some semblance of her?'

'How would I know? The man's disturbed. He can't bear to be parted from her, but if she was left to decay on her own, can you imagine the insects, the putrefaction, the smell?'

'Okay, we'll accept that the man had lost it, mentally that is, but what does this tell us about how the woman died?'

'It doesn't, not yet. We're taking what remains to Pathology today. Give them a few days, more than the two hours you normally do, and maybe they'll come up with something.'

Isaac knew Windsor was right. As the senior investigating officer, an arrest and a conviction always looked good on his CV. The only problem was that the last three murder cases his department had investigated had extended, not only in time but also in the number of deaths. The current investigation had all the hallmarks of being another one. And what did they have: a body, no more than a skeleton, a body in the garden with a knife in its back, a family at war, although it was more of an uneasy truce. Isaac hoped he was wrong in his summation, but he was sure he was not.

Wendy had liked Emma Lawrence, an elderly woman with a healthy outlook on life, a woman who had embraced the flower generation, free love, and no doubt transcendental meditation and a few drugs not on prescription. Regardless, she still looked sprightly, more so than Wendy, and she knew it.

Caddick, when he had temporarily occupied Goddard's seat, had been desperate to get Wendy out of Homicide by way of a rigorous medical, showing that she could no longer keep up with the workload. Wendy knew it was rubbish, using whatever he could to get rid of her.

She didn't need to be able to run a hundred yards in under twenty seconds, and she didn't need to be able to scale a wall in one bound. But Caddick had been desperate to undermine Isaac's support mechanism of loyal staff: Bridget Halloran, the lead admin person in Homicide, Wendy Gladstone, who had known Isaac longer than anyone, even from when he had been on the beat in uniform, and then there was Detective Inspector Larry Hill. He had handled himself well on an earlier murder investigation, and Chief Superintendent Goddard had brought him across to Challis Street at Isaac's request.

'There would still have been some smell during the process,' Larry said to Windsor outside Lawrence's house.

'Contained, at least within the house,' Windsor said. 'No idea how the housekeeper could have avoided catching a whiff occasionally. Lawrence had done it well, almost professional. Burying the body in the cellar. In time, the body could be removed, and placed in with the beetles. It's all a bit weird for me, but who knows how the man thought. Apparently, he was into real estate,' Windsor said.

'A lot of it, from what we're told. Bridget's doing the research, and we're on our way to meet with the solicitor. No idea about him, but it appears that he was the only one who spoke to Gilbert Lawrence.'

Chapter 4

Leonard Dundas occupied a suite of offices in Pimlico. Isaac had to admit that he was impressed. But then, it was Pimlico, he thought, and definitely upmarket and costly.

'Can I help you?' a young woman asked. She was sitting behind a glass-topped reception desk. It looked expensive. In fact, the whole office did, what with its leather chairs in reception, the open plan office, a man watering the plants around the place.

'Mr Dundas, he's expecting us. DCI Cook, DI Hill, Challis Street Homicide,' Isaac said.

'It's a shame about Mr Lawrence,' the woman said.

'You knew him?'

'As good as. He was our only client.'

'You must have thirty people here.'

'Thirty-four. One's off sick, and another two are out on business. I'll let Mr Dundas know you're here.'

Isaac and Larry made themselves comfortable, but not for long. An elderly man came into reception. He was wearing a suit, his greying hair parted in the middle, a sullen expression.

'Tragic about Gilbert,' he said.

'Mr Dundas?' Isaac said.

'Yes, of course. My apologies. Mr Lawrence's death has thrown us all out of kilter.'

'We're told he was your only client.'

'He was, but that's not surprising. You're aware of his substantial holdings?'

'Not in detail. We're researching them now.'

'Not all of them are in this country. He was a canny man, purchased when the market was low, never sold, or rarely. There's more money in having the properties rented out than buying and selling. The costs only multiply, stamp duty, taxes. I'm sure you know how it is.'

Isaac didn't, as he still had his flat in Willesden, and he had no intention of moving. Larry did, as his wife was determined to buy somewhere larger. The only problem was that she could only envisage the furniture that she would need to buy, the colour of the curtains, the marble-topped counters in the kitchen. She did not consider what Dundas had just mentioned: the hidden costs, the removal company, the increased payment on the mortgage, the solicitor's fees. He knew she would not stop talking about the move, and he knew that without promotion he would struggle with the payments.

'What do you plan to do now?' Isaac asked.

'For me, I'm past my retirement age. I only stayed on with the firm because of Gilbert. My daughter is the junior partner. She looks after the day-to-day operations.'

'What can you tell us about Gilbert Lawrence?'

'Where to start? He was a brilliant man, although after Dorothy died, he changed, so much so that I barely recognised him towards the end.'

'But you met with him. We're assuming he spoke to you.'

'He did, but only in truncated sentences, as he would have a prepared list of actions to follow. I would give him a report, the template we had agreed on many years ago. Our conversations were normally short, no more than a few sentences spoken by either, no mention of the weather, or the family.'

31

'Are you saying he never asked after his family?'

'Never. Howard Hughes syndrome some would call it, although with Gilbert it wasn't a fear of germs, but the loss of his wife.'

'You're aware of what was in the house?'

'I am now. What can I say? I never went into the house, never through that door with its bolt.'

'Where did you meet him?'

'In the kitchen. He made sure that the back door was bolted and the blinds were down. He didn't want Molly Dempster to come in.'

'But he kept her on.'

'She had been with the family for a long time. As far as he was concerned, she was the only person he could trust.'

'And you?'

'He didn't trust me. He needed me, and he knew what I did, and how much I should charge. He also entrusted me with buying property for him.'

'Easy to cheat?'

'You can see the office here. He paid for it, the renovations, everything. The man has made me rich. Why would I have cheated him?'

'And now?'

'I have his will and his power of attorney. In the meantime, his empire needs to be tended, and in time sold off, or passed on to those who inherit.'

'Are you able to tell us the contents of his will?' Larry asked.

'Not at this time. It is sealed in a bank vault, duly witnessed. I will read it out to his family and other interested parties in due course. You have to remember that Gilbert, regardless of how he lived, was not a fool. He had amassed over two hundred and thirty properties around the world: shopping centres, office blocks, residential and commercial. We have in this office the deeds to over two billion pounds worth of real estate. He was a tough negotiator, a tough landlord. Such men make enemies, even within their own family.'

'Ralph and Caroline, his children?'

'Ralph was a disappointment, although he would not be capable of murder.'

'Why not?'

'The man would rather scrounge off others. He's a charismatic man, managed to charm a few women out of their savings. But murder, not Ralph.'

'Caroline?'

'She would be capable, but unlikely. She has a good life, and her husband is doing well.'

'Well enough? There are hundreds of millions of pounds at stake here. Irresistible to a lot of people.'

'Not so easy to get hold of. There are overseas trusts, offshore accounts, umbrella companies. Unravelling those, if we have to, will take a long time. We, as a company, will be fully occupied with Gilbert Lawrence for many years.'

'His death doesn't appear to concern you?'

'It does. The man was a friend, even before his wife died, even after he became a recluse.'

'He had what he wanted, his wife with him.'

'Is it related to his death?'

'We don't know. We had hoped you could enlighten us.'

'Not me,' Dundas said. 'I never went in there. The first I knew, the first any of us knew, was when your people found her. She was an attractive woman when she was alive. I suppose she isn't now?'

'Unrecognisable.'

33

***

'DCI Isaac Cook, what took you so long?' Graham Picket, the pathologist, said. To Isaac, it was a muted welcome, in that the man was usually more vocal when he and Larry walked into Pathology.

'I thought you'd appreciate some more time with Mrs Lawrence.'

'Rubbish. You were busy elsewhere. Otherwise, I would have been chasing you out of here.'

'Maybe. What do you have?'

'Female. No sign of major trauma. From what I can see the woman died of natural causes, although with just a skeleton, it's not possible to be conclusive. No sign of a bullet or a knife or a blunt weapon on the bones.'

'Is that all you can tell us?'

'You've given me nothing to work with. We've confirmed that it's Dorothy Lawrence. Dental records, a DNA swab from the daughter. Apart from that, there's nothing more. The only way you'll know what happened is if the husband wrote it down somewhere.'

The result from Pathology was not unexpected, and the woman's death was not the primary consideration, Gilbert Lawrence was. The two police officers returned to Homicide. It was time for a meeting with the team.

'What about the son?' Isaac asked. It was the first time he had sat down in his office for some time. Wendy Gladstone was in the office, as were Larry Hill and Bridget Halloran.

'Ralph Lawrence has a history of failed businesses, broken marriages, and a troubled son along the way,' Bridget said. Office-bound, and glad of it, she was the person who could find her way around a search engine. Isaac had asked her to put together a profile of Gilbert Lawrence, a dossier on him and his family. 'Ralph Lawrence is in Spain, speculative real estate sales to English tourists. I contacted the local police there, and the man's been released from jail on the understanding that he leaves the country immediately.'

'To where?'

'London. I assumed you would want to talk to him.'

'Is he being picked up?'

'He is. I've organised someone from the station.'

That's what Isaac liked about his team, always thinking ahead, taking the initiative. And yes, Ralph was a person of interest, although if, as it seemed, he was in Spain, he could not be the murderer.

'What else?' Larry said. He was standing, his usual pose. Both Wendy and Bridget were sitting down.

'You and DCI Cook have met with Leonard Dundas. Is he providing you with a list of Lawrence's assets?'

'He is, but we would rather hear it from you. Dundas will be considering what to tell us, and what not to.'

'Very well,' Bridget said. 'This is what we have. Gilbert Lawrence, eighty-two years of age. He purchased his first property when he was nineteen, a small studio flat in Clapham. Nothing special and it was rented out. By the time of his twenty-fifth birthday, he had sixty-three properties throughout London. Some were shops, others were offices, although the majority were residential. From what I can gather, he was cutting a swathe through London, and I've found newspaper articles showing the young property magnate. Their words, not mine. He had met and married his wife when he was twenty-two, purchased the house where he died when he was twenty-nine. Before that, it had been converted into flats. He had it renovated, and Dorothy decorated it. It featured in a couple of magazines at the time. I've included copies of what it looked like back then, although I suppose it looks vastly different now.'

Larry looked at the magazine article. 'It does,' he said.

'Any history on Dorothy Lawrence?' Isaac asked.

'If you're referring to her bouts of madness, there's very little. She was born in the north of the country, went to school there. I've managed to obtain a birth certificate. After her marriage to Gilbert, two children, Caroline and Ralph. You've met one, the other is due in the next few hours. I'm checking with the private hospitals around the country that deal with people who have her condition.'

'Why private?'

'Gilbert Lawrence was a private man. He would not have wanted any more people than necessary to know if his wife was ill.'

'She could always have been signed in under a false name.'

'How many properties did Dundas tell you about?' Bridget said.

'Over two hundred.'

'I've found close to one hundred and fifty through companies that are registered in his name or companies that he controls in the UK. The other properties may be overseas or hidden from view. Also, in the thirty years that he remained reclusive, he has expanded his empire considerably. He may have retreated from the world, but he continued to make money.'

'Which means that whatever the reason he decided to hide in that house with his dead wife, he was still mentally astute.'

'It makes you wonder what makes people tick,' Larry said.

'Or how they can form enemies who want to kill them.'

'That makes no sense. Gilbert Lawrence spoke to no one, offended no one, and he didn't get involved with his son and daughter, and yet he's killed. The man was old and frail. He couldn't have lasted much longer anyway.'

'Long enough if you're to inherit.'

'Ralph?'

'Or Caroline. And what about Ralph's son?' Isaac said. 'Where is he?'

'The last we have on him is an arrest for drug possession six months ago. After that, nothing.'

'Wendy,' Isaac said.

'Leave him to me.'

'What about Gilbert and Dorothy's daughter?'

'Caroline married Desmond Dickson thirty-three years ago.'

'Were Gilbert and Dorothy at the wedding?'

'It's in the files I've given to all of you. Yes, they were. It's also the last record I can find of Dorothy.'

Larry studied the newspaper article. 'The two Rolls Royces in the garage,' he said. 'They were used at the wedding.'

'Caroline and Desmond Dickson have two children,' Isaac said. 'What do we know about them?'

'Both are employed, steady jobs. The daughter is married with a child under one. The son is single. Neither has been in trouble with the law.'

'And Desmond Dickson?'

'A fine arts dealer, well respected. We've nothing against him.'

'Statistically, it's a family member or someone Gilbert knew,' Isaac said.

'Ralph or his son. They're the most likely,' Wendy said.

'The most obvious, although Ralph wasn't in the country, and the grandson is a junkie.'

Chapter 5

Wendy Gladstone, from when she had been a constable in the north of England finding child runaways to tracking down persons of interest in a murder investigation in London, had an enviable reputation. Her skill, she knew, honed over the years, was to adopt the mindset of those she was looking for. A rich person is not about to hide in a derelict property, a drug addict is not likely to check into a five-star hotel.

Ralph's son Michael, Wendy knew, was dossing down somewhere with his addicted friends, sharing needles, and whatever food they could scrounge or steal. And he was not likely to be close to his grandfather's house, the area too upmarket for derelict properties, or squatters.

Of more immediate importance was that Ralph Lawrence had arrived in London on a flight from Barcelona, and he had failed to meet up with the constable sent from Challis Street to pick him up at Heathrow. He, Wendy thought, would be easier to find.

From what they knew, Ralph Lawrence was a man who appreciated the finer things in life, regardless of whether he could afford them, or whether they belonged to someone else. He would either be at a friend's house if he had not outstayed his welcome on previous occasions, or he would have checked in under a false name at a quality hotel, enjoying the minibar and the restaurant, using an invalid credit card if needed. He was a slippery character, everyone in the department knew, although his criminal record had amounted to no more than passing false cheques in his teens. Since then, some investigations into the fraudulent use of credit cards overseas, unpaid hotel bills, and a litany of other misdemeanours, although none had been substantiated.

The upside was that Ralph had no record, except for a miserable credit rating. The downside was that he could not be escorted off the plane at Heathrow. He had left Spain as an undesirable, but in England, he was English, and he was free.

Bridget was assigned the task of checking with the other police stations in London, contacting the homeless agencies and other charities, in the hope of locating Michael Lawrence. As with Ralph, he was a person of interest only. No one in Homicide felt that he was responsible for the death of Gilbert Lawrence. Whoever had killed the old man had been careful to leave no incriminating evidence. Apart from a smudged fingerprint on the knife, the only other evidence at the scene was a crushed plant in the garden where the murderer had placed his boot, and a trace of blood on the gate handle as he exited the property. The blood had been found to be that of Gilbert Lawrence. Another trace of blood had been discovered ten yards south down the street. The traffic camera mounted on the corner of the road had failed to identify the individual, as the area was busy at the approximate time of the man's death, and besides, what were they looking for? Was it a man or a woman, tall, short, fat, thin? Did they have on a coat or not, and what about their age? The reality was that Isaac and his team had very little.

And the woman upstairs had apparently died of natural causes, although that did not obviate her being poisoned, a skeleton unable to reveal that possibility.

'It's the inheritance,' Isaac said. In the office, Larry Hill and Chief Superintendent Goddard, his uniform proudly worn.

'It's for the presentation of a gallantry medal to the constable who was shot when he was protecting a woman from an irate husband,' the chief superintendent said.

Anything to promote himself, Isaac thought. Goddard was looking to take over Counter Terrorism Command when the time was right, although that wasn't likely to happen as long as Alwyn Davies was the commissioner of the London Metropolitan Police, and the man wasn't in a hurry to vacate his post.

Davies, the man who was going to reform the Met, bring it into the twenty-first century, but instead had proven himself to be an adroit political animal, had done little in the way of reformation, more in demoralising. At least that was the opinion of Isaac and Goddard, although there were others who had prospered.

'No chance of an early arrest?' Goddard said.

'Not yet. We've not got a motive for the murder. Sure, the man had money, but not in the house, and no one's gained anything yet. Once the man's last will and testament is read, we'll have a better idea.'

'And when's that?'

'Tomorrow. The family will be gathering at Leonard Dundas's office at ten in the morning. I'll be in Dundas's office, although I'll probably not be at the reading. However, I will be given a copy afterwards.'

'Not all the family will be there,' Goddard said.

'Ralph probably won't be. The father may not have liked him, but he's probably included in the will somewhere.'

41

'No guarantees. It would help if you were in when the will is read.'

'Outside will be fine. I'll see the people as they come out from Dundas's office.'

***

Ralph Lawrence prowled up and down in his hotel room in Kensington. It had cost plenty, more than he could afford, but what did it matter. He would either pay for it with one of the cards he possessed or he wouldn't. He knew that his return to England, not that he had any option, was a necessary risk, and there were some people not far away who wanted money in cash, and he could not pay. And he knew how they dealt with those who crossed them.

'One month from now you will be in here, or we will find you,' they had said. And now he was back in their part of the world, and he still remembered the man with his shattered kneecaps groaning in agony, their idea of a warning.

'Just so you don't forget, take a close look at him,' one of the three had said. Criminal nobility, that was what Ralph Lawrence knew their lead man to be.

If only I hadn't tried to cheat those men in Spain. How was I to know that the British tourists, a sweet and gullible husband and wife team, were part of a sting to trap me? Ralph Lawrence thought in a moment of introspection.

And now he was in England, and the repayment to the man and his thugs could not be avoided. He knew being here was a risk, but his father's death had been providence from heaven. A chance for the miserable old skinflint of a father to pay for all the suffering he had caused him, and as for the others, his son, his sister and her husband, what did they matter. Once the gangsters had been paid off, he was going straight, straight from Heathrow and back out to where it was warm, to purchase himself a good house, a good car, and find himself a willing woman. Ralph Lawrence was not a vain man; he knew that he had the gift of the gab, and this time, he would not need to pretend with the woman. This time he would be rich.

***

Molly Dempster, for the first time in her adult life, found herself without a routine. She did not like it, having been used to her twice-weekly visits to the Lawrence mansion. She did not know why she had been invited to the office of Leonard Dundas on the following day. She knew it had to be important, but she had never asked for anything from her employers and had never once been tempted to take anything from the house: not a bar of soap, nor washing up liquid, nor even some money occasionally. All that she purchased for the home she accounted for in her neat and meticulous handwriting. She felt great sorrow for the man who had died, even sadness for a woman who had died decades before. She could only imagine the anguish that her husband must have gone through. If she had known, she would have made an effort to soothe the man.

Caroline, she knew, was a compassionate woman. She'd ask her tomorrow at Dundas's for three months to move out of the house that Gilbert Lawrence had let her live in. She had saved some money and could afford to pay the rent for a while. After that, she could live with her sister, though she didn't want to. Molly knew that as much as she loved her sister, the woman could drive her mad

43

with her untidiness, her need to smoke in the house. Gilbert's death had signalled to Molly the closing of her life, and all she could do was resign herself to the inevitable. She sat down again on the kitchen chair and shed a tear, not only for Gilbert and Dorothy but for herself.

Chapter 6

An auspicious occasion, the reading of the last will and testament of Gilbert Aloysius Lawrence: recluse, property magnate.

Isaac knew that the accolade of philanthropist would not be used in any obituary, not even at the man's funeral, as he had never given much to anyone outside of his family, and only to charity when it came with a sizeable reduction in tax.

Bridget, in the office, had checked back for any press cuttings in the last thirty years and had found very little. The name of Lawrence had appeared in the financial sections of the newspapers from time to time, but apart from that, there was not much of interest.

Ralph Lawrence had more column inches devoted to him, due to his behaviour in his teens, starting with drunken and loutish and culminating in appearing in court on a charge of passing fake cheques.

As Bridget had said to Isaac, the man's a habitual conman, no perceivable morals, good or bad, a rotten egg as her father would have said. All that could be found about Caroline Dickson, née Lawrence, were the details of her wedding, as well as a photo.

Isaac sat in the reception area of Leonard Dundas's office; he was early. The young woman at reception had given him a coffee and a magazine to read, although those coming in through the door were of more interest. Jill Dundas, Leonard's daughter, came over and introduced herself. Isaac found her to be polite, but not friendly, purely professional. He judged her to be in her forties. She was wearing a dark blue jacket with matching trousers, a white blouse. If her look was anything to go by, she was a worthy person to take over from her father, Leonard, who had come into the office looking tired, more so than the first time Isaac had met him.

'It's a nightmare,' Leonard Dundas said. 'When Gilbert was alive, he kept his finger on the pulse. But now, his death has left a lot of people anxious.'

'What sort of people?'

'Tenants, lending institutions, overseas banks.'

'Why? Surely everything is secured.'

'Secured, yes, but people are people, they panic. And besides, what's to worry about? Gilbert was solvent, and no lease agreements have been impacted.'

'Was Lawrence still buying?'

'He never stopped.'

'New instructions?'

'It depends who inherits.'

'Ralph gave us the slip at Heathrow. We're trying to find him and his son,' Isaac said.

Caroline Dickson entered the office, nodded at Isaac. Her husband accompanied her, as did Emma, Gilbert's sister. Molly Dempster came in looking a little unsure of the surroundings. The receptionist gave her a cup of tea, and showed her where to go, and ensured she was seated comfortably. Isaac could see through the open door that Caroline gave the housekeeper a brief hug.

The door to where Dundas was to read the will closed soon after. Isaac strained to listen but could hear nothing. A man walked into the solicitor's office. He was puffing, and he looked as though he had had a rough night. Isaac knew that he was face-to-face with Ralph Lawrence.

'Where's the meeting?' Ralph said to the receptionist.

'Your name?'

'Ralph Lawrence. Sorry for being late, traffic.'

'I'm Detective Chief Inspector Cook,' Isaac said, standing up to introduce himself. 'We missed you at Heathrow.'

'You didn't miss me. I missed you. Subtle difference.'

'There are some questions we have for you.'

'After we've dealt with finding out who my father has given his money to. He was a difficult man, we never got on, although I suppose you know that. And my mother upstairs in the house. I thought he was smarter than that. Did he kill her?'

'Not that we can prove. Is there any reason he would have?'

'None that I can think off. I liked him when we were young, but then he became remote, thought that throwing money at our education, paying for overseas trips, was the solution.'

'Challis Street Police Station after the reading, okay?'

'As long as he hasn't given it all to the Battersea Dogs Home, that'll be fine.'

Ralph Lawrence rushed away, entering through the door into the room where the rest of the family, as well as Molly Dempster, sat. Isaac craned his neck to see the reaction of the others but could see little. The one man who had remained elusive, the one man that his family had not wanted to see, and for whom Wendy had been searching, had walked into the solicitor's office.

Isaac took his phone out of his pocket. 'Wendy, Ralph is at Dundas's. Get down here, take a good look at him, and make sure he doesn't give us the slip again.'

***

Leonard Dundas rose to speak. The others in the room held their breath, looked nervously around them, all except Molly who sipped her tea. She would have admitted to being baffled as to why she was there, and what was being said. She had an aunt who had left her a teapot once when she had died, but the handle had fallen off long ago, and all she received from her parents, who had been as poor as church mice, was a demand from the council to pay the electricity or it would be cut off.

And there in that room was Ralph, looking much older than the last time she had seen him, vaguely smelling of aftershave and alcohol.

Such an attractive young man, she remembered, always trying to sneak a girl into the house, never getting past his father, but he had charmed Molly as well as the girls, and if the coast was clear, she had turned the occasional blind eye – not that she approved. She was strict Presbyterian, and they didn't do such things, not before marriage. Not that it stopped a few in the congregation, she knew that.

Caroline sat on the other side of the room. She was clutching her husband's hand, hard.

I, Gilbert Aloysius Lawrence, presently of 47 Atherton Street, Kensington, London, England, hereby revoke all former testamentary dispositions made by me and declare this to be my last will.

Those present listened as the preliminary declarations were made, and the nomination of Leonard Dundas as the man's executor. In the event of his being unable to complete his duties, then Jill Dundas was to take the role of executor. Caroline Dickson and Ralph Lawrence waited for the distribution of the estate. The fact that their father's solicitor had been nominated as the executor concerned Caroline, not so much Ralph, as long as he received his fair share.

To Molly Dempster, a person who has shown great loyalty to the family, I extend my thanks.

The housekeeper looked up when her name was mentioned. Ralph was instantly suspicious that Molly and her father had been involved, but he took a further look, and realised that both of them had been too old, and Molly had always been the eternal spinster, but...

The house that she currently occupies will be signed over to her. The deeds will be made available in her name, and she is to continue to receive her salary until her death. Also, all costs relating to council rates, electricity, gas, and maintenance will be paid out of my estate. A fund will be established to cover this. As well, a one-off payment of one million pounds will be deposited in a savings account for her use.

One house down, over two hundred more properties, Caroline and Ralph thought. Neither of them had any problem with Molly receiving the house and the money. Molly sat stunned, not sure what to make of what had been said. Ralph leaned over and whispered in her ear. 'He's given you the house,' he said.

'Does that mean I don't have to go and live with my sister?'

'You're rich. You don't have to go anywhere. Our father has looked after you well.'

'Oh, good. I am pleased,' Molly said. Leonard Dundas could see that the woman was confused. He would have a word with her before she left.

Dundas continued.

To my son Ralph, a disappointment, in that he has frittered away an excellent education, a stable upbringing, and chosen not to embrace frugality and sound business practices, I bequeath nothing.

'What the …?' Ralph jumped to his feet. 'He can't do this, not to me. I have debts to pay, people with demands.'

'Sit down, Ralph,' Caroline said. 'Hear what Mr Dundas has to say.'

'I can't leave here with nothing, I can't.'

'Mr Lawrence, Ralph, if I could have your forbearance, there is more,' Dundas said. Jill Dundas sat quietly taking in the interactions of the people. It would be her who would have to deal with them afterwards.

However, he is to be offered redemption. If he can hold down suitable employment for one year, with no cheating, no harebrained get-rich schemes, and no seduction of gullible women, then subject to the recommendation of a group of eminent persons that I have assembled, a sum of five million pounds is to be given to him. That money will be transferred to him over a five-year period in monthly instalments.

'Who came up with that?' Ralph said.

'Your father,' Dundas said. 'I believe the term is that you've been snookered.'

'I'll challenge the will.'

'At the end of this reading, it will be necessary for those present to sign that they will not contest the will. If they do not, then all monies to them will be forfeited.'

'And given to who?'

'The money will be held in trust for another generation. Mr Lawrence was an astute man. He had thought this through very carefully, and with my advice.'

'He was mad, mentally incapable. There's no court in the country would believe that he was a sane man, thirty years in that house with our mother, a corpse. What kind of man does that, and did he kill her? We don't know that yet.'

'Be quiet,' Caroline said. Ralph sat down, a scowl on his face. Desmond Dickson looked at the man, remembered him from when they had last met, eleven years ago at least. He hadn't liked the man then, he liked him even less now.

Michael Lawrence, my grandson, through Ralph, has become a person of weak character. A fund sufficient for his rehabilitation has been set up, and he will voluntarily check into a private facility that will treat his addiction. He is an intelligent young man, poorly guided by a father of low repute. If, after one year, Ralph's son, with Ralph's active encouragement, is still clean and contributing to society, then Ralph will receive an additional payment of one million pounds. Michael will also receive one million pounds at that time. If, as I expect, he has not re-entered society, then Ralph will not receive either the five million pounds or the additional one million pounds. I will further add that I do not believe that any of the money bequeathed to Ralph and his son will ever be paid. I cannot, in death, profess to like my son and my grandson any more than I did when I was alive.

Ralph sat quietly. He knew people who would deal with the high-and-mighty Leonard Dundas.

To Caroline, my daughter, a person that I have missed over the years, but could not bear to see, on account of her mother, I bequeath five million pounds. An additional one million pounds are bequeathed to each of her and Desmond Dickson's children. Both of them have taken their place in society, and I can only express my admiration for them. Unfortunately, I have never met either, except when they were very young, but I have received regular reports, as I have on all those present here today.

'What does that mean?' Emma Lawrence asked. So far, she had sat quietly.

'Yearly reports were prepared by a private investigator, a discreet man. Mr Lawrence led the life of a recluse, but he was well aware of what went on. His mind was still alert, his business acumen was sound.'

'He was as mad as a hatter, locked up in that house,' Ralph said. He had been quietly seething, knowing full well that a will was invalid if signed by an incapacitated person. And he knew madness when it was there staring everyone in the face.

'Gilbert Lawrence's will has been updated every year. He was a sane man, and tests were conducted to prove that he was.'

'The man never left the house. How can he be sane?'

'Proof will be supplied if required.'

'Whoever did these so-called sanity checks, did they know that my father had his wife upstairs, a skeleton that he had prepared in the cellar of the house?'

'That knowledge was not available,' Dundas said.

'Then we are wasting our time here. I've better things to do than sit here and listen to the last words of a madman,' Ralph said.

'Under the terms of the last will and testament of Gilbert Lawrence, you will forfeit any claim on his estate if you do not sign your agreement here today.'

'Let me remind you, Dundas. My father was mad, and his will is worthless. I will find someone competent to deal with its legality. I am entitled to half of what he's worth, not a measly five million pounds, and then only if I hold down a job. What do you, what did he expect me to do? Get a job in a shop, work in an office? I'm an entrepreneur, not someone's lackey.' With that, Ralph Lawrence stormed out of the room.

'Mr Lawrence,' Wendy said, as the man tried to exit the building.

'Yes, what do you want?'

'Sergeant Wendy Gladstone. We have a few questions for you.'

'Not now. I'm busy.'

Wendy could see the anger in the man's face. His eyes were bulging, his cheeks were flushed, his hands were shaking. 'Unfortunately, I must insist.'

'Not now. Can't you see that I have other things to do.'

'It's either voluntarily or in handcuffs.'

Lawrence looked at the two uniforms standing by. 'Very well, but I will lodge a formal complaint.'

'That's your prerogative. I'll give you the contact details once we get to Challis Street. Mind your head as you get in the back seat of the police car.'

After a short break, while everyone calmed down after the disruption by Ralph Lawrence, Leonard Dundas continued.

To my sister Emma, I bequeath one million pounds. I cannot say that I approved of some of her decisions in life, but they were hers, and I respect her for that. The money is hers to use, wisely or otherwise, although with age comes wisdom.

Leonard Dundas and his daughter will maintain my property portfolio. To Leonard, one million pounds. To Jill Dundas, one million pounds. Caroline and Desmond Dickson will take responsibility for my property portfolio, in consultation with Leonard Dundas and his daughter, although Caroline will be the only one given voting rights. They will not be able to liquidate more than five per cent of the assets in any two-year period. The children of Caroline will be asked to join the committee in time, and with voting rights. What has been set up will remain with the Lawrence family.

'What about the mansion in Atherton Street?' Caroline asked.

'It will become part of the Lawrence property portfolio. What is inside belongs to you.'

'The cars?'

'They are yours,' Leonard Dundas said.

Chapter 7

Ralph Lawrence slouched in a chair at Challis Street Police Station.

The information received from Spain had shown that with an excellent website and his charm Ralph Lawrence had managed to induce British holidaymakers enamoured of the sun and the local culture to place down payments on a speculative property development venture. It was a scam. The Spanish knew it, as did Homicide at Challis Street, but that was a technicality in as much that he had not broken any laws in England.

Isaac looked at the man, well aware that he had been dealt a body blow at the reading of the will. Leonard Dundas had updated the DCI about the contents of the will, and the reactions of the people present. He explained that even in death, Gilbert Lawrence had no intention to give his fortune to non-deserving causes. And according to the father, the son was not deserving.

'Mr Lawrence,' Isaac said. 'We're investigating the death of your father, Gilbert Lawrence.' Wendy Gladstone sat next to Isaac. Ralph Lawrence sat on the other side of the table. He did not have legal representation.

'That bastard screwed me.'

'I have been updated by Leonard Dundas,' Isaac said. 'The conditions placed on you are harsh. It is understandable that you are angry, although it does not obviate the fact that the man was murdered. That is what concerns us, not your enmity towards him.'

'I didn't dislike the man, only the way he lived, even when we were young.'

'According to your sister, he fulfilled his responsibilities, and neither of you suffered.'

'She's right, but she was always the favourite. He would confide in her, even ask her advice sometimes.'

'Did he take it?'

'Who knows? Probably not. With me, nothing.'

'Your childhood, unsatisfactory as it may have been to you, does not have any bearing on the death of your father, or does it?'

'What does that mean? I was in Spain, you know that, so do the Spanish police.'

'Along with some unfortunate tourists who put down payments on property they'll never own. How much did you make there?'

'We broke no laws. And besides, what do people go on holiday for if it's not to waste money?'

'Mr Lawrence, your reputation precedes you. Whether you conned them does not affect our enquiry. Your father was murdered, and we need to find who was responsible.'

'Why am I here? It can't be me, and I hadn't seen the man for decades.'

'But you know people who are capable of murder. Did you expect to receive half of your father's property portfolio?'

'I did.'

'Had that been promised to you? Had you seen a will to that effect?'

'No, but what else was he going to do with all his money? He couldn't take it with him, although he would have if it were possible.'

'You've been told what was in the will. Your father has placed his trust in Leonard Dundas.'

'My father trusted no one. If Dundas has the assets, he's there now figuring out how to realise on them. I know what the promise of easy money does to people. The holidaymakers in Spain, believing that they are getting a special deal from another Brit. Do you think they considered the poor soul who was losing money? Do you think they worried if someone else and their family were to be reduced to begging on the street?'

'I doubt if they did,' Isaac said.

'That's what makes it so easy. Greed, the most powerful human emotion, and my father has given Leonard Dundas the keys to the vault. That man and his daughter will cream the money, not that anyone will ever know.'

'Smart?'

'Smarter than me. They'll never be caught.'

'According to Mr Dundas, your father was of sound mind, and had been checked each year for his mental stability,' Wendy said.

'How? You tell me. My father never left the house, apart from once a week to walk down to the off-licence. He has our mother upstairs, a skeleton, and everyone says he's sane and the great financial mind.'

'Are you suggesting we check on his mental condition?'

'It's highly suspicious to me. Okay, in that room at Dundas's, I blew it, but I'm right, and everyone knows it, even my sister.'

'She's happy with your father's bequest,' Isaac said.

'And why not? She's got voting rights, and no doubt access to any decisions that Dundas and his daughter make. With all that property, maybe it doesn't need to be sold. I've been cheated by others who want the fortune for themselves. Believe me, there's skulduggery involved, and Leonard Dundas is a large part of it. Caroline maybe, although I wouldn't trust that husband of hers.'

'Desmond Dickson. You have your suspicions?'

'Not as such, but the man knows the value of money. He'll make sure he and Caroline have plenty.'

'Molly Dempster?'

'Let her have what my father bequeathed her. She deserves it.'

'We have difficulty believing that she did not know what was going on in the house,' Isaac said.

'When I was younger, I used to suspect her and my father.'

'An affair?'

'We used to see more of Molly than our mother sometimes. It was just a childish fantasy, that's all.'

'Your father and Molly were friendly?'

'Forget I said it. To me, Molly is the one good person. I'll not hear a word against her.'

'In the meeting at Dundas's, you stood up and stated that people have demands on you. What did that mean?'

Wendy noticed Ralph Lawrence shift uncomfortably in his seat.

'I needed the money, that's all.'

'What will you do now?'

'Find someone to contest the will.'

'That will cost money. If Dundas and his daughter are as smart as you say they are, they'll have covered their tracks well. According to Dundas, a lot of the money is tied up in overseas banks, trusts, offshore-registered companies. Not so easy to get hold of.'

'That's why I need a good solicitor. They're out there.'

'I suggest you do not break the law, Mr Lawrence. The English police are not as forgiving as the Spanish.'

'They weren't forgiving either. Strings were pulled.'

'What does that mean?'

'What I said. Do you think they would release me just because my father died?'

'Why are you telling us this?'

'Insurance.'

'Against whom?'

'Just remember that whatever happens, I didn't kill my father and that Leonard Dundas is not to be trusted.'

'These people? The sort that kill to get what they want?'

'Yes.'

'Did they kill your father?'

'I don't know, and that's the honest truth.'

'We need to stay in touch. As much for your protection as for our investigation.'

'Your son, where is he?' Wendy said.

'I've no idea. I've not seen him for a few years.'

'Is he in trouble?'

'Not to my knowledge. I found alcohol when I was younger, he found heroin.'

'Does that upset you?'

'He's an adult. My father was a self-made man. I wanted to be, but my son, he's a hopeless case.'

'His mother?'

'No idea where she is now. A few wives, a few other women since then.'

***

The interview with Ralph Lawrence had brought a new element into his father's death. Chief Superintendent Goddard had joined the scheduled meeting in Homicide.

It now looked as if the investigation was going to be prolonged, and this time with the addition of possible organised crime interference.

'Ralph Lawrence is in trouble,' Isaac said.

'You could see that he was putting on a brave face, but he was frightened,' Wendy said. 'He's going to disappear again.'

'You've got a watch on him?'

'I have, but if he's in deep with the loan sharks, they'll not wait long.'

'What are you suggesting?' Goddard said.

'Either Ralph has borrowed money beyond his ability to repay, and the father's death came as a godsend, or else he's borrowed against his perceived inheritance,' Wendy said.

'If organised crime had killed Gilbert, that would explain the lack of clues,' Isaac said.

'Are we suggesting that the man's death was prearranged, murder to order?' Larry said.

'It's possible. Ralph may have known that entering an arrangement with the loan sharks came with some conditions: pay the money back with interest, we'll deal with your father.'

'Would he have entered into such an agreement?'

'Is Ralph the type of person to read the small print or to care about his father?'

'Unlikely,' Wendy said.

'According to Leonard Dundas, the man has survived by charming gullible and rich women.'

'And once he had his money and tired of them?'

'Cast off, flotsam to the sea. Tell us, Bridget and Wendy, you're both mature women. Wendy, you've met the man, Bridget, you've seen him. Pretend you're rich and lonely, and Ralph Lawrence comes up to you and lays on the charm.'

'Twenty years too old for me, and the man's going to seed,' Wendy said.

'He didn't appeal, not from what I could see,' Bridget said.

'That's it,' Isaac said. 'The man's survived due to his charisma, his good manners, his expensive education and his posh voice. He's never needed to borrow heavily before, but now he's getting old, and Spain was the make or break. He also knew he only needed a few more years before his father died of natural causes.'

'Men like Gilbert Lawrence don't die that easy,' Goddard said. 'They refuse to accept the possibility. He could have lasted another five, ten, maybe fifteen years.'

'Okay, we'll concede the possibility, but Ralph's aware that one day he'll be fine. And he's a chancer. He's had a litany of failed ventures. It could be that he wanted to settle down, get a house in the country, a garden, grow vegetables.'

'Conjecture, short on facts,' Goddard said.

'That's the problem,' Isaac said. 'We don't have facts. We have a dead man knifed in his garden, no clues of any significance. We have a great deal of money, and according to the man's solicitor, a great deal of property.'

'But not going to the man's children.'

'Not in itself. Caroline, the daughter, received a five million pound one-off payment.'

'Enough?'

'Not if you expected a great deal more. Greed, yet again. Caroline Dickson and her family are stable people. No reason to suspect them at this present time.'

'Money corrupts, you know it,' Goddard said. 'I suggest you don't leave anyone out of your investigation.'

'We won't.'

'An early arrest?'

'Not looking good,' Isaac said.

'I was hopeful. You've got my confidence but be careful. If the son is involved with dangerous people, who knows where it will end up.'

With Goddard leaving, Isaac turned to Wendy. 'Ralph Lawrence's son, any updates?'

'I've got one,' Bridget said. 'I did some searching on the internet.'

'And?'

'He's moved on from being a layabout squatting somewhere or other. He's now an anarchist, committed to the overthrow of capitalism, and the redistribution of wealth to the needy.'

'With him being one of the needy. Where do we find him?'

'Idiots Incorporated,' Bridget said.

'Apart from that, do they have a title?'

'Anarchist Revolutionaries of England. Their address belies the fancy title. You'll find them in a lockup garage down in Putney. Wendy's got the address.'

'Violent?' Isaac said.

'Their website states that they are committed to the overthrow of the current government. By any means, according to them.'

'It's either rent-a-crowd who do little except philosophise or people who believe that murder is acceptable.'

'And Ralph Lawrence's son had a grandfather who represented the worst excess of what they abhor.'

***

There was one thing that concerned Isaac, the sanity of Gilbert Lawrence.

Isaac phoned Jill Dundas, made an appointment to meet with her later that day. Meanwhile, Larry Hill and Wendy Gladstone were getting acquainted with London's very own anarchists. Not that Wendy, a committed socialist, had any problems with people who wanted a better deal for themselves, but violence and extremism did not sit well with her. Larry had formed his opinion the moment they drew up alongside the ramshackle lockup garage, pre-war by the look of it, with its two wooden doors literally falling off their hinges. Outside on the street, four men stood. One was tall, and academic in appearance. 'All he needs is a soapbox and a spot down at Speaker's Corner in Hyde Park,' Larry said.

Wendy switched off the car engine and looked to where Larry had been pointing. She could see what he was talking about. The academic, judging by his corduroy jacket and his faded jeans, had the other three assembled around him. He was making a speech.

'The workers need us, and they need us now. For too long they have been downtrodden and made to feel the boots of the capitalist overlords on their backsides. That will change when we take control. When we ensure the distribution of the wealth amongst the people. I live for that day, and so must you.'

'Sorry to disturb you,' Wendy said, although she wasn't concerned if they were upset. A check on the Anarchist Revolutionaries of England website had identified the academic as Professor Giles Helmsley, faculty member of the London School of Economics until he staged a demonstration inside the main building complaining about the disparity in salaries between the teaching faculty and those working in administration. Once evicted from the LSE – Bridget had done the research – he had drifted from organisation to organisation, demonstration to demonstration, until he had founded the ARE.

'A smart man, once,' Larry said.

'Disturbed,' Wendy said.

Helmsley had taken no notice of her the first time. 'Mr Helmsley, a moment of your time,' Wendy shouted again.

Helmsley, temporarily interrupted, looked Wendy straight in the eye. 'The filth, I suppose,' he said to his audience of three.

'If, by that, you mean a police officer charged with protecting you and every other ratbag from themselves and others, then I am. Sergeant Wendy Gladstone. A few minutes of your time, if you please.'

'We do not recognise your right to be here. We have dispensed with the need for the capitalist lackeys.'

'No doubt you haven't dispensed with their fortnightly handouts of money for the unemployed, the vacuous, and the just plain stupid. And a public footpath is open to all people, even the police.'

'Is that an insult? If it is, I will be forced to take action.'

'What? Sue me? Threaten me with violence?'

'I will defend my rights as a citizen of this country. Neither you nor anyone else has a right to criticise me or take action against me.'

'Freedom of the masses, is that it?'

'If you understood our manifesto, you would agree.'

Helmsley, realising that he had met his match, turned away from the three converts and came over to where Wendy and Larry stood.

'What do you want? I've not broken any law,' Helmsley said.

'We're not saying you have,' Wendy said. 'We need to find Michael Lawrence.'

'Never heard of him.'

'He's on your website. Five feet eight inches, dark hair, spikey. He's got a tattoo on his arm of an eagle.'

'I've no idea who you're talking about.'

'That's fine,' Larry said as he took out his phone. '16 Grantly Street, Putney. A lockup garage, currently occupied by the Anarchist Revolutionaries of England. Check it for class A and B drugs, weapons, subversive literature, incitement to riot. You know the drill.'

'You can't do that,' Helmsley said.

'Do you want me to cancel it? It's up to you.'

'Okay, I know him. One of our most fervent.'

'Where is he?'

'I don't know.'

Larry reached for his phone again.

'Very well. 246 Hazelmere Road. It's a five-minute walk from here. He shares with some of the other comrades.'

'You've been there?'

'Not me. I've got a place not far from here.'

'No doubt you share it with your fellow revolutionaries.'

'I do my bit.'

'And what bit is that? The bit where you incite them to violence? The bit where you take a share of their benefits? Mr Helmsley, you've never been arrested, other than for causing a minor affray. Fifty pound fine, is that the limit of your anarchy?'

'You don't understand what we are trying to achieve. Some of us need to remain at a distance, to provide leadership and guidance.'

'And have a good time,' Wendy said. 'Is Michael Lawrence having a good time?'

'He's into heroin, a hopeless drug addict.'

'Do you know of his family?'

'I do.'

'Did you kill his grandfather? You must have hated what he represents.'

'One of the elites. I am glad that he is dead, but no, I did not kill him, nor did any of our members.'

'And what's going to happen when you succeed?' Larry said. 'Tumbrels taking the capitalists to the guillotine? The women sitting there knitting, the men cheering?'

'It won't be like that. The people will welcome us, even those who oppose us now.'

'Mr Helmsley, you're full of hot air. If we don't find Michael Lawrence, we'll be back, and this time, not only to your headquarters but also the house you own. You're no different from Lenin driving around in a Rolls Royce: just a hypocrite. We'll meet again, Mr Helmsley, and soon.'

Chapter 8

Ralph Lawrence, free of Challis Street Police Station, realised there were imponderables for which he had no solution. He made two phone calls. The first was to a psychiatrist whom he had known from his school days, an eminent man in his field now. The second was to a man who would either assist him or would see that he never walked again. Ralph plotted his course very carefully.

If, as he suspected, his father with only a corpse to keep him company, had been irrational and eccentric, then the man's sanity could be disputed. But even if the will was invalidated, how much of his father's wealth would come to him, and how much would remain hidden? After all, Leonard Dundas and his daughter had had a long time to distort the truth and to hide the whereabouts of swathes of property and legal documents.

The first call revealed that a case could be made to dispute Gilbert Lawrence's sanity, although it would be costly and prolonged. If Dundas had been controlling his father for many years, then his father had been merely a shell, rubber-stamping Dundas's instructions. He knew that he needed the truth, he needed allies.

'Caroline, we need to talk,' Ralph said as he stood at the door of his sister's house. He had in his pockets the sum of one thousand five hundred and fifty-two pounds. Not much to show for a lifetime of playing the game, he knew, but he had hoped for a fortune.

'Come in, if you must,' Caroline said.

Once inside the elegantly decorated terrace house of Caroline and Desmond Dickson, Ralph quickly found a radiator and sat down close to it, removing his suit jacket. He had to admit that his sister had done well for herself, but then, she was the more sensible of the two. She had always looked for stability in her life, whereas he had searched for adventure.

'Life's taken a turn for the worse for you,' Caroline said. They had been close when they were young, and seeing him down and out, a body blow straight in the chest after the reading of their father's last will and testament, she could only feel compassion.

Before Desmond had come along, the most important man in her life had been her brother, even if he had not been the best influence or the most honest.

'Our father was not sane, you know that,' Ralph said as he slowly warmed in the heat.

'I know it, but what can we do?'

'Leonard Dundas controlled our father for years.'

'I've spoken to Desmond about it. We will accept the money offered, and I'll take up the offer that Dundas made at our father's request.'

'That's a smoke screen. You're to be given voting rights. Voting on what? The truth? Will you be given full visibility?'

'It will give us five million pounds, our children one million pounds each, and more importantly, it will give us time.'

'Time for what?'

'Time to find out the truth.'

'I've received nothing, not unless I agree to conditions that cannot be met.'

'We can only sympathise with your predicament.'

'Sympathy will not help,' Ralph said. He moved away from the radiator and sat in an armchair near to his sister. 'I need money, and I need it now. Holding down a steady job is not going to work, and as for Michael, he's barking mad.'

'What do you know about him? Where is he? What is he doing?'

'The last I heard he was into heroin. He was looking for money from me.'

'Did you give him some?'

'I sent him ten thousand pounds. What else could I do?'

'He is your son. His mother?'

'No idea.'

'Did you come here for money, or just to complain about how your life has turned out?'

'I'm desperate. What we were working on in Spain hasn't worked out. The police down there are tough. They've seized our assets.'

'Assets?'

'Okay, just a rented office, a couple of cars, and our laptops.'

'The money you had managed to part from the gullible?'

'That as well. It was a sound business proposal. They would have had secured tenure.'

'Ralph, save the advertising for others. You've lost your money, probably borrowed plenty. And now you're looking for a handout, and support to take on our father, is that it?'

'That's what I said before.'

'We will take no further action at this time until we have more knowledge of the intricacies of what our father and Dundas have been doing for the last three decades. We have time on our side, you do not. What do you intend to do?'

'I'll fight.'

'With what?'

'Whatever I've got.'

'You're playing with fire, not for the first time, but fire nonetheless. You're going to get burnt, not by Desmond and me, but by others. Did you kill our father? You'd be capable.'

'Not me. I was incarcerated in Spain, you know that.'

'What about Michael? He was in England.'

'Not him. He's barely capable of looking after himself.'

Ralph knew his sister would not help him, and he did not intend to plead. His situation was precarious, and he had been in tight jams before. He would get himself out of this one.

***

The young anarchist Michael Lawrence was found at the address given by Giles Helmsley. In keeping with the beliefs of the organisation, or because they were just bone-lazy, the house that three of the anarchists occupied was only fit for keeping animals.

'Mr Lawrence, we've a few questions,' Wendy said. She stood back more than ten paces on account of the mess. The man who wanted to right the wrongs of the capitalist state was lying on a mattress on the floor. It looked neither clean nor hygienic. To one side, there was a syringe and a bottle of beer.

'If you're the filth?'

'Sergeant Wendy Gladstone and Detective Inspector Larry Hill,' Wendy said as the two officers showed their warrant cards.

'I've nothing to say.'

'That's fine. We can continue our discussion down at the police station.'

'You can't come in here and tell us what to do,' one of the others said.

Larry moved over close to the man who was dressed in a tee-shirt with the words 'Down with the Capitalist State' emblazoned across the front of it. 'Now, look here, my anarchist friend,' Larry said, enunciating his words, 'if you want to be arrested and charged for having heroin in here, a firearm on the shelf behind you, then I suggest you shut up and leave us to deal with your friend.'

'There are no guns here,' the would-be tough man said. Wendy could see that Larry was ready to give him a swift kick in the stomach and a slap across the face.

The other anarchist remained curled up, fast asleep. On the arm of a chair next to where he slept, an empty bottle of whisky.

'Not much revolution today from that one,' Larry said, looking over at the man.

Wendy returned to Michael Lawrence. 'What is it? Here or down at the police station?'

'I've done nothing wrong.' Wendy could see the similarities between him and his father. She imagined that the young man could even be handsome underneath the tattoos and all the rings, some in his ears, one in his nose, another in his left eyebrow. If he was an indication of what the end of capitalism was to bring, then she was glad it was not going to happen anytime soon. One of her two sons had come home with a tattoo once. She remembered hitting the roof, not that he had taken too much notice as he had been drunk, but the next day, he felt her tongue. After that, she had to put up with the occasional tattoo, liking some, not liking others.

Then she and Bridget on holiday in Italy had dared each other, and both had had a small butterfly tattooed on their left ankle. It had been down to too much of the local vino, and Wendy's sons had given her hell when she got back to England.

'Okay, here, if you must,' Michael said, attempting to sit up and to lean against the wall.

'We've spoken to your father,' Larry said.

'Him? What for?'

'What do you know of your grandfather, Gilbert?'

'Not much. I've never met the man.'

'What else do you know?'

'According to my father, my grandfather is rich.'

'He's one of those that you're against.'

'It won't be long before you and your masters will be gone. Plenty for everyone.'

'Someone will need to work. Will it be you?' Larry said.

'Not me. Giles says the revolution will need soldiers.'

'I thought it was to occur when the people of England embraced the cause. There'd be no need for you then. Mr Lawrence, you're just a layabout, spouting nonsense as long as you are able to doss here. Helmsley told us where you were. He's done a con trick on you and the others, but that's not why we're here.'

'My grandfather. What about him?'

'Do you know where he lives.'

'No. Should I?'

'Your grandfather was killed.'

'Should I be sorry? Shed a tear? Is that what you want?'

'Mr Lawrence, did you kill him?' Wendy said.

'Are you joking?'

'Did you know anything about him?'

'Giles wanted me to find out more. He asked lots of questions.'

'What did you tell him?'

'I knew where he lived, that's all. I never went to the house or spoke to anyone.'

'Your father's sister?'

'I left home at fourteen. I've been on the street ever since. I may have met her when I was a child.'

'What would you do for some of your grandfather's money?'

'Anything.'

'Including detoxing from drugs, finding a job?'

'Anything.'

'Mr Lawrence, your grandfather has offered you one million pounds if you are willing to enter into a private drug rehabilitation clinic to sort yourself out. After that a job. Will you do it?'

'Yes, for a million pounds.'

'Very well. Make a phone call to this number,' Wendy said as she handed Michael Lawrence the number written on a piece of paper.

Outside on the street, the figure of Giles Helmsley. 'Not willing to go in, is that it?' Larry said.

'I'm here to ensure that the comrades are not subjected to police brutality.'

'What would you do if they were? Wise up, Helmsley. You're a charlatan preying on vulnerable people who neither understand nor care about what you're talking about, as long as they have their drugs and a place to sleep.'

'Did you feed that errant nonsense to the comrades?'

'Don't worry. The comrades are beyond caring about what we have to say,' Larry said.

Wendy and Larry walked to their vehicle.

'You were pushing it,' Wendy said.

'Michael Lawrence could have killed his grandfather, but it would have needed Helmsley to make him.'

'A blow for the cause?'

'Helmsley's cause. He could have hatched a plan to kill the old man, assuming that the grandson would get some money. And then he'd convince Michael to hand it over.

'It's a possibility, but far-fetched.'

'It's no worse than any other scenario.'

'No better, though.'

***

Two weeks after the death of Gilbert Lawrence, five letters were sent. Two days later, four of them were signed for. The first recipient, Molly Dempster, opened hers and almost collapsed to the ground. The second, Caroline Dickson, phoned her husband. The third was delivered to Emma Lawrence. She was disturbed to receive it, not altogether surprised. The fourth was received by Leonard Dundas. He was shocked by the thoroughness of what he read. The fifth, to Ralph Lawrence, was not delivered due to the man not being at the hotel where he was staying.

The first that Homicide heard of the letters was when Molly Dempster appeared at Challis Street Police Station. It was Wendy who escorted the nervous and shaking woman up to Homicide.

Isaac and Larry, who had been out following up on the few leads they had, returned to the station as fast as they could.

Once back, the team sat with Gilbert Lawrence's former housekeeper.

'When did you receive it?' Larry said.

'This morning. It's from Mr Lawrence, from his grave.'

The team studied the envelope. It was from another solicitor in London. It was dated two days previously. On the outside the details of the person it was addressed to, and in the far-right corner in capital letters, 'TO BE OPENED AFTER MY DEATH'. Inside, three sheets of paper. The letter was dated 28th April 2017. Only one year old.

'I couldn't read it,' Molly said. 'It's as if he's writing to me from beyond.'

'Bridget, phone up the solicitor that sent this after this meeting,' Isaac said. 'Either they come in here, or we'll go out there.'

No doubt you are all wondering what to make of me, and whether I was sane or not. My death, whether it was in my sleep or after an illness, or whether my end was violent, I cannot know, as I cannot predict the future. Those who have received this letter will know by now what they have been bequeathed. Some will be pleased, others will be neutral, and some will be angry. The question about my beloved wife, Dorothy, is also a question that must be answered.

But first, my reasons for the division of my assets. I was a careful man in life, generous to those I loved, difficult and belligerent to those I did not. While I have tried to be scrupulous in my business dealings, I have at times been forced to deal with unsavoury characters. These are not people of my choosing, and I have always kept them away from my family. Some of them have been villains, no doubt some of them would be capable of murder. That explains the reference to my death and the possibility that it could be violent. I have never sought the company of dishonest people or criminals, but with some of my more significant acquisitions, it was sometimes inevitable. I should say that this letter has been updated annually since I first put pen to paper over twenty-five years ago. Nobody, not even Leonard Dundas, knows of this letter and its contents. It has changed to some extent as the years have moved forward, as has my will.

If you are reading this now, then I am dead. Molly is no doubt confused, but the remainder of her life will be as agreeable as I can make it. Caroline, my daughter, is also provided for. Ralph, my son, has become a disappointment. I had hoped to give him and Caroline the control of my empire, but, alas, it was not to be. I know that I could have given it to Caroline instead, but I wanted the family to control it. Desmond Dickson is a good man, I've no doubt of that, but he is not of my blood. I could not give all that I have strived for to others. Caroline's children will be eventually brought in, when and if they show the necessary acumen. I have engaged another firm to monitor their progress. By necessity, I am forced to rely on others, but I have put checks and counter-checks in place to ensure compliance and accountability of those charged with the responsibility. An additional letter will have been sent to Leonard Dundas and his daughter with full details of the auditing process, as well as the auditing of Dundas and his company.

Leonard Dundas has served me well over the years, and whereas I could trust him when I was alive, I cannot give him my unqualified trust when I am dead. His daughter, Jill, will take over the reins soon, and those checks will apply to her too. Caroline will have the most significant role in the years to come, and that is why there is to be a strict liquidation of assets policy in place. No doubt my directives will dissipate in time, yet I hope in death, as I did in life, my legacy will continue.

My beloved wife, Dorothy. I grant that some may see my isolation from the world and my reclusive behaviour as symptoms of madness. They are not. Dorothy had suffered all her adult life with a debilitating mental condition. It had become worse in the last six months before she vanished from the world. She was a proud woman who did not want people to know. If she had died, there would have been an autopsy. Such is the burden of men as successful as I have been. There was also a substantial life insurance policy in her name. Suspicion would naturally have arisen. On the day my wife died of natural causes, I closed all the shutters in the house and placed my wife in the cellar. The possibility of her vanishing from the house and dying as a result of misadventure was plausible and ultimately accepted.

It is strange to reflect that the preparation of my wife to allow her to be placed in her bed was a calming experience. She was there with me, and I wanted nothing more. Some people will see it as macabre, others as a sure sign of madness, but believe me, it was neither. It was a sign of love.

I had never been a sociable man and the attention that I received as I became all the more successful did not sit easily with me. Being reclusive in the house with Dorothy suited me admirably. Molly continued to look after me and was never involved in any way with Dorothy's disappearance.

In time, as I aged, I have become more careless in my appearance and my health. I contacted three companies of psychoanalysts. Their names are with Caroline and Dundas. I did not meet them, although I would speak to them once a year, and go through their questionnaires, their attempts to understand the state of a person's mind. They will attest to my sanity. Of the three companies, one is in the UK, one is in the USA, and the final one is in Australia. If an attempt is made to dispute my sanity, a well-honed team of lawyers is in place to deal with it, and a fund in place to pay for their services. Yet again, a process of checks and counter-checks between the companies has been set up. Collusion by anybody or any group will not be possible.

I cannot allow my legacy and the love of my wife to be destroyed by unfettered greed. That is all. Gilbert Lawrence.

Chapter 9

Ralph Lawrence rarely regretted any decisions that he had made in his life. He was a man with an unrelenting belief that life was what you made it, and luck had nothing to do with it.

As he sat on the chair in the back room of a disused warehouse in the east end of London, he was beginning to regret his philosophy. He had returned to England primarily because the Spanish authorities wanted him out of their country, but secondly because his father had died.

Not that he had felt any sadness. On the contrary, the man's death, tinged with intrigue about how he died, gave him the best hope for the future. Yet now he was in trouble, and he knew it was not going to be so easy. The man sitting opposite him in the seedy back room that smelt of damp and decay was not likely to be swayed by smooth words.

'Lawrence, I staked you money for your venture in the sun. Where is it?' Gary Frost said.

'I need time. There's been a problem,' Ralph said. On either side of him were two men who looked as though they were used to beating people for a living.

'Gilbert Lawrence, a relative of yours?' Frost said. He was a small man, quietly spoken. He was dressed in a navy-blue suit, a red tie, and a white shirt. He looked like a banker, and that was what he was: the banker of last resort.

Ralph had done the sums. The cost to set up the scam in Spain was more than four hundred thousand pounds. No use skimping on a cheap website, and then there were the advertisements, and transferring the money overseas, and the bribes, a lot of money in themselves. His Spanish partner, another charmer, still languished in a cell in Spain. He had also borrowed money, and it had been going well. They had managed to sucker over one and a half million out of the tourists, another two million to be followed up on. And the money was not there. Lawrence was not sure why, although he suspected the bribes they had been paying hadn't been enough. No doubt his Spanish partner would be making a deal to get himself out of jail.

One of the men standing over Ralph grabbed hold of his shoulder, almost lifted him out of the chair. 'You never answered the boss's question.'

'He was my father.'

'Then why are we here having this unpleasantness,' Frost said. 'Let go of Mr Lawrence. He is our honoured guest. And what is four hundred thousand? How much was your father worth?'

'Somewhere close to seven hundred million pounds, probably more.'

'And your share?'

'It'll take time to realise on his money, but it should be three hundred million pounds.'

'Why didn't you tell us before? I was prepared to let my boys go to work on you. You know what that would have meant?'

Ralph flexed his legs, imagining the pain of a low-velocity bullet penetrating his kneecaps. 'It may take time to get the money.'

'What does it matter. We can wait. Six weeks, is that long enough for you?'

'It is,' Ralph said, hoping that it was long enough to get out of the country.

'Give our guest a whisky,' Frost said.

One of the heavies poured the drink and gave it to Ralph. The man now receiving the VIP treatment was shaking so much he was barely able to hold it.

'I'm a reasonable man. It's only business, you know that.'

Lawrence knew it wasn't. It was sheer desperation on his part that had led him into the clutches of the loan shark. He was shaking now because he had just been saved from a savage beating, and his kneecaps possibly being shattered. He knew that once he was free of Frost and his men, he would be shaking until he had distanced himself from them. But what to do for money: he had none.

***

Caroline Dickson realised that her father had made a strategic error. A possible indication that the man had been slipping in his later years. It would have been understandable, given his advancing years and his morbid account as to what he had done to her mother, and how he had kept her in her room. She could imagine him up there with her, discussing business, updating her on the economy and what was outside, and how she was better off where she was.

Ralph may be a fool, and his outburst when the will had been read had not endeared him to anyone, but Caroline knew that the brother she had not seen for eight years had been right. Their father had been mad, but the medical and psychoanalytical reports showed clearly that the checks had been conducted correctly, and her father's responses had been above average. *How could that be?* Caroline thought. *Do I want to rock the boat?*

She knew she had voting rights, and as a direct descendant of the dead man she had precedence over Dundas, but the man and his daughter had control. She had had to look up where the Marshall Islands were, as there were five million two hundred and fifty-nine thousand dollars in an investment fund there. The Cayman Islands she knew, as well as Cyprus and Mauritius. She needed the accounts in her name, and that had not occurred yet. She could see the hands of the Dundases pulling strings. They had access to all the bank accounts, the title deeds of all the properties, and yet they were all in the name of Gilbert Lawrence and the companies that he had set up. Caroline knew that it would be a battle royal.

Desmond, her husband, was an honest man, and he would help, but he was used to dealing with trustworthy people, not with Leonard and Jill Dundas. But Ralph knew crooks, and he knew how to deal with them. She needed him as her special adviser.

***

Isaac Cook and his team in Homicide studied Gilbert Lawrence's letter from beyond the grave. The distribution of the wealth was not the primary concern, although it was important. What concerned them more was what the dead man had revealed about the death of his wife, Dorothy. Wendy Gladstone and Bridget Halloran abhorred the cavalier manner with which he had described his wife in the cellar. Larry Hill was more intrigued by the process. All, including Isaac, could not believe it was the behaviour of a rational man, a man capable of satisfying three respectable psychoanalysts on three continents that he was sane.

The experts' results were of no concern if they were legitimate, but what if the tests had been falsified? If they had been, as seemed possible, then it would invalidate Lawrence's will, which in turn would throw the motives behind the man's death into confusion.

'How do we prove this?' Bridget said.

'Research these companies, see what they have to say.'

'I've done some research, not of the companies, but what constitutes insanity.'

'And?' Isaac said, knowing full well that Bridget would have been thorough.

'If the will is to be contested…'

'Assume it is,' Isaac said. 'Ralph Lawrence has been left out of any immediate money, and Caroline Lawrence is only to receive a minor amount.'

'Five million pounds, minor?' Larry said. He was struggling with finding fifty thousand for his wife's house-hunting plans. To him, Caroline Lawrence had received a fortune.

'The dead man had a property portfolio in the billions. And it's still with Leonard Dundas. If that man has concealed some of his client's money and property holdings, there's no way that anyone could find out the full extent of what the man owned.'

'He's either the greatest crook or naively honest,' Wendy said.

'Have you met any honest men lately?' Larry said.

'My husband was, but he could only lay claim to a small pension and a bungalow. Apart from him, there aren't too many, especially if they're worth hundreds of millions.'

'We can debate this ad infinitum,' Isaac said, 'but what is important is whether Gilbert Lawrence was sane.'

'As I was saying,' Bridget said.

'Apologies, we digressed.'

'This what I've found out. The person must be of "sound mind, memory, and understanding" when making a will. That person must understand the nature of the act and its effects, the extent of the property of which he/she is disposing and must be able to comprehend and appreciate the claims to which he/she ought to give effect.'

'Is that it?' Larry said. He had had an aunt who had died and had given her money to the church instead of her family. He remembered his mother, his aunt's sister, saying over the dining room table that the woman was mad, but the money remained with the church.

'There's one more clause. It's in legalese. "And must not be affected by any disorder of the mind that shall poison his affections, pervert his sense of right, or prevent the exercise of his natural faculties and that no insane delusion shall influence his will in disposing of this property and bring about a disposal of it which, if the mind had been sound, would not be made."'

'The précised version,' Larry said.

'If he had been declared sane and he had the necessary proofs at the signing of his will, then it's valid. Remember, most people don't get their sanity verified while they're alive. It's up to the beneficiaries, or those who believe they should receive something from the person's estate, to contest it afterwards.'

'Are the three certificates valid?'

'They are.'

'Did they have all the facts?'

'How could they? Nobody knew about Dorothy Lawrence upstairs in the house.'

'The will is contestable?'

'Without a doubt. And if Gilbert Lawrence was so smart, he wouldn't have left loopholes in the will.'

'There was a clause at the end for those present to sign their agreement,' Isaac said.

'That may have been legally binding, but Ralph Lawrence didn't sign.'

***

Ralph Lawrence made contact with his sister one day after his encounter with Gary Frost, a man who had an unenviable reputation as to how he called in his debts. Ralph had not wanted to use the man, regretted it now, but he had been down on his luck, and he needed out from the predicament he had found himself in. The first day he had made contact with Frost was the first time for a very long time that he felt trepidation about what he was doing.

Ralph Lawrence knew himself to be a supreme optimist, fully aware that not many ventures had turned out bad. Some, his sister and their father included, would have said that a failed business venture was indeed that, a failure. To Ralph, his definition was that if you lost money, it was. But he had not lost money; others had. On every venture he had been creaming off the top and squirrelling the money where no one else could get hold of it, including his ex-wives, bloodsuckers all of them. But he had chosen them for their youth and beauty, or for their money. The last woman had been smarter than most and had seen through him early on. She had found some of his bank accounts, the cryptic passwords, and had helped herself to over two hundred thousand pounds before sending him a letter from an unknown destination: 'The weather's fine, so is the hotel and the man I picked up in the bar last night. And don't expect me to wish you were here.'

'Where have you been? I've been trying to contact you,' Caroline said.

The siblings met at a restaurant. Caroline knew she would be paying.

'I was occupied,' Ralph said.

'You didn't pay for the hotel. I phoned them.'

'Did you pay?'

'Hell, I did. What sort of trouble are you in?'

'Money trouble, the usual.'

'Where are you staying?' Caroline could see that her brother was looking the worse for wear and that he had a tired, faraway look about him.

'A cheap hotel. It's not much good.'

'Why? You could always check into somewhere better.'

'The deal in Spain has gone all wrong. It's left me in a predicament.'

'You're hiding out. Why?'

'Some people want their money. The sort of people who don't take no for an answer.'

'I need your help,' Caroline said. 'Dundas has got us over a barrel.'

'Didn't you figure that out when he was reading the will?'

'I wanted the five million first.'

'You signed the clause at the bottom, no contesting the will?'

'It's not enforceable. The tests of our father's sanity are invalid. We can dispute that.'

'Caroline, supposing I agree to go in with you, what's in it for me?'

'Two hundred thousand pounds today, and forty per cent of whatever we find.'

'Assuming the will is invalidated, and we become the sole beneficiaries?'

'We'll never find it all. Dundas will have covered his tracks well. That's why we need you,' Caroline said.

She called the waiter over. 'Another bottle of wine, please,' she said. This was a time to celebrate.

'We? You and Desmond?'

'Regardless of what you and he may think of each other, he realises that he's not up to what's required.'

'And I am?'

'You know the tricks, what Dundas could have done. Where the titles to the properties are, the bank accounts.'

'It will cost.'

'I've offered you two hundred thousand pounds.'

'We'll need a top-notch computer hacker, someone to go through Dundas's office, check the files, take copies.'

'Illegal?'

'Do you think he'll respond to a legal demand?'

'We need to know before we force him. How much for the additional help?'

'Probably another three hundred thousand pounds.'

Caroline was suspicious. He was her brother, and she knew him better than anyone else. Give the man an inch, he would take a mile, and then disappear, brother or no brother. 'You want me to give you more money?' she said.

'Not this time. Our father owes us a lot more than a pittance. I'll play it by the book, but I need your assurance that you'll help out if I can't fend off the money lenders.'

'Violent?'

'I was desperate. I had no option. But now, with you and me, we'll deal with Dundas. Our father was crazy, you know that?'

'I know it. Our mother up there in that room. Have you seen the body?' Caroline said.

'I'm not sure if I want to.'

'I have. It's ghoulish. Whether it was her death or not that turned him, there's no way to know. And are we sure he was making the decisions all these years, with Dundas implementing them?'

'How can we be? How can anyone be?'

'We'll never know. The will, we are assuming, is genuine.'

'Maybe it is, maybe it isn't, but whatever you do, don't dispute it for now. You, Caroline, need to be with Dundas. He must never know of our meeting here today.'

'Agreed. I'll transfer the money to your account when I have the details. Play this fair, and we'll deal with that bastard Dundas and his scheming daughter.'

Chapter 10

Homicide still wrestled with where Molly Dempster fitted into the investigation. There was no reason to believe that she was involved in her employer's death or that of his wife, but she had spent more time in the house than any person other than Gilbert.

Isaac and Larry found her at her house. There were signs of her new-found wealth: the two men at the front of the house painting the windows and the door, another man tending to the garden.

'I had to do something,' Molly said. 'Mr Lawrence gave me the money to look after myself.'

She seemed to be unaffected by the wealth of her lifelong employer and spoke of him and his children in a loving, almost childlike manner, as though they were her family. Not unusual, he supposed, as checks into the woman had revealed a life of modest means: no man in her life, no pets, nothing.

Inside the house, also being subjected to modest renovations, Molly Dempster sat in the small living room. Isaac and Larry sat nearby. A tray of tea and biscuits on a table in front of all three.

'Miss Dempster, for all those years you were in that house with Mrs Lawrence upstairs,' Isaac said. He had helped himself to a cup of tea and a biscuit. Larry, conscious of the need to keep his weight down, only had a cup of tea.

'I know. Somehow, I find it romantic, but then I was always the first to cry if there was a love story on the television, you know the type, where one of them dies young, the other left on their own.'

'Do you understand why Mr Lawrence would have wanted his wife there?'

'Oh, yes. They never wanted to be apart, neither of them. If he was late coming home, or she was, the other one would be fretting.'

'But what concerns us is that you were there twice a week, and Mrs Lawrence was buried in the cellar. After that, Mr Lawrence had to prepare his wife's body, and that is not the easiest of the processes. There must have been some odours, and not pleasant either.'

'Maybe there were, but I wouldn't have taken any notice.'

'Why's that?'

'Hyposmia, virtually no ability to smell. I've had it since I was young. It's no use talking to me about the smell of a flower. Once, I nearly gassed myself. The oven hadn't lit, and I was trying to find out why. I almost passed out until Mrs Lawrence came and pulled me free.'

'Your friendship with Mr Lawrence?' Larry said.

'Ralph was trying to make something out of it, but he was young and adolescent. His hormones and his imagination were getting the better of him. And besides, I had no need of a man or a woman. Never have, never wanted to. I just want my routine, the chance to sit down at the end of the day and turn on the television.'

'How could the man have kept away from you? You must have seen him occasionally.'

'Maybe I did, but he wanted to be alone. Once he left the door unbolted, so I snuck in for a quick look.'

'How long after he had gone into seclusion?'

'One, two years. I don't remember exactly, but it was a long time ago.'

'And what did you see?'

'Nothing. It was dark with the shutters closed and very dusty. I might not be able to smell very well, but my hearing was fine. I could hear a sound from upstairs, so I returned to my part of the house. After that, I never tried to look again.'

'Did he know you'd been in there?'

'It was never mentioned, although, as I said, he always wrote his instructions down for me. The door was never open again while I was in the house.'

Both Isaac and Larry could not fault the woman, although no physical contact, no conversation, made no sense.

'Let's go back to when he needed a dentist. What did he sound like, look like?'

'He was quiet, as though he hadn't spoken in a long time, which I suppose he hadn't. I made the appointment, and he left when I wasn't in the house. All I know is that three hours later, he was back in the house. After that, I never spoke to him again.'

'The dentist?'

'Brian Garrett. I've got his phone number. I suppose he must have seen more of Mr Lawrence than me.'

***

Gary Frost, unscrupulous and on the periphery of crime, knew what he had with Ralph Lawrence. A man who had come to him five months earlier needing money. It wasn't the first time he'd seen men such as Lawrence, men who lived on the edge, scoundrels more than criminals.

Frost understood that Ralph Lawrence was weak, not like his father, Gilbert. He did not tell the son that he already knew of the father. Frost had done further research, not difficult considering the amount of interest in the man's murder. It made for great headlines – England's own Howard Hughes, dead with a knife in the back. The reclusive billionaire with his wife dead in her bed, the battle for his fortune.

The estimates of the dead man's wealth varied from one billion up to somewhere close to infinity. No one, certainly not Ralph and his sister, knew precisely how much. The only person who seemed to have any idea was the father's former solicitor and his only confidante.

Frost was reclining on a chair, taking in the sun through the window in his penthouse flat. The flat was big enough to double as his accommodation and his place of work. It was on two levels, the lower one for his office and his support staff. With Frost, an agreement to lend money came with a handshake and an email setting out the terms and conditions: the money to be transferred to any nominated location, either a deposit into a bank account or cash. The payment schedule, principal plus interest of ten per cent per week, payable on demand. Default penalties, not included in the email but given in person or by phone, were simple. Non-payments or delays in adhering to the agreement would be settled by extreme violence.

'It's sure-fire, can't lose,' Ralph had said when told of the conditions of the loan.

Frost remembered his words only too well. If it was sure-fire, it could only mean that it was not strictly legal, and it would either make a fortune or it wouldn't. But then men such as Lawrence were all too ready to play into the hands of men such as him. And now he had the son of Gilbert Lawrence. What could be achieved? He needed his man in the prime seat, but there were problems. Even without the media, Frost could see delays, also the possibility of Ralph being sidelined and receiving none of the fortune, or so little as to render him irrelevant. Frost could not allow that to happen. If Lawrence was entitled to half of his father's wealth, then that was what he would get.

Ted Samson, small, barely five feet four inches, his name not indicative of the man, stood before his boss. He was dressed casually, yet expensively. The ideal man for going here and there without raising suspicion.

'I've got a job for you,' Frost said.

'Whatever you want,' Samson said.

'Ralph Lawrence. He's not seen you, has he?'

'Nobody sees me unless I want them to.'

'Good. I want you to keep a watch on him, never let him out of your sight.'

'Twenty-four hours, seven days a week?'

'Exactly. Your brother can take over when you need a break.'

'And what do you want, boss?'

'Don't let him out of your sight, report back all that he does. And if he attempts to do a runner, well, you know.'

'Call you, and then grab him.'

'Exactly, but don't let him know that you're keeping watch.'

'You can trust me, boss.'

***

Chief Superintendent Goddard was under pressure, which meant that Isaac Cook and the entire Homicide team were as well.

'It's like this,' Goddard said as he sat in Isaac's office. 'Gilbert Lawrence is receiving a lot of press interest, understandable given the man's lifestyle, and his wife upstairs.'

'Not to mention the fact that he owned a lot of property,' Isaac said.

'The man's will, has it been resolved?'

'Not to everyone's satisfaction. The only problem is that the main beneficiary appears to be Lawrence's solicitor.'

'Complicated, but why? Normally the children would inherit the majority.'

'That's the problem. Lawrence wasn't normal, was he?'

'Who gained from the man's death?'

'The solicitor. Lawrence's daughter inherited five million pounds, and her two children one million each. Ralph Lawrence, his son, nothing, although there were conditions under which he could inherit.'

'Cut out of the will?'

'Without question, and Ralph's son is an anarchist, as well as a drug addict.'

'Dead within a month, if the drug addict got hold of some of the money. Anarchists would have no issue with Gilbert Lawrence being murdered.' Goddard said.

'They're only pretend anarchists. A brick thrown at a bank, a demonstration somewhere else. Just assorted ratbags, although their leader, Professor Giles Helmsley, is a unusual character.'

'What do you mean?'

'Academic, well-spoken, and up until six years ago, a member of the faculty of the London School of Economics.'

'Any reason to suspect him of the murder of Gilbert Lawrence?'

'No proof. That's the problem, the man is killed, nobody sees anything, nobody hears anything. The housekeeper comes in later and discovers the body, but she's hardly a suspect.'

'Why not?'

'No motive. She's been working for the family for decades, even before Lawrence went crazy. And she received a million pounds in the will.'

'If she knew about the wife upstairs, she could have felt the need to do something.'

'No one had been up there, not for a very long time, apart from the dead man. The CSIs have been over the place with a fine-tooth comb. We had a concern about what Molly Dempster may have known, but we've not come up with anything. The off-licence where he used to go once a week is not in the best area. Someone could have followed him home, seen the opportunity to accost the man, steal some money.'

'Did the people in the street, the off-licence, know who he was?' Goddard asked.

'Some would have.'

'And nothing from the CSIs?'

'There was a clear sign where the housekeeper had walked, as well as the postman, but nothing more.'

'Then it's not someone off the street, is it?'

'Gilbert Lawrence sent a letter to everyone important outlining certain facts, including why his wife was upstairs. No document has been received with accounts, real estate holdings, passwords. Everything is with Dundas.'

'And Lawrence is certified as sane?' Goddard said.

'We're checking, but we're expecting Ralph Lawrence to dispute the will. He may be a con artist, but he's got a point. An evaluation of sanity can only be based on the facts presented. And not one of these experts knew about how he had taken his wife, buried her in the ground underneath the cellar floor for some months, and then exhumed her, removed what he could of the excess skin and internals, and then had her remaining body eaten by dermestid beetles until she was virtually only bone.'

'But she could have been murdered?'

'It's possible. Unprovable, though.'

Isaac realised he'd given his senior very little. As soon as he'd left he called in his team.

'What do we have?' Isaac said.

'Ralph Lawrence met with his sister,' Wendy said.

'How do we know?'

'I've been keeping a watch on him after I found him at another hotel. Since meeting with her – they met at a restaurant – he's moved out of the hotel and back into something decent.'

'What about Dundas and his daughter? Any movement there?'

'They've done nothing wrong that we can see,' Larry said.

'Yet they have gained the most from this.'

'On the face of it.'

'Larry, we need to go and interview the postman who found Gilbert Lawrence,' Isaac said.

Chapter 11

'I still had to deliver the mail,' was not the comment that Isaac and Larry were looking for.

Jim Porter, the postman, had been found at his home five miles from where he had discovered the body of Gilbert Lawrence. Judging by the condition of the flat he lived in, he was a slovenly man. He had not been pleased to see two police officers at his door, although it was a block of flats which the local police would have been only too familiar with. It was grim, low rent, and definitely not the sort of place that Isaac liked. His small flat in Willesden was not much larger than the postman's, but it did have a pleasant outlook, whereas the view from where the three men stood was of an old industrial site.

'They're putting up some fancy high-rise for the wealthy, not for us,' Porter said as he looked out of the window.

'Gilbert Lawrence was wealthy,' Isaac said. 'You must have been tempted.'

'Who wouldn't be? I'd heard stories about the man: reclusive, never spoke, the smell of rotting fish.'

'Rotting fish?'

'That's what they said at the off-licence.'

'Who else have you spoken to about him?' Larry said. He looked around the flat, realised his wife wouldn't have crossed the threshold. He had to admit his wife looked after him, the children, and the house well, and with her, there were no dirty cups in the sink, no magazines thrown haphazardly across any vacant space.

'Nobody, not really, but sometimes people liked to talk, and old man Lawrence was as good a subject as any other.'

'Molly Dempster?'

'She liked to talk, but if I asked about him inside, she'd clam up. I was never sure what to make of her.'

'What do you mean?'

'You've been in the house; didn't you feel it?'

'Feel what?'

'As though it was evil, which I suppose it was.'

'You had been in?'

'Only as far as the kitchen. Sometimes she'd ask me in for a cup of tea. I always got the impression that she was glad of the company.'

'Did you ever see Lawrence?'

'Not me. Once I heard a noise from inside, as though something had fallen over and smashed on the floor, and once or twice the sound of footsteps. I'm not squeamish, far from it, but I never wanted to stay there for long. Do you reckon Molly's all there?'

'What do you mean?'

'I don't know. It's just the feeling that something wasn't right. Now we know it wasn't, but Molly, she must have known something.'

'According to her, she hadn't. She served the family all her adult life, that was all.'

'I read in the newspaper that Lawrence had given her a house and money.'

'He had. For loyal service to him and his family.'

'But he never saw his children.'

'Not since he locked himself away. Had you ever seen them there?'

'I saw the daughter once or twice, but she only ever spoke to Molly from the footpath outside the front gate. The son, Ralph, he never came around, but Molly said he was a lovely child, not so good when he grew up.'

'You never saw him?'

'Not me. Molly may have, but she didn't say much, although I could tell she was fond of the man inside the house. Supposedly at night, he'd come out into the kitchen, eat his meal and then retreat back to his place.'

'For a postman, you seem to know a lot about Gilbert Lawrence and his family history.'

'Just snippets over a few years. I saw him once shuffling down to the off-licence. I walked past him, said hello, but nothing.'

'Why did you talk to him?'

'Just curious. He didn't reply, didn't even look my way. What would have happened if someone got in his way? Would he have reacted?'

'Porter, at some time we'll find out the full story of Gilbert Lawrence, who killed him and why. We'll also find out if you've been lying or failing to tell us the full story. If you didn't kill him, then it would be better to be honest now. Later on, you could be charged with obstructing justice. Do you understand this?' Isaac said.

'I understand, but I'm just the postman, a bit too nosy sometimes for my own good. You'd be surprised what I've seen over the years, but Lawrence, I don't know what to say. I didn't kill him, and no doubt you've checked, but there's no criminal record against me.'

'We've checked. You're clean, but you must have seen something of the man, seen something that would help us with our enquiry.'

'Once or twice, when I was delivering letters along Lawrence's street, I'd see a man standing by the post box, looking in the direction of his house.'

'Checking the house?'

'I don't know. It only happened a few times in the weeks before his death, and it wasn't always the same man. I know what I saw, but why they were there, and what they were after, I can't tell you.'

'Would you recognise these men if you saw them again?'

'Probably, but if one of them is a murderer, I'm not too keen.'

'We'll give you protection if it's needed.'

'And when's that? When you find me dead? Whoever they were, they weren't there to make sure the old man was well and in good spirits.'

'It's more than that,' Larry said. 'The man did leave the house on an occasional basis. If they had wanted to do him harm, they could have then.'

'Anything else?' Isaac asked.

'His letterbox used to fill up occasionally, and I always pushed the letters through. I couldn't go back to the post office and say that I couldn't deliver them when there was a letterbox in the door of the house, could I?'

'You could have given them to Molly Dempster.'

'I could have if she would have accepted them, but she wouldn't.'

'Any idea why?'

'She never said. Anyway, there was this one time. It was about a year ago, and don't ask me the date, as I can't remember back that far. The letterbox was full, and I've got a letter to push through. It's thick and in a padded bag. So I give the letters a shove, and they fall out of the back of it and onto the floor inside. I kneel down to hold up the flap on the letterbox to push the letter through. Now, most letterboxes have a weak spring on them, but Lawrence's is heavy duty, and it's hard to hold open.'

'What happened?'

'I've got the flap open, and I have the letter halfway through when it was snatched from me.'

'Gilbert Lawrence?'

'It had to be.'

'Did you see him?'

'I did. He was kneeling down on his side. Our eyes made contact. Nothing was said, he grabbed the letter, the flap closed, and I grabbed my bag and beat a hasty retreat. Not before I took a second look, though.'

'Why?'

'Maybe it's too many horror movies, maybe not, but I was scared.'

'But nothing happened.'

'I know it didn't but looking back at those eyes scared me.'

'Did you see anything else?'

'He swore, but to himself, not to me. I had seen inside the house, and I saw him standing ten feet, maybe fifteen, back from the letterbox.'

'Why didn't you just put the letter through and leave?'

'Curiosity. I couldn't help myself. I kept looking, and then he disappeared. After that, I never looked again.'

'The men across the road, what about them?'

'There's not much more I can say. I'm paid to deliver the mail, not to speculate on who's watching him.'

'Molly Dempster, do you think she knows more than she's saying?'

'I would have thought so.'

***

Ralph realised that with his sister he had to play it by the book. With her, he would act honourably, but he still had the issue with Gary Frost and that little man who appeared at regular intervals. If he was to assist his sister, he needed Frost off his back. He needed to meet with the man.

Ralph had spent most of his adult life in the shadows between legal and illegal, and it wasn't the first time that someone had been after him. He'd seen the man watching him outside the restaurant where he had met Caroline, and then at the bank, and the last time in the foyer of the hotel where he was now staying.

'I'm not about to take a runner,' Ralph said as he sat down next to Ted Samson on the seat in the hotel foyer.

'I beg your pardon,' Samson said.

'Tell Frost I want to meet with him in public. I don't fancy my chances with his heavies.'

'When, where?'

'Here, two this afternoon. I could do with his help.'

With that, the little man walked out of the front door of the hotel and melded into the crowd outside. Ralph walked up to the bar and ordered a whisky. He knew he was taking a risk, but he and Caroline needed help. They needed to understand what Dundas was up to, and they needed to follow up on the trail of deception he had created.

Caroline had attended one of the meetings with Dundas; her voting rights were not needed. All Dundas and his daughter had spoken of were taxation liabilities for the current year, rental increases, and maintenance issues. It had been a smokescreen to confuse her,

Caroline knew that, with superfluous nonsense, and yet the full extent of her father's assets still eluded her.

She had signed at the end of the will reading, agreed to take no further action to contest it. It had to be Ralph who would contest the will, and he had little credibility. It was a narrow line that they walked, Caroline and him. It was all or nothing. The thought of her mother propped up in her bed still gave her occasional sleepless nights.

***

Leonard Dundas knew the truth, having spent more time with the reclusive man than anyone else, and now Ralph was threatening to cause trouble.

'Father, we cannot let this collapse. All that you have built up, gone in an instant,' Jill Dundas said.

'How can it? You know the subterfuge that we have created, the false trails, the hidden bank accounts.'

'Admittedly it will be difficult, and we are open to criminal investigation.'

'We are open to legal challenges, that is all. It will take them more than my lifetime, probably more than yours, to get to the truth, and then it will only be what we allow them to see.'

'Caroline Dickson?'

'We'll ensure she has the sweeteners that we have agreed on. She'll not want for money.'

'Ralph?'

'An idiot, dangerous though. The man's savvier than his sister. He could cause us trouble.'

'Are you suggesting…?'

'Not yet. We have enough to deal with at this time,' Leonard said. He knew that he had schooled his

103

daughter well. Gilbert Lawrence may well have made a fortune, but that did not mean that it belonged to his offspring. It was a dog-eat-dog world, and he, Leonard, had been tutored by the best, by Gilbert Lawrence. When he had been at his peak he had been unassailable, and many had fallen foul of him, forced to sell their properties below their true value.

Sometimes it had been Gilbert who had created the situation, sometimes it was the economy, but the man had profited at the expense of others, not caring as to their fate. Why should he, Leonard Dundas, a man who had put up with that dishevelled man of few words for the last thirty years, care if the man's children were deprived of their inheritance? Caroline, he knew he could deal with. Ralph, he was not so sure. He would wait and see, but not for too long.

Chapter 12

Gary Frost did not appreciate being summoned to a meeting by someone he considered of little worth. 'Lawrence, what is it?' he said disparagingly once the two men were seated in chairs close to the hotel bar.

'I believe the situation has changed, don't you?' Ralph said. 'It is no longer me that needs you, it is you that needs me.' Caroline would not approve of what he was doing, but then she was naïve in so many ways. Too many years of affluence had weakened her ability to see what they were up against.

'I don't see how,' Frost said.

'The money I owe you is unimportant,' Ralph said with bravado. It was a habitual error on his part that had got him into trouble on a few occasions. He should have remembered Spain and what had happened there. But there he had been giving the spiel about how investing in Spain was low-risk, an easy way to secure a financial nest egg at a discount price, not knowing that the couple attentively listening to his advice were English civil servants, and not only that, from the inland revenue. Bob and Deidre Marshall, a couple in their forties, had considered buying a small house in Spain, not far from Barcelona. Deidre had the money from a favourite aunt who had just died, and they had researched the subject thoroughly. They understood the legal aspects of a foreign purchase, the taxation implications, and above all, the real cost, not what the man with the smooth tongue was telling them.

It was they who had reported Ralph and his partner to the English authorities, who then passed on the information to their Spanish counterparts. The end result was that Ralph and his partner had been arrested and flung into a damp cell where the mosquitoes kept them awake at night, as well as the cockroaches that scurried over them once the light went off.

'It's still my money that I want from you, plus the interest,' Frost said. He did not appreciate or trust people who were overly confident. They were the most likely to let him down. 'I've given you time on account of who your father was.'

'And what you could hope to gain from it,' Ralph said.

'I know Dundas has got you and your sister tied up. The man's smart, smarter than the two of you.'

'That's why I've summoned you here.'

'*Summoned.* I suggest you be very careful in how you talk to me. Your position is still tenuous.'

'Okay, I'll concede that you've come to see me at my request,' Ralph said. 'The problem is that Dundas had somehow managed to obtain certification that my father was sane.'

'Your mother upstairs propped up in the bed, is that it?'

'Not the act of a rational man, and then he signed over control of his fortune to Leonard Dundas.'

'How much do you know of your father's holdings?'

'Not enough.'

'And your sister?'

'She will not play her hand at this time. I intend to contest the will, but Dundas has all the information, not me or my sister. We need to know more.'

'What do you want me to do?'

'Five per cent of whatever you find over and above what we have already. Remember that not all can be liquidated quickly.'

'Do you intend to liquidate?'

'I want money, not property. If I have enough, then I'll be overseas and enjoying life.'

'Hustling?'

'Not for me. I'll be an upright citizen, may even settle down.'

Frost knew the money that he was owed was inconsequential compared to what was on offer. 'What do you want from me?' he said.

'Call off your dwarf, and then help me to chase what's out there.'

'It's a deal.'

'And cancel the money I owe you.'

'It's a lot of money.'

'I'm offering you a fortune.'

'Or nothing?'

'As you said. It's a risk on your part, on mine.'

'Where's the risk to you?' Frost said.

'I don't trust you, Frost. You're a man who succeeds through thuggery and intimidation. You could still have me kneecapped or killed.'

'There's no risk from me. You're too valuable now. Keeping you alive is my only concern.'

Ralph ordered a bottle of champagne to celebrate. For the time being, he and Gary Frost were united. But behind the smiles and the polite conversation both men knew that the other was treacherous, and neither would relax until their business arrangement had come to a conclusion.

***

Caroline Lawrence attended the next meeting at Dundas's office. It was clear that it was to be a repeat of the previous one: the minutes read, an update from Jill Dundas on profit and loss, tax liability, the year ahead. Caroline could see that she needed Ralph in the meetings.

Caroline listened as Jill Dundas droned on about provisions for the next year's projected downturn in rentals, and the possible selling of five per cent of the real estate, a shopping centre not far from London, where the vacancy rate was higher than the national average and only likely to get worse.

'How much?' Caroline asked. It was the first item in the otherwise dull meeting that interested her.

'Forty million pounds, if we act now. If, as we suspect, the major tenant, a supermarket, pulls out, the value could go down five million.'

'Won't any purchaser know that?'

'Not yet. The supermarket chain will not reveal what their long-term plans are.'

'But you know?'

'We pay to know.'

'Someone on the inside?'

'Someone who will keep it under wraps for the time being,' Jill said.

'How much will that cost?'

'A lot less than the five million drop in value if we don't act now.'

'And the proceeds?'

'After costs, twenty per cent to you.'

'And the eighty per cent?' Caroline asked. She had to admit that close to five million pounds excited her.

'That will be invested, probably into another property, and then there are our costs.'

'How much to you?'

'It will be documented. After costs of sale, then approximately ten per cent to our account.'

'The bribe?'

'That will not be recorded.'

'Illegal?'

'Debatable, but Caroline, do you care? We are offering you a lot a money.'

'But when and how often?'

'The sale will take some time, maybe four to five months. After that, we will make a payment to you.'

'And after this, what then?'

'Your father's instructions were clear, no more than five per cent divesting of assets in any two-year period,' Jill said.

'But how can that be valid? He's dead, and I am his daughter. Surely that decision belongs with me.'

'Not according to your father's instructions,' Leonard said. 'He named me as the executor of his will and his legacy, and I, as his friend, will uphold what he has requested.'

'Even if it's not legally binding?'

'Any attempt to interfere will result in your immediate exclusion from this meeting and any subsequent ones.'

'Are you taking over from my father,' Caroline said.

'The empire that he created will continue, and you, Gilbert's daughter, will be provided for, but let us be clear here and now: it will be me and my daughter and this company that make the decisions.'

'Is this legal?' Caroline said meekly.

109

'It is. I've spent half my life with your father. I know what he wanted, what I believe is correct. There is no further discussion. You, Caroline, in accordance with your father's wishes, are welcome at these meetings. You will receive substantial sums of money for your compliance, but any attempt to take over from me and my daughter will result in your non-attendance, and no information as to what we are doing,' Dundas said.

'Which means you will make the decisions. It is for me to rubber stamp them.'

'Stamp or otherwise, it makes little difference to us.'

'You certainly screwed my father, and you say he was sane.'

'He was, ask the experts. Let me know what your decision is. Either you are with us, or you are not, but I have had a long time to ensure that the Dundas family is in control. You may regard this as a hostile takeover if you like, but remember, the law is on my side, not yours.'

Caroline looked over at Jill Dundas, could see the smug look on her face. Now, Caroline knew the truth. For all those years, as her father had slowly declined, her mother propped up in her bed upstairs, Leonard Dundas had been subtly engineering his control of the empire her father had set up. She could not speak, other than to weakly nod her head.

Chapter 13

Michael Lawrence, now under the tutelage of Giles Helmsley, the eccentric leader of the Anarchist Revolutionaries of England, was, for once, not drunk or drugged. He was coherent and feeling as sick as a dog.

He was in Helmsley's flat, not the dosshouse which was more in keeping with the disreputable state of the grandson of the property mogul: his lank hair, the tattoos, the smell of alcohol, and the years of living rough.

'Michael, it's our chance to strike a blow for the cause,' Helmsley said. If the young man had been awake and aware, he would have noticed the insincerity in the tone of his leader's voice, the man almost choking as he spoke what he did not believe.

'Go away, I'm ill. I need a fix,' Michael said as he retched, his stomach incapable of emitting any more.

'You need to stand up and be counted. It is time for us to strike at the system.'

Michael Lawrence moved away from the chair where he had been sitting and leant over the kitchen sink. His head throbbed, his body shook, and he was shivering, even though the flat was warm. Helmsley knew he needed Michael functional, although he was not sure how he could use him, or how long it would take. He did not relish the man occupying the bed in the second bedroom, but for the cause, his cause, he would suffer.

'I need a fix,' the young man said yet again. Helmsley knew he had a poor specimen of manhood, but he had no option but to use him.

Within his group of degenerates, one or two were committed to the cause, the others were only interested in banging whatever drum it was that gave them what they wanted, which in the case of Michael Lawrence was a ready supply of heroin and alcohol, coupled with the occasional woman. And now Helmsley could see the way to move his cause forward, while at the same time embellishing his bank account.

Luckily for him, he knew, he had within their midst the grandson of a wealthy and dead man, a grandson who must surely be entitled to some money. Not that the complaining youth cared, but Helmsley was a man of strong personal convictions, a man who had dedicated his life to the less fortunate and found most of them lacking in the moral fibre and tenacity that he possessed.

'I need you to stand up and claim your inheritance,' Helmsley said. He thrust Lawrence under a hot shower and liberally applied the soap to him. It was not the first time that the leader of the Anarchist Revolutionaries of England had been excited by the sight of a naked man, but now was not the time and the place.

Once Michael was out of the shower and dry, Helmsley removed his earrings and studs. Not much could be done with the tattoos, only a long-sleeved shirt to cover them the best he could. Once he looked more normal, Helmsley took him to a hairdresser to get his hair cut into a more conventional style.

Two days later, a man entered the office of Leonard Dundas and his daughter. It was Jill, the daughter, who invited him into her office after he had said who he was.

'I believe that my grandfather has died,' Michael Lawrence said.

'You were mentioned in his will, but how did you know?' Jill said. She looked at the man in front of her. If this was the Michael Lawrence that they had been told about, then either the information had been wrong, or the man had changed.

'I believe there are conditions placed on me.' He was dressed in a red-striped shirt, a pair of blue trousers, and a navy jacket. He did not like the look, but Helmsley had explained it all to him carefully.

'Play your part, help the cause,' Helmsley's repetitive chant over the last few days. He, Michael Lawrence, knew what was required of him, and if it was dressing in clothes that he did not like, pretending to be one of those he despised, then that was what he would do.

'How do you know about the conditions?'

'I was told. It doesn't matter, does it?' It did to Jill Dundas, but she chose not to comment.

'Are you still on drugs?'

'I'm clean, although I need help.'

'One of the conditions is that you will check into a drug rehabilitation centre. Is that acceptable?'

'Yes.'

'Today?'

'I'll need money for expenses.'

'At the centre, you will need nothing, but I will authorise payment of five thousand pounds to your bank account.'

'Thank you.'

'It is not for drugs.'

'I will adhere to the conditions,' Michael said, his stomach cramping.

Michael Lawrence had prior to meeting with Jill Dundas, and with Helmsley's prompting, contacted his aunt, Caroline, who had told him what was required. She had then phoned Ralph to update him. 'It's playing into our hands,' Caroline had said, although she was not sure if it was or how.

Ralph was suspicious of his son's resurrection, not having had any contact with him for several years, and the last time they had met, he had deemed his son a hopeless case. But according to his sister, who had met him, her nephew looked presentable, although pale and definitely undernourished.

Jill Dundas booked the young man into the Waverley Hills Centre, a stately home on the outskirts of London, in an area complete with rolling hills and fresh air. Michael, driven down by Caroline, looked at the place as they drove through the main gates and up the sweeping driveway. He did not look forward to it, having attempted to get off the drugs a few years earlier. But that had been a detox centre alongside a charitable institution in one of the rougher parts of London. That hadn't worked; he wasn't sure if this would, but he had Caroline in one ear, Helmsley in the other, both offering encouragement, although neither had met and were unlikely to.

'Good to see you, Mr Lawrence,' Ian Grantly, the medical director at the drug rehabilitation centre, said. The sign outside made no mention of its function, or that it catered to the rich and famous. Caroline saw one of her favourite singers as she walked through the building with Michael and Grantly. At another time and place, she would have felt inclined to stop and talk to him, but as Grantly had said, 'We're all equal here.'

'Leave me, Caroline,' Michael said. 'I'll play the game.'

'It's up to you,' Caroline said. She had to admit that after so many years of not seeing her nephew, she had been surprised by his better than expected appearance. He was also polite, and he had inherited the charm that his father had in abundance.

'Once an addict, always an addict,' Grantly said as he escorted Caroline off the premises. 'Visiting hours, Monday and Wednesday, 2 p.m.'

'Can you get him off the drugs?'

'We can control him in here, but outside, that's when the problems start. He looks as though he's had it rough.'

'There's not been a lot of guidance from his father, and as for his mother...'

'Long gone?'

'The mother, no idea where she is. His father is here, although he's been absent for more years than I can remember.'

'That's the problem. Michael needs a support mechanism.'

'I'll try, but I'm not going to be a nursemaid.'

'I'm informed that all costs will be borne by his grandfather's estate.'

'They will, although you'll be submitting them to a Leonard Dundas. He's as careful with money as my father was. I'd suggest that you don't commit to any treatment out of the ordinary unless you've run it past Dundas.'

'I read about your father,' Grantly said.

'No doubt you formed your own opinion.'

'Your mother, that's what I assume you're referring to. Hardly the actions of a rational man, but I suppose you don't need me to tell you that.'

'I don't. Ralph, my brother, Michael's father, is also not always easy to understand.'

'It doesn't make it easier when there's eccentricity in the family.'

'But you'll try. I need Michael on my side,' Caroline said.

'And his father?'

'If you have a centre for stupidity, he could do with a few weeks there.'

'Bad decisions?'

'In the past. I just hope he's wiser now.'

'Do you think he is?'

'No.'

***

For once, Ralph was welcomed into Caroline and Desmond Dickson's house, but not because the two men liked each other. On the contrary, Ralph regarded Desmond as a pompous snob; Desmond considered his brother-in-law worthless.

'The situation's changed,' Caroline said. She was holding a glass of red wine and leaning back on the dining room chair. She had to admit that she was slightly tipsy.

'Not to me, it hasn't,' Ralph said. He had drunk as much as his sister, but he was a regular drinker, Caroline was not. 'Dundas is still in control.'

'But your son is attempting to reform.'

'He's a weak man, a major disappointment.'

'The pot calling the kettle black,' Desmond said in a moment of derision. For the last few hours he had been civil to Ralph, but now, when all three were winding down after a meal prepared by Caroline and three bottles of the best wine from the house's cellar, the reluctance to speak their minds had dissipated.

'Desmond, you may be married to my sister, but it doesn't stop you being a pain in the rear end.'

'Please,' Caroline interceded, not very successfully as the effects of the alcohol were impairing her usually coherent speech. 'We need to work together. The enemy is Leonard and Jill Dundas, not each other.'

'Caroline is right,' Desmond conceded. 'I spoke in error. Ralph, please accept my apologies.'

'There is no more to say. My son will assist or he won't. It doesn't stop the issue with Dundas and his scheming daughter, and what they have control of. Caroline, you've attended their meetings. Are you able to update us with any more than what you have already told us?'

'Not really. We can assume there are more properties than we know of, more bank accounts, but unless Dundas tells us, we're blind.'

The three of them moved to another room. Caroline prepared coffee, black for everyone, and she made it strong.

'I have a contact. I don't trust him,' Ralph said.

'A criminal?' Desmond said. He didn't like where the conversation was heading. He did not need to walk on the dark side. He had a successful business, upstanding members of society as his customers. He had met the occasional villain, realised to what lengths they would go to maintain their importance or to achieve their aim.

'We need to hack Dundas's computers, check out the files in his office.'

'We need someone on the inside, not a crook,' Caroline said.

'Anyone in mind?' Ralph said. He was about to suggest bringing in Gary Frost, but he knew the man could not be trusted.

'Someone in Dundas's office must be willing to help if we pay enough.'

'That's the easiest way to get yourself evicted from the meetings.'

'Your contact?' Caroline said. She wanted the money from the sale of the shopping centre, but that was months away, even more time for the Dundases to put additional blockers in place.

'What do we know?' Desmond said.

'We know of three bank accounts in the UK, two overseas.'

'Passwords?'

'Not to any of them.'

'And how much in total?'

'Seven million pounds approximately.'

'So where is the rest? There must be more cash,' Ralph said. He couldn't see how they could progress further by talking about it. There was a time to bring in help, and that time was now.

The three studied the figures that had been presented to Caroline by Leonard Dundas. According to what they had in front of them, there were twenty-five million pounds deposited in various bank accounts, the locations not specified, as well as a total of one hundred and eighty-three properties, the majority in the UK, others around the world. Nobody believed that what they were being shown was the true situation, purely what had been prepared for them to see, and an independent audit of Gilbert Lawrence's assets would not reveal much more, cleverly concealed as they would be.

'I don't trust my person,' Ralph said.

'Then we need someone in Dundas's office,' Desmond said. For once he found his brother-in-law making sense. 'Your son, Michael?' he said.

'I've not seen him yet. Caroline, what did you reckon?'

'It may be time for you to reacquaint yourself with him. His return may be suspicious.'

'What do you mean?'

'He was, according to what I've gleaned from the police, involved with anarchists.'

'Do we have them in this country?'

'Apparently we do. They call themselves the Anarchist Revolutionaries of England. It's run by Giles Helmsley, a disgraced academic.'

'Him?' Ralph said.

'Do you know him?'

'We were at school together. Back then he wasn't an anarchist, just odd.'

'What do you mean?'

'He always saw himself as superior. Academically brilliant, always on about the ruling classes.'

'But you went to an elitist school, even members of the aristocracy in your year.'

'But Helmsley was different. He was working class, won himself a scholarship. Supposedly an attempt by the school to make itself out to be egalitarian.'

'Was it?'

'Not at all, but I suppose there were brownie points to be gained for those in charge. Anyway, Helmsley was there and he was keen, keener than any of us. He always sat up the front of the class, looking for an opportunity to show us how smart he was.'

'Was he?'

'He was. We were at the back of the class, only interested in playing up, getting a few drinks in, making plans to meet up with the local girls.'

'Helmsley?'

'Not him. We always thought he was gay, not that there was any proof, but it was unnatural. Teenage males are hot for anything in a skirt, but Helmsley, he'd be there, his face in a book.'

'You've not changed,' Desmond said.

'Thankfully, I haven't,' Ralph said. 'Anyway, Michael. What's he up to?'

'Are you suspicious?'

'Of Michael? Like father, like son. If he's willing to sort himself out, it can only be with someone at his back. I was always weak if temptation was there, but Michael, he was worse. If there was alcohol, he'd down the lot, and then he was into drugs, running with the crowd. Quite frankly, I assumed he'd OD at some stage.'

'It didn't concern you?' Caroline said.

'It did, but he's an adult, and even if I was more responsible, I couldn't take him on. I have enough trouble looking after myself.'

'And his mother?'

'The last I heard, she was swanning around the Caribbean. A beautiful woman in her day, probably still is, but she was never the maternal type.'

'Not much of an upbringing for your son,' Caroline said.

'No worse than ours. The first thing that our parents did was to ship us off to boarding school, come home at long weekends, holidays, and even then, we were soon sent off on an activity somewhere.'

'That was our mother and father, devoted to each other.'

'Not normal, though.'

'We survived.'

'Who knows if what they did was right or wrong. And besides, it's Michael that we're talking about. The man is sorting himself out, a weak and feeble person susceptible to drugs. The condition of our father's will was that he had to stay clean for a year, get himself a job. I can't see him doing that.'

'What if he's cleaned up? What are the chances of getting him into Dundas's office? Could we trust him? Would Dundas let him in, give him a job?'

'If I agree to Dundas's conditions, he might,' Caroline said.

'What conditions?'

'If I agree to rubber stamp everything that charlatan and his daughter do, then maybe they'll agree.'

'Try it on,' Desmond said, 'and Ralph, go and see your son, make your peace.'

'And Helmsley?' Ralph said.

'Let's see what he does. If he becomes a nuisance, we'll need to neutralise him.'

Chapter 14

'No, we never met Mr Lawrence,' Kingsley Wilde, the senior psychoanalyst, said. He was broad-shouldered, with grey hair and a beard trimmed short.

Isaac and Larry were in the offices of Wyvern Psychiatrists, one of the organisations that had declared Gilbert Lawrence sane and able to sign his will.

'If you never met the man, how can you declare him to be of sound mind?' Isaac asked.

'It was an unusual request,' Wilde said, as he sat upright, looking at the two police officers with a keen eye.

'We're not here for evaluation,' Larry said. He found the man unnerving.

'Apologies. I'm not conducting an analysis of you. No doubt you're both subjected to vigorous checks of your physical and mental status by the police doctor.'

'We are,' Isaac said. 'We're concerned that for the last twelve years you have given Gilbert Lawrence a clean bill of health, when the man lived an unusual life and, as we now know, his dead wife was upstairs in the house.'

'How a person lives does not decree whether he or she is mentally impaired. We had realised that he was eccentric, but our tests are not there to deal with what we would believe to be unusual. Our requirement was to ascertain whether the man was capable of signing his last will and testament, that is all.'

'Are you saying that living in that house as a recluse does not indicate a person with severe mental issues?' Isaac said, not sure if Wilde was on the defensive and trying to justify his position or whether he genuinely believed what he was saying.

'We conducted standard tests in writing and via phone.'

'No video?' Larry said.

'At the request of his solicitor, it was only audio.'

'And how did the man sound?'

'He sounded like a man of advanced years. He was coherent if a little slow in his responses. Apart from that, he was found to be in control of his faculties. And let me make this clear. If the man's last will and testament is to be contested, it is up to those contesting it to prove that he did not have the required mental capacity or did not properly understand and approve the content of the will.'

'Will you stand up in court and defend your position?' Isaac said.

'Detective Chief Inspector Cook, we are a reputable organisation. There is no need for us to defend what we have stated. The standard tests were conducted, the results were appropriate. As far as we are concerned, the man was sane.'

'Even with his wife upstairs in her bed for thirty years.'

'Even then, although we did not know of that. A murderer, a rapist, those who commit outrageous and disturbing abuses against other people or commit terrorist acts could all be sane. It may be that others will say they are not, but the tests are specific in so far as Mr Lawrence was concerned. His wife in her bed will no doubt sway the general public, but in law it will have little bearing. If others wish to dispute the will the man signed, then they can, but the law is not on their side in this matter. I realise that is not what people would expect, but the onus of proving mental incapacity is on those disputing.'

Wilde, no doubt, had a list of clients impressed by the letters after his name. To be associated with a disputed will, with him having to argue in a court of law that a man who he had declared sane had in fact been living with the skeletal remains of his wife, was not going to be well regarded in the media.

Isaac could only imagine the headlines in the press: 'Billionaire sane even though his dead wife was propped up in their bed,' says a prominent psychoanalyst. Other media outlets might not be so kind, running quizzes on how to determine your sanity: 'Do you have your dead wife upstairs? If you do, then you're sane'; 'If she's in the kitchen making you tea, then suspect borderline mad'. Facebook could well have a field day, with the amateur pundits providing comedy.

'Mr Wilde,' Larry said, 'are you seriously expecting us or anybody else to believe that your tests, as detailed as they may have been and even if they were in line with agreed procedures, were not impacted by his dead wife being upstairs? And before you answer, remember that not only did he put her in the bed, he had previously buried her for some months and stripped her carcass, cutting chunks off her body, before putting her in with flesh-eating beetles. Can we be expected to believe that the man was sane, can any court of law, can you?'

'I hold by what I said,' Wilde said. He sat down, a dejected look on his face. 'I know what you're saying. There are some who still regard what we do as charlatanism, an opportunity for the criminally insane to get off serving a sentence in a normal prison, to be confined to a mental institution with three meals a day and daytime television, even after they've murdered or committed other ghastly crimes.'

'We intend to contact two other psychoanalysts,' Isaac said. 'One in America, the other in Australia. Will they answer the same as you?'

'They will.'

'Any gain to yourself?' Larry said.

'We were paid for our services, that is all.'

'A lot of money?'

'Yes, but that's to be expected. Any legal challenges to the man's inheritance were expected to be rigorous. Anything other than total diligence on our part would have left us open.'

'And Leonard Dundas?' Isaac said.

'I have no idea what Dundas's arrangements were. All I know is that Gilbert Lawrence understood what he was signing and that he had the mental faculties to do so. Regardless of how your investigations turn out, we acted correctly.'

'And if he murdered his wife?'

'Did he?'

'We have no proof, but if he did?'

'The tests were conducted according to accepted criteria.'

***

A father and son meeting after so many years should under normal circumstances be a cause for celebration, Ralph Lawrence realised, although he could not see it that way. He had never been paternal, no more than the mother of the boy had been maternal. It had always been agreed between Ralph and the then Mrs Lawrence that no child should result from their union. However, when

Ralph had been flush with money, and the alcohol had flowed, as well as ganja, in Negril, Jamaica, the one-time hippy resort that had become the playground of the rich and famous, Yolanda had become pregnant. Neither she nor Ralph had been excited at the time, each blaming the other, but nine months later the boy had been born on a rainy day in London.

A cause of celebration it should have been, but Ralph had taken one look and decided fatherhood wasn't for him. His wife had taken a look as well and felt maternal love for what she had produced. For the sake of the child, active and healthy with a fine pair of lungs as he went through teething, the reluctant parents had tried their best, even ensuring that their son was well looked after. By the time of his fifth birthday, the young Michael was sent off to school. With him out of the way for most of the day, Ralph reverted to type and started to stay out longer, Yolanda also finding herself another lover.

Ralph had known that his wife was easy, the reason he had been attracted to her in the first place. He had never wanted the perennial wallflower, the stay-at-home wife, the meal on the table at dinnertime sort of woman. He had wanted someone wild and free, the same as him.

Both Ralph and Yolanda looked across the table one night, as the young Michael sat in his chair eating his meal.

'We're not cut out for this,' Ralph said. It was the first time in several months that he had said something that his wife could agree with, the arguments, the separate beds, having become the norm.

'He's still our son,' Yolanda said.

'What do you suggest?'

'When he reaches seven we can send him to a boarding school. In his holidays, he can come and stay with either of us.'

And that was that, so much so that in the years from his seventh birthday up until he was eighteen, father and son had not seen each other more than a handful of times. And even then it had always been for short periods, and neither felt comfortable in each other's presence. Not that Yolanda, the mother, had been any better: always off here and there with one wealthy lover or another. Very soon the periods away from boarding school became a succession of brief contacts for the young Lawrence with his parents, intersected with activities such as hiking in Scotland or learning to surf in Hawaii, or whatever else the wealthy did with their children until they grew up.

The drugs came about after a weekend with the son of a banker at his house in the north of England. Two friends who had boarded together for the last five years, each looking out for the other. Michael Lawrence, extrovert and charming, his friend Billy, shy and introvert. It was the former who secured the two women, both eighteen and attractive, working class. With an empty house, the two friends seduced the women, not difficult given the amount of alcohol in the house, and it was them who introduced Michael and Billy to heroin.

Neither had been able to resist the descent into hell. Billy had died at the age of twenty-three, alone and destitute, after his father, desperate to protect his reputation, had thrown him and Michael out of the house after coming home early and finding the two of them cavorting with the women in the indoor swimming pool.

And now Ralph Lawrence found himself in the same room as his son. Each looked at the other, and then out of the window at the rehabilitation centre. Outside the weather was frosty and overcast, reflective of the mood in the room.

'It has been a long time,' Ralph said.

'Time moves on,' Michael said. He stood calmly, sedated or whatever the centre did to a person; Ralph didn't know, didn't want to either. He had spent a lifetime drinking, never once succumbing to anything more harmful than cocaine, the occasional joint of marijuana, and as for injecting into a vein, that wasn't for him. He had seen it, who hadn't in the circles he had moved in, but a fear of needles and an aversion to the sight of blood had served him well.

'You're looking well,' Ralph said.

Both men struggled to come to terms with the current situation, and neither was enamoured of the other. Even when Michael had been growing up, and on the rare occasions that they had met, it had been difficult. A few hours away from the school at the weekend, a meal at a restaurant, a brief chat about school and what the other was up to, and then back to the school, both of them breathing a sigh of relief.

And now the two of them together, one older and supposedly wiser, the other in his thirties. It was the only time in nearly twenty years that both had been sober or detoxed. An uneasy stillness filled the room. Eventually, Michael took the initiative and approached his father, his right hand held out. Both men shook before Ralph put his arms around his son and embraced him. 'Sorry,' he said. 'We've both stuffed up, but now's our chance to put it right.'

The two men left the room and walked down the corridor outside. Both of them felt a little embarrassed about their momentary show of emotion. Ralph had to admit to feeling good for the embrace, Michael was not so sure. To him, this was the man who had deserted him, had thrown his mother away. Whatever Yolanda Lawrence may have been, Michael, through the years at boarding school, had maintained a vision of his mother as someone of loveliness, someone who would come and rescue him. But she had never come, and Michael could only blame the man at his side.

'It wasn't wise, you coming here,' Michael said as the two men sat down next to a coffee machine in the centre's dining room. Ralph took two coffees and gave one to his son.

'I wasn't sure if I should, but Caroline said it was important. How is the treatment?'

'The need remains.'

'Unpleasant?'

'It has been, but there is a greater cause.'

'My father's fortune,' Ralph said.

'I cannot wait a year.'

'The drugs will return?'

'I don't know. I'm not used to feeling normal. Is this what it's like?'

'If you mean boring and uneventful, then yes,' Ralph said. 'Normality is that. I miss my previous life, but then I'm older.'

'My mother?'

'We'll find her. The last I heard she was in the Caribbean, but that's a few years ago.'

'Why are you here, father? To gloat?'

Ralph shifted uncomfortably on his seat. The man he was talking to was a stranger, although the resemblance between the two men was noticeable. 'You went to Caroline and then to Dundas, why?'

'There were two police officers.'

'DCI Cook?'

'He was one of them. They told me about the one million pounds if I straightened myself out.'

'The money would not have convinced you to change.'

'It didn't, but Giles Helmsley encouraged me.'

'I know him, did you know?'

'He never mentioned it.'

'No doubt he wouldn't. I was told that he was an anarchist.'

'He is. He understands what needs to happen, and the cause needs money.'

'Giles Helmsley needs money. Is he still the same malignant worm?'

'He is a great man.'

Ralph realised that even without drugs, his son had fallen under the influence of Helmsley, a man who had few redeeming features.

'Then we must disagree as to what you want, but it is still possible for us to work together for our mutual benefit, would you agree?' Ralph said. As much as his son was alien to him, he had to admit that he liked the man, even if his attachment to Helmsley was of great concern.

'For our benefit, then yes. But you, father, must do your part. If I am to work with you and my aunt, then you must agree to mend your ways.'

'I'll not get a job in an office, but let's see. I can still sell, maybe there are opportunities for me in this country.'

'And no hustling, breaking the law. We must be beyond reproach.'

'We will be. It is strange, Michael. I almost feel excited at the prospect.'

'I do not. It will be hard for me, but with you and Giles, I will persevere. I also want to see my mother one more time.'

'Why only one?' Ralph said.

'Neither of us was put on this earth to live to a ripe old age, and neither of us has a woman who is devoted to us, we to them.'

Ralph said nothing, only thought to himself that Yolanda, wherever she was and whoever she was with, would look good dead and in bed. His son had reopened wounds that had been closed for too long.

Chapter 15

The atmosphere in Homicide was tense. It had been six weeks, and not one person had been put forward as the possible murderer of Gilbert Lawrence. The question of Dorothy Lawrence was still unresolved, and her remains had not been released for burial.

'Update,' Isaac Cook said. His mood had worsened in the last week, understandable given the current situation. In the past, the DCI's temperament had remained constant even when the pressure was on, but now he could see unresolved questions begging for an answer.

Larry Hill was standing, his usual pose, Bridget grasped a file of papers in her hand, and Wendy Gladstone nursed her left leg, not wanting to show that her arthritis was giving her trouble, not fully conscious that rubbing the sore area only made her pain more noticeable to the others.

'Ralph Lawrence is visible,' Wendy said.

'Doing what?' Larry asked.

'He's moved out of the hotel and into a small flat in Bayswater.'

'Not his style, is it?'

'Not at all, but the man's inheritance is conditional on him and his son sorting themselves out.'

'That was for one year,' Isaac said. 'Neither of them is going to last that long. The son's a hopeless junkie.'

'He's still in rehabilitation and doing well by all accounts,' Bridget said.

'How do you know?'

'I phoned them up.'

'They may have just given you the standard response,' Larry said.

'They may have, but you can check, can't you?'

'We can.'

Wendy was unsure what to do. In the past, she would have been involved looking for someone who was missing, but now all the main players were visible. Leonard Dundas and his daughter were most days at their office, Caroline Dickson and her husband, Desmond, were to be found at Desmond's place of business or at home, and Ralph Lawrence was either at his flat or out at the son's rehabilitation centre. And Molly Dempster could be found at her small house most days of the week.

'Bridget, the papers you're holding?' Isaac said.

'I've checked with the psychoanalysts in Australia and America. They've applied similar tests to Kingsley Wilde, and I've checked on the internet to see if there have been similar cases to this that would set a precedent.'

'Have there been any?'

'Not with a dead wife upstairs. Disputed wills can take years to resolve and a great deal of money. There was one case in the United States where so much money was spent to secure the inheritance that the legal costs were more than the money the complainant ultimately received.'

'Has a case been registered yet by any of Lawrence's family?' Isaac said.

'Not yet. They have twelve years to dispute the will, indefinite if fraud is proven.'

'Ralph Lawrence has to stay out of trouble for a year, the same as the son. Neither of them is capable. Is Giles Helmsley still around?'

'He's visited Michael on a couple of occasions. On the third, he was ejected after making a scene about his right to see his friend whenever he wanted without visiting hours.'

'Quoting the anarchist bible?'

'According to the person I spoke to,' Bridget said, 'he made a fool of himself, spoke about the upcoming revolution when he and his people would take over, and he would remember those who had removed him from the building.'

'If he took Wilde's tests, what do you reckon?' Isaac said.

'He'd pass.'

***

Leonard Dundas, almost as old as Gilbert Lawrence, knew that his days as a solicitor were numbered, even his days on earth. Not a spiritual man, he could only reflect on what he had achieved. The son of a minor civil servant, a man who punched the time clock at work every morning, a newspaper under his arm. And then at the end of the day, he punched out and took the bus to his council house in a nondescript suburb, with a non-descript wife, only to sit by the radio of an evening smoking his pipe.

Dundas remembered it only too well: the sheer drudgery, the infinite boredom of a father who every year took his two-week holiday and booked into the same boarding house in the same seaside resort. And there would be the man with his wife and children, strolling up and down the promenade, sitting on the beach in rented deck chairs, and then, for a treat, fish and chips.

The one positive, Leonard Dundas realised as he sat at his desk, that his father had been a disciplined man, a trait inherited by the son. His father was a creature of circumstance, the son was as well, but he had had the benefit of an education and the chance to see some of the world. His mind was not closed to the opportunities, and a chance encounter with a young man about town by the name of Gilbert Lawrence had been opportune for both of them. To Dundas, Gilbert was a friend, as was his wife, but the children, Caroline and Ralph, were of little consequence.

He judged Caroline to be competent, although financially not astute. Ralph had been the bane of Gilbert's life, and neither father nor son had much in common apart from a mutual disdain for each other, not like his daughter, Jill. To Leonard, his daughter was a person of great worth, even to Gilbert who had expressed his admiration for her. And now, Leonard knew, as he sat calmly in an attempt to slow the shaking of his hand, to ease the aching in his back and the throbbing in his chest, he had complete confidence that Jill would maintain Gilbert's legacy, and his as well.

'What is it, Father?' Jill said as she came into his office. She had seen the glazed look in the man's eyes, and him sitting motionless, almost like a statue. She also knew that he had pushed himself too hard in the last month securing Gilbert Lawrence's fortune, making sure that the loose ends were tied up, and that his daughter had signing rights to all the accounts around the world, and that her name had been given on any proxies needed.

'I've done what I can,' Dundas said. And with that, his head fell forward. Ten minutes later, Leonard

Dundas was in the back of an ambulance and on the way to the hospital, a mere formality, as he had been declared dead by the medic who had arrived with the ambulance.

The first that Homicide heard was a phone call from Caroline Dickson. 'Leonard Dundas has suffered a heart attack. He's dead,' she said. It had been just five minutes after he had left for the hospital that she had arrived at his office for another of the scheduled meetings.

Bridget contacted the hospital to confirm it and then informed Pathology that they had another body to check.

***

With Leonard Dundas dead, the scheduled meeting at his office was cancelled indefinitely. Not that either the man's death or deferring the meeting concerned Caroline. To her, he had been the devil incarnate, the man who had engineered himself into her father's confidence and then stolen everything he could lay his hands on. She knew how Dundas and his daughter lived, very well in fact. A house in town, better than hers, and a place in the country.

With the senior Dundas out of the way, Caroline met with Ralph and Desmond to discuss the way forward. Desmond had to admit that his brother-in-law had changed. No more the flamboyance, the endless patter of the 'what I can do for you' and 'to our mutual benefit' jargon that he was usually only too keen to roll out.

'It's Michael,' Ralph said. 'He's getting out in a few days.'

'A problem?' Desmond said.

'You know it is. He needs somewhere to stay, and I don't think that he and I should share, do you?'

'Not here, if that's what you are suggesting.'

'We need Michael the way he is now. I went and saw him a couple of days ago. He's straightened himself out, and he's sure got my gift of the gab. He was charming one of the young nurses. I wouldn't be surprised if the two of them haven't got a thing going on when the lights are low.'

'I thought there were rules about fraternising with the patients,' Caroline said.

'It's not a hospital. More like a hotel with rules, that's all. Good luck to him if he is. She was a cracker to look at.'

'Has he said that he wants to stay with you?'

'It's either me or he'll be back with Helmsley. He was back out there again, and this time they let him in.'

'Why?'

'He played their game, apologised for his previous outburst. Even gave them some cock and bull story about him suffering from an addiction.'

'And they believed it?'

'No reason not to. The man's an oddball, and he can talk. No doubt they weren't checking too hard either. There was another celebrity checking in, one of those holier-than-thou types. Outside there were some reporters and cameras. The centre was under pressure, and Helmsley took the opportunity.'

'Any damage?'

'To the centre?'

'To your son?'

'Michael started on about the cause again. I don't know why, as he was a smart enough lad when he was young, and then there's the nurse. If he could stay on the straight and narrow, she would do him a world of good, but there you are.'

'Like father, like son,' Caroline said. 'You had it made with Ralph's mother, but you blew it.'

'There was more to it than that. You only saw one side. She used to play around, did you know?'

'So did a lot of people back then, especially the crowd you hung around with.'

'Maybe, but she left us high and dry. Michael wants to see her.'

'What have you done about it?'

'I found her. I don't know why, but I thought she may have calmed down, not that I want to see her, but I had spoken to Michael's doctor out at Waverley Hills Centre. He agreed, even spoke to her on the phone. She's arriving in the country in two days' time.'

'Where's she staying? Not with you, I hope.'

'She's booked herself into a hotel. Apparently, she's got money, although not much else. She sounded upbeat, but it was a pretence.'

'Is she pleased to be seeing her son?'

'With Yolanda, it's hard to tell. Maybe she regrets what happened.'

'And maybe she realises that you're on the cusp of a financial windfall,' Caroline said.

'Am I?'

'Dundas is dead, his daughter's in charge. We can deal with her.'

'How? She's been schooled by her father, and she's no pushover.'

'We'll find out. The next meeting, you're coming as my adviser.'

'And Michael?'

'One week at the same hotel as his mother. We have the funds to do that. After that, we'll meet with him, as well as Yolanda if necessary. Leonard Dundas's death couldn't have come at a better time.'

'We still need to know where the money and the assets are,' Ralph said.

'We can afford to give it a couple of weeks. Jill Dundas may prove to be more flexible.'

Chapter 16

Graham Picket raised his eyes from the desk and let out a deep sigh. There, standing in front of him, DCI Isaac Cook and DI Larry Hill.

'Wouldn't it have just been easier for me to send you an email with my report attached?' Picket, a humourless man of few words, said.

'Probably, but you're a busy man. Rather than waiting for the full report, we were just interested in your professional opinion,' Isaac said. Neither Picket nor Isaac had much in common. Isaac was personable, the sort of person that people opened up to; with Picket, most people turned away, and the man knew it, but he had come from a dour family, and he wasn't going to change, the reason he was a lifelong bachelor.

'Seeing that you're here. If Dorothy Lawrence had been murdered, there's no way that I can ascertain the truth. Analysis of the bones reveals nothing, other than she had broken her left arm as a child and a leg in her thirties. Approximations though, and no doubt you can check the records. But you'll not bring a case against her husband even if you wanted to. Unless you have any reason to delay, it would be possible to release what remains of her for burial.'

'Cremation? Larry said.

'I would suggest burial,' Picket said. 'That way if you need to exhume her remains, they'll still be there. Gives me the creeps thinking about her in that house.'

'Hold off for now with Dorothy Lawrence. What about Leonard Dundas?'

'Apart from the normal ailments of a man in his late seventies, Leonard Dundas was in good health. He suffered a heart attack, nothing more. I'll send you a report, more technical, but his death is not suspicious.'

'His body can be released?' Isaac said.

'I'll sign a death certificate and release the body to his family if that is what you want.'

***

It was clear that Leonard Dundas's death was going to have repercussions. As had been suspected by Homicide and the Lawrence family, the man had been calling the shots for a long time.

Isaac and Larry visited Dundas's house, found the man's daughter dressed in black. 'Sorry about your loss,' Isaac said.

'He was a great man, always cared for his family,' Jill Dundas said. It was the first time for the two police officers in the house, and it was, as expected, impressive.

The woman was on her own in the house, save for a cat asleep in one corner of the room.

'You live here on your own?' Isaac said.

'With my father. I'm not married, but you know that already.'

'Your career took precedence?'

'I was married once, but it didn't work out. He wanted children, I didn't. Nothing sinister, and we keep in contact, the occasional weekend away together.'

'It's unusual.'

'Not to us, it isn't. He's still single, so am I. We should never have married, stayed as lovers.'

'And his wanting children?'

'He had them with another woman, but it was me he wanted, not her. She was purely the vessel.'

'It sounds cold-hearted.'

'I suppose you harbour illusions of romantic love, happy families, the children with their friends, birthday parties. None of that drives me, apart from the romantic love, and I have that from Carl.'

'Do you have someone coming over to be with you?' Isaac said. He had met the woman on a couple of occasions, but this time she seemed hard, as if she was pretending to be strong and resilient when she wasn't. He wasn't sure what to make of her, but then he had never been sure of her father.

'My father knew his time was up. He had completed what needed to be done, and we had spoken about his death. It is not a time for overt displays of sadness or joy, just time to reflect on his passing, and what he and Gilbert Lawrence had achieved.'

'Gilbert and your father?'

'Yes. What else did you think? Gilbert was another great man, but as with Alexander the Great and Hephaestion, or as with Lennon and McCartney if you want a more contemporary reference, he needed someone with whom he had an infinity to implement his ideas, to deal with the legalities, the financial controls.'

'And now you have the most complete knowledge of what Gilbert and your father set up.'

'I do, and if the Lawrence family thinks I'm an easy touch, then they are very wrong. I was schooled by two great men. They taught me well and believe me when I say that I was a great student.'

'Which means you'll be walking into the lion's den the next time you meet with them.'

'With them, I'm the lion.'

'Why are you telling us this?' Larry said.

'I'm telling you because you will be talking to Caroline and Ralph Lawrence, and no doubt Michael. If the young anarchist thinks he's going to get special treatment because he's cleaned himself up and because he's a charmer, he can think again.'

'You seem to know a lot about Michael,' Isaac said.

'It pays to know who you're dealing with, their foibles, their strengths, although with Michael, he'll soon turn back to the easy road, even with Giles Helmsley in his ear.'

'You know Helmsley?'

'I know everything. Even Caroline and Ralph meeting, planning on how to take control, but it's not going to happen.'

'It's a big challenge for you. Aren't you frightened that whoever killed Gilbert Lawrence could target you.'

'Why? I have the key to the vault, no one else. Gilbert never did, but his death brings the murderer closer to me, I realise that.'

'Are you convinced that Gilbert was murdered for his money?'

'What else? And none of the Lawrence family knew of the man's will.'

'You did, so did your father.'

'Why would we kill him? We had access to every facet of the man's empire.'

'The man was getting older, possibly senile, dementia setting in. At some stage there was a risk that he wouldn't be able to pass the sanity checks, and even if he did, they don't hold much weight in law,' Isaac said.

'They've kept the family at bay, and even though Gilbert had met with no one for many years, except for my father, he was well aware that the rats were ready to pick over the bones.'

'Did you ever speak to him?'

'Yes. My father always said it was only him, but sometimes we would receive instructions, and I would speak to him, but only on the phone, never in person.'

'And what did he sound like?'

'Lucid, although a little slow, but his mind was sharp. Sometimes he'd even share a joke with me. He may have been eccentric, but he and I got on well. He once said that he wished I had been his daughter.'

'Derogatory about Caroline and Ralph?'

'Don't get the impression that we had long conversations. They were always formal, business-related, but sometimes… It was almost as if he regretted the life he led, and he would make a personal comment.'

'Such as his respect for you?'

'Yes. And one day you'll be in my office, or down at your police station, trying to get me to admit to the murder.'

'Why would we do that?'

'I'm innocent, and you would be clutching at straws. No one had any immediate gain on Gilbert's death, and there was no clear direction as to who would benefit. The only two people who knew the contents of the will were my father and me. My father wouldn't have killed him, but I could have.'

'Is this pre-emptive? Assuming that by giving us the scenario we would have come up with, it will somehow exclude you from our investigation.'

'In part. I did not kill Gilbert, I'm just letting you know. If you take me in for questioning, you will need to be sure of your facts. And now, if you don't mind, I would prefer to be on my own.'

'She would be capable of murder,' Larry said once he and Isaac had left.

'I liked her,' Isaac replied. 'The woman may be hard, but there's a vulnerability about her. She misses her father greatly, and regardless of what she says, she is a woman who has forgone a lot for her ambition. In her quiet moments she must be very sad.'

'She could still be a murderer.'

'It's possible that she is. She is, as she said, the person with the strongest motive.'

Chapter 17

Gary Frost, a man who had lent money to Ralph Lawrence when he was high-risk, did not relish taking a back seat. But that was what had happened. So much so that the man had chosen not to answer his phone calls. Ted Samson, the short man who had been tailing Lawrence, had been replaced. Now there were two, sometimes three and they were varying their schedules. Now his tails were a housewife in her forties, a retired army officer, and a schoolboy in his teens, all appreciative of the extra cash in hand.

Frost phoned his men downstairs. 'Bring Lawrence in but be careful. No witnesses, nothing suspicious, and no roughing up.'

Yolanda, the former Mrs Ralph Lawrence, sat in her hotel room; she was bored. She had been in London for two days: the first, jet-lagged, the second talking to her former husband and preparing to meet a son she had not seen for a long time. As she walked down Oxford Street, her eager eyes on every shop window, her gold-plated credit card firmly in her handbag, Gucci, of course, she had to admit to feeling slightly better, although the climate was not to her liking.

Easily solved, she thought, as she deviated from her route and entered one of the shops. Forty minutes later, a uniformed doorman opened the door as she left. She walked further on, no more feeling the cold, a fur-lined coat wrapped around her. She cared little for the man she had left behind in Antigua, but his credit card had not let her down. She knew she was callous, but if Ralph were about to secure the golden egg, to become almost as rich as Midas if he had his way, then she could see a change in her affections.

Ralph had a talent for spotting people keeping tabs on his movements, his wife did not. From across the road, at two different vantage points, two people kept watch.

It had been Frost who had seen the complication. The word was that Yolanda was no pushover. Ralph had made his money through his charm and his ability to set up plausible if ultimately worthless investment strategies. Yolanda had the looks and the ability, even in her early fifties, to seduce men, the richer, the better. The man in Antigua, pushing seventy, was barely able to keep her satisfied, but it was not what drove her. The fortune he had made in shipping or transport or something – she was never sure what, never cared either – came with a credit card, the best jewellery, and an expensive car wherever she was. In London, the car wasn't critical, although the jewellery was first-rate, and the credit card glinted each time she showed it. A jewellery shop beckoned, and she went inside. Outside were two people, neither aware of the other. Both took their phones out and made their calls.

***

While Yolanda enjoyed herself, or as much as she could, knowing that the meeting with her son was scheduled for the following day, Ralph could not say the same for himself.

As he left his flat in Bayswater a man that he knew came up to him. 'Mr Frost wants to see you,' he

147

said. He was big, at least a head and shoulders taller than Ralph.

'I said I would be in contact. Things are progressing,' Ralph said, knowing full well that his dismissal of Frost's request would have little effect.

'Mr Frost, he doesn't like to be kept waiting.' The tone was polite but menacing.

'Tomorrow.'

The firm hand on the collar, the bundling into the back seat of a BMW 7 Series was not violent, although sitting wedged between two burly men who looked like they were wrestlers at the weekend was not welcome.

'I'll have something to say about this to your boss,' Ralph said, more sheepishly than when he had been standing out on the street.

'Do what you want. We're following orders. Mr Frost, he doesn't like to be kept waiting.'

No more was said until the car pulled up outside Frost's place. This time Ralph got out of the car on his own, no hands on him, and walked to the lift. He pressed the button for the penthouse.

'Ralph, good to see you,' Frost said as the door opened on Ralph's arrival. 'It's been some time since we sat down for a chat.'

'I thought we had an arrangement.'

'And so we do.' The man was effusive and overly friendly. Ralph knew that this was when he was at his most dangerous.

The two men sat on comfortable chairs in the living room. A view of the River Thames, the skyscrapers of Canary Wharf on the other side of the river. Each man held a glass of red wine. Ralph Lawrence feigned relaxed; he was not. He knew the man to be vicious and able to impart pain through his heavies at any time.

148

Frost sat nearby, attempting to assess the man opposite. Was he a major player? Was he trustworthy? Would he ever get any of his father's money, or should he just break one of his legs now and squeeze him for whatever was owing? Or should he pressure the son, even the new-found ex-wife?

'What do you want?' Ralph said as he put his drink to one side.

'What I always want: money. And your friendship.'

'Frost, you're not the sort of man who wants or needs friends. You enjoy threatening people, gaining an advantage, and having them thrown into the back of a car and brought to you here.'

'There was no throwing, just gentle coercion. You've kept away, Ralph, not even answering my phone calls. I was worried, thought you may be ill, coming down with a cold.'

'Cut it out, Frost, and get to the point.' Ralph knew that acting firmly with the man was risky, but he had little to lose, and besides, he had leverage, money leverage. With his sister and him working together, even his brother-in-law, there was a possibility that they might bring it off. Now they only had Jill Dundas to deal with, given that her father had done them all a favour and keeled over with a heart attack.

'You're pushing your luck here, Ralph.' That was one thing about Frost's intimidating tactics, he always maintained the same calm manner of speaking. No bad language, no raising of his voice, no leaning over the hapless fool who had got into his clutches. It was more frightening than a thug looking you in the face from one foot away and shouting at you, Ralph knew that. He wanted to leave, but he couldn't.

'I still intend to pay you back. The situation's changed.'

'I know that. Dundas has died, and your wife is back in town.'

'Ex-wife. We haven't had anything to do with each other for many years.'

'She's a gold-digger from what I've been told.'

'Just you leave her alone. Our arrangement is between you and me, not Yolanda, not Michael, and definitely not my sister. Is that clear?'

'You still owe me money.'

'If I pay you now?'

'The original four hundred thousand plus interest.'

'How much?' Frost's offer seemed the preferred option to Ralph, but he wasn't sure how to get the money. Gilbert Lawrence's fortune would take years to sort out, although with the money he had been given by Caroline, plus a share of the shopping centre sale, another three to four hundred thousand, then it may be possible.

'Pay me today, and it's just over one million two hundred thousand.'

'How? That's outrageous!' Ralph said, getting up from his chair and pacing around the room. 'I can give you two hundred thousand now, more when the sale of one of the properties goes through.'

'How much and how long?'

'Four to five months, and then I can only give you another four hundred thousand.'

'What a shame,' Frost said. 'Such a pleasant meeting and you go and ruin it by giving me bad news.'

'What do you mean? You're ahead on the deal.'

'You're forgetting the interest. It's ten per cent per week.'

'I never agreed to that. That means I can never pay you.'

'Pay me now what I want, or in four months when we have another conversation, it will be at least five million, probably closer to six.'

Ralph had been feeling good that morning when he had woken. The first meeting since Dundas's death had been scheduled for the following day, and he was going along as Caroline's adviser, not that Jill Dundas would approve. She'd complain, both he and his sister knew that, but not as effectively as her father. And now, as he sat with Frost, Ralph knew that he was back where he had been before. In Spain, he had had the money, or he did until his partner upon release from prison had absconded with the lot. It was either pay Frost what he wanted now, and only Caroline could help, or he could not afford to wait for his father's fortune. He'd have to make a run for it, hope that Frost and his men could not find him, and then somehow ensure he could maintain his stake on his father's fortune. And then there was the added complication of Michael and his association with the anarchist fool Helmsley. And what about Yolanda? She still looked lovely, though mercenary, and when he had picked her up at the airport, he had recognised that she was still fond of him, and he of her. It had only been money that parted them, but now he had the chance for that money. He had known when she had come out from customs that he wanted her back in his life.

But Frost was in the way, and if Caroline wouldn't help with the money, then Yolanda wasn't possible.

Ralph knew he was compromised. He had to act quickly and decisively. He was afraid. 'One week,' he said. 'The money in full.'

Chapter 18

Michael Lawrence met up with his mother on a Tuesday in a restaurant not far from the Waverley Hills Centre. Neither was comfortable in the presence of the other.

'Mother, a long time,' Michael said.

A pregnant pause before Yolanda responded. 'You're looking well,' she said. She looked inside herself for the emotions that she knew a mother should have for her child.

'Twelve years since I've seen you.'

'A long time.'

Ralph Lawrence, who had driven Yolanda to the meeting of mother and son, watched from outside. It was not intended that he join them, as he had made his peace with his son, difficult as it had been. It was now time for the mother, but he knew it would not be easy. Yolanda had left her son in the care of others, mainly the various boarding schools he had attended, and apart from the occasional difficult weeks during holidays when it had been impossible to avoid, they had barely sat down together. But now they were two adults, the son older than the mother had been when she had abrogated her responsibilities.

Yolanda moved forward and wrapped her arms around her son. A brief embrace, followed by a longer and more sincere one, though neither felt the warmth that should exist. Ralph watched as they sat down at their table. He then returned to his car to wait and ponder his next move.

'Why did you come?' Michael said.

'Your father told me that you wanted to see me,' Yolanda replied, realising that the child she had emotionally rejected as a babe in her arms had grown into a good-looking man. She liked what she saw, unable to make the connection between mother and son. It had been a rainy day the last time they had met in a café in Hyde Park, not far from Buckingham Palace. Michael had been at his worst, his speech slurred, a new tattoo showing the redness of being freshly inked. On his arms she had noticed the needle marks, the sign of the tie-off that had been wrapped around his upper arm to make the vein more pronounced. Then she had been ashamed of him, and apart from having a cup of tea and a sandwich neither had said much to the other. Their parting had been no more than a brief embrace, as one shuffled off looking for somewhere to sleep, the other to find a taxi to take her to Heathrow and the first-class cabin on the flight to the Caribbean. She remembered that she had shed a tear in the taxi cab.

And now, here was a person to be proud of, a son to show to her friends. 'It is hard to answer. I had not heard from your father for many years. He phoned, I came,' Yolanda said, her voice choking with unexpected emotion.

'Not for my grandfather's fortune?'

'I don't need it, and that's the truth,' Yolanda said, but it meant staying with a man in Antigua who did not move her the way that he should. Ralph still did, although he was older and definitely fatter, and the innate charm he'd had when he was younger had diminished. She knew that she would choose him over her current man. Ralph had been a dreamer who was always living on the edge, one day rich, another poor, but if he could secure some of his father's fortune, then maybe…

'I sorted myself out for it,' Michael said.

'You were in a bad way the last time I saw you.'

'Once an addict, always an addict.'

'And this Giles Helmsley that your father mentioned?'

'I'm not sure now although he made sense before.'

The two, if they would admit it, would have said that they were enjoying talking to each other. Ralph Lawrence took another quick look through the window of the restaurant, anxious to ensure he wasn't seen by Michael. He returned to his car and made a phone call.

'People like Helmsley prey on the weak and vulnerable,' Yolanda said. 'Are you vulnerable?'

'If I hadn't been neglected, then maybe it would have been different.'

'Don't lay your guilt on me.'

'I'm not. Off the drugs, I realise that life is not certain. Sometimes, certain events are for the better, sometimes they aren't. If we had lived a conventional life, you and my father, as well as me, it still would have given no guarantees.'

'It wouldn't, and you've fared well, although you've made some bad decisions, so has your father.'

'Have you, mother?'

'Your father still moves me, but he was not a steady provider. He could have made something of himself, but in the end, he only managed to stay one step ahead of the law, and to bed as many women as he could.'

'Mother, you've bedded enough men from what I've heard.'

'I'm not innocent, none of us is, but I'm here in England. What are we going to do? Can you forgive? Can I love you as I should?'

'We can try,' Michael said.

Neither drank alcohol, ordering instead orange juice. Yolanda knew that she had been drinking more than she should in recent months, an attempt to compensate for the boredom of living in a hot country, and friends who judged you by the money in your bank, not your worth as a person.

'Then we need to help your father,' Yolanda said.

'If I have money, I'll weaken. You must know that?'

The two finally ordered a meal and made idle conversation. Yolanda talked about her travels, not mentioning all of the men, even the ones who had treated her badly, one who had even hit her. Michael talked about his time on the street, his attempts to sort himself out, the places he had slept, the people he had met. Even the woman he had wanted to be with, but she had overdosed on heroin one night, and he had watched her die.

It was late when they left the restaurant, Yolanda walking with her son to the centre, leaving him at the door and kissing him on the cheek, Michael responding by putting his arms around his mother and holding her close.

Outside on the road, Ralph waited. Once she was in the car, they spoke, but not for very long. Yolanda, emotionally drained, soon succumbed to sleep as Ralph drove. At the hotel, Ralph escorted her to her room. He did not return to his car that night.

***

Molly Dempster walked into Challis Street Police Station. She was well dressed and had applied make-up. Isaac and Larry did not recognise her at first, although Wendy did.

'Miss Dempster, what brings you here?' Wendy said.

'I've got a confession to make,' Molly replied, her voice quivering.

Wendy feared for the worst and called over Isaac. 'It's not that,' Molly said. 'Is there somewhere we can sit?'

An interview room was found along the corridor. It was not intimidating, and it was just the three of them. Isaac felt obliged to follow the correct procedure and to advise the woman that her conversation was being recorded. She acknowledged the fact.

'You spoke of a confession,' Wendy said.

'I'm embarrassed to tell you. It complicates your enquiries.'

Apart from the standard activities, the investigation into the death of Gilbert Lawrence had stalled, and it was causing problems, not only within Homicide and for Detective Chief Superintendent Goddard but with Commissioner Alwyn Davies, the head of the London Met. Neither Isaac nor Goddard had any time for Davies, with both regarding him as the worst head of that august organisation in living memory, but he couldn't be ignored.

'Take it nice and slow,' Wendy said. In another situation, she would have gone and sat with the woman, but in the interview room, she sat alongside her DCI.

The two police officers waited while the woman composed herself.

'Ralph is my son,' Molly said. Wendy almost fell off her seat, Isaac's mouth opened with a gasp.

'This comes as a great surprise,' Isaac said.

'It's something I've lived with for many years. Nobody knew except for Gilbert and Dorothy, and now they're both dead, the secret could have gone to my grave.'

'You'd better take your time,' Wendy said. She felt a flush of emotions come over her: horror, disgust, love, confusion. She didn't know which one was prevalent, although she had always regarded the housekeeper as one of life's gentle souls, a person who never sought attention or fame or wealth but completed her daily tasks and went home to watch the television or to read a book. And in one sentence, the woman had changed totally, no longer the innocent, but a woman with a history.

'I had been with Gilbert and Dorothy for a year, and Caroline was there, a lovely little girl, similar in so many ways to her father, but she had her mother's looks. I never wanted much out of life, just somewhere to live. My father had been a good man, hard-working, but with a reckless streak. That explains Ralph's impulsive behaviour. My mother was the same as me, a stay-at-home mother who always ensured we were clothed, and there was a meal on the table when my father came in. It was a good life, but when I was seventeen, they both died suddenly. My father from too many years down the coal mine, my mother from grief. I was distraught and had nowhere to go. I thought to go into service, work in a grand house somewhere, a domestic. I found an agency, and they put me in contact with Dorothy. We hit it off straight away, and I moved in above the garage. I was happy. I knew my place and they treated me well. Gilbert was always exceedingly polite to me, not abusing his position, no pushing up against me in the house, pinching my bottom. Always the perfect gentleman. I grew to love them both very much.

157

'One day, Dorothy was in the kitchen. She was sad. I went over to her, and she told me what the problem was. It seemed that Gilbert was desperate for a son, but Dorothy couldn't give him one. She had had a difficult birth with Caroline, and she was incapable of bearing another child.'

Wendy sat transfixed by the story, Isaac couldn't say a word, only to listen to Molly recount an incredible tale.

'I had never considered motherhood, not for myself. All I wanted was a quiet and simple life, but I could see the anguish in Dorothy. I offered myself.'

'Her reaction?'

'Shock, what else? To me, it seemed the ideal solution. They were my family, and I was always a practical person. I could see a way out of any dilemma.'

'She agreed?'

'Not then, but over a few months she'd occasionally raise the subject, and I would always reply in the positive. It was a great deal of trust we placed in each other, in Gilbert. Not once did the bond break between the three of us. Eventually, we all sat down and discussed the matter. It was me who convinced them that I was the best, the only opportunity for them to have a son. No guarantees you realise, as it could have been a daughter.'

'Any legal agreement between you and them?'

'I would never have accepted it. They were family. This was my gift to them.'

'You became pregnant how?' Isaac said.

'Men, they always see the difficulties,' Molly said to Wendy. 'It was a long time ago, no visits to a fertility clinic. I slept with Gilbert on three separate occasions, Dorothy and me calculating the optimum times.'

'Dorothy?'

'She wasn't there when I slept with Gilbert. She always went out those times. Anyway, the third time I'm pregnant. six months later, I left the house and checked into a place up north, Dorothy coming with me. Caroline was at a boarding school for two months, and then she spent the next holiday with Gilbert and then a cousin in Cornwall. After the birth, Dorothy and I returned with Ralph, his mother holding him close to her body.'

'Dorothy was now the mother?' Wendy said.

'Oh, yes. I was delighted in that I had given birth to Gilbert's son. You must have realised that I always loved him. Dorothy was pleased, and her husband now had a son.'

'After that day?'

'I was there as my son grew up, although he never knew, and I never spoke to Gilbert and Dorothy about the matter. Nothing changed after our return, and I loved them both all the more.'

'Did you…?'

'Never. Apart from becoming pregnant, Gilbert and I never slept together again.'

'Yet Ralph became trouble, a disappointment to his father.'

'It was my side of the family, don't you see. My father could be reckless, but I still loved Ralph regardless. He was a lovely boy, a charming man, and he has never found out the truth.'

'Why have you told us this?' Isaac said.

'I had to. My friends are dead, and I am slowing down. One day it will be my turn to pass on. I need, at least once, to hold my son and for him to recognise me for who I am. It's the foolish request of an old woman, and it might cause complications, but I had to tell you first.'

159

'Why?' Wendy said, a lump in her throat, a tear forming in her eyes.

'Someone murdered Gilbert. Your investigations need the facts, and my relationship with Gilbert and Dorothy may have some bearing on your investigation.'

'Do you think anyone else knows the truth?'

'It was a long time ago, and none of us ever spoke of the matter. It was always our secret. You must understand why I have come here today.'

'We do,' Isaac said, feeling the same emotions that Wendy did.

Chapter 19

Michael checked out of the rehabilitation centre, and after a few days at Yolanda's hotel, moved in with Ralph. It was not an ideal situation. For one thing, both men still felt uneasy in the other's presence, and also Michael proved to be untidy, open toothpaste tube in the bathroom, dirty clothes thrust into the washing machine looking for someone else to wash and dry them.

Ralph prided himself on his appearance, his clothes arranged on hangers in his wardrobe, his washing done by a lady who came in once a week. And she was now complaining, wanting more money, not to mention having to clean the sheets after Michael had brought a young woman over for the night. Although Ralph, who had been with Yolanda, a not infrequent occurrence, had to admit on his return to the flat that apart from the signs of debauchery, there were no signs of drugs and alcohol.

Yolanda still stayed in her hotel, her gold-plated credit card working fine, although regular phone calls to Antigua were a requisite, and even a long weekend back there to ensure maintenance was carried out on the benefactor. The day she left, Ralph had driven her to the airport. He had felt a pang of sorrow that she was going to give herself to someone other than him in exchange for money. Not that he hadn't been guilty in the past of such indiscretions, but with Yolanda he felt comfortable, as if somehow it was meant to be, and the years apart had been a mistake best forgotten. But then, he remembered as he bade her farewell, the two of them had been a lot younger, and the fire had burnt stronger then.

Ralph, conscious that he was in his fifties and not in peak physical condition, took to exercising, a few laps in a swimming pool each day as well as walking three times around a park across the road from the flat that he and Michael occupied. Yolanda kept fit walking around London with her credit card. Michael, sober and responsive, looked for work, one of the conditions in his grandfather's will, not that the thought inspired him. He was, he knew, an inherently lazy person, although he could see a future in sales, given that his natural charm and his looks made him likeable, but he had no track record.

'I'm in a spot of bother,' Ralph said as he sat down with Caroline at a pub not far from her house. At any other time, Ralph would have appreciated the open fire, the bonhomie of the place, the horseshoes nailed to the timber beams of the sixteenth-century former coach house. But he could see the look on his sister's face, the look that clearly said no.

'It's money, this loan shark that you got yourself involved with, isn't it,' Caroline said. She was keeping to mineral water, Ralph had a glass of red wine in his hand. Neither was smiling.

'If I don't pay him, it's a broken leg, maybe worse.'

'How much?'

'It's over one million pounds.'

'Give him what I gave you and pay the remainder when you can.'

'It's not that easy. There's the compound interest.'

'You're not going to be much use to Desmond and me, are you? If you can't keep out of trouble, how are you going to keep Michael off drugs, and is he working? I've got some sway with Jill Dundas, but you're going to destroy this, you know that?'

'I'll pay you back once the shopping centre sale goes through,' Ralph said.

'It's still not enough, is it? And loan sharks don't lend money at five per cent per annum, do they?'

'That's the problem. The deal in Spain was going well. We had the money, but my business associate took the lot.'

'I saw promise in you, I really did. Now you are back with Yolanda, and Michael is making an attempt, but yet again you're a loser.'

Ralph could see that the bond between him and his sister was not there. She had needed him, still did, but she was going to throw him to the wolves. The evening ended badly, and neither felt the need to wish the other a good night.

***

Back at the flat, Michael was occupied filling out another job application, the third in as many days. To one side of him on the sofa was Giles Helmsley. Ralph, alarmed at seeing the man on his return but remembering when they had been younger, initially felt the need to be polite, but soon realised that the eccentric former professor was not there for his son's benefit; he was there for himself.

'What are you doing here? This is my place, not yours,' Ralph said. He sensed his temperature rising, the short temper that he had possessed since he was a young boy coming to the fore. It had not been a good day. His sister had rejected him, his son too now from what he could see, and Yolanda was in Antigua sleeping with another man. And then his phone rang.

Absentmindedly, without first checking, he brought the phone to his ear. 'Ralph, I was expecting you to come and see me,' Frost said. In sheer terror, Ralph pressed the off button on his phone and lurched forward at Helmsley, grabbing him by the collar, causing a cup of coffee on the small table in the centre of the room to tip over.

'Lawrence, what do you think you're doing?' Helmsley said. He knew that if Ralph hit him, it would hurt, but it was good, better than he had hoped, the chance to begin bringing back Michael to him.

'Giles is helping me to get a job. We are not talking anarchy or politics at all. He is here as a friend,' Michael said, hoping to calm the situation.

Ralph, beside himself with anger and frustration and not sure what to do, took a seat to one side of the room. He looked across at the now-smiling face of Helmsley, wanting to punch him in the face, but realising that he was not the problem, it was his sister. She had more than enough money to pay off Frost.

'My apologies,' Ralph said. 'Helmsley, I don't trust you, you know that. I don't even like you, never have, but you have a right to my son's friendship.' He didn't know why he had said what he had. He did not believe it for one minute.

'Michael needs our help, and you need mine,' Helmsley said, going into charm mode.

Ralph left the flat and went downstairs and out onto the street. It was a bright night, and he looked up at the sky.

A car pulled up alongside him, the same BMW 7 Series that he had been in once before. Ralph reacted with alarm and attempted to move away and back to the safety of his flat. As he approached the main door to the building, an arm blocked his way. 'Mr Frost wants to see you,' its owner said.

Ralph looked around and then up at where the voice had come from. It was one of Frost's heavies. 'I have an arrangement with Mr Frost. My time's not up.'

'Mr Frost, he wants to have a little chat, remind you of the seriousness of the situation. That's what he told me, anyway.'

'Tomorrow.'

'Today. He said you needed reminding.'

Ralph could only remember the first blow that hit him in his stomach outside his block of flats. After that, a blur as he was manhandled into the back of the BMW, his head pressed firmly down into the footwell.

'Ralph, you hung up on me,' Frost said when Ralph regained consciousness.

Ralph realised that he could not move. He struggled, felt ropes binding his arms that were stretched skywards. He could see the beam above him. He felt the wetness in the crotch of his trousers.

'What is this? What have I done?'

'You've forgotten our agreement, haven't you? I've been told that you and your ex-wife are getting cosy.'

'You've been spying on me,' Ralph said. He was feeling distinctly uncomfortable, his feet barely touching the ground, his right leg cramping up, the rope biting into his wrists.

'Protecting my investment, that's all.'

Ralph wanted to tell the man he was a liar, but he knew that his situation was precarious. He was strung up as if he were a side of beef in a butcher's shop, or maybe freshly slaughtered and in an abattoir. He was confused, not sure what to do, not sure if he would leave the warehouse alive, or if he did, if he would be able to walk again.

'You've soiled yourself,' Frost said. 'We're only here for a little chat, nothing more.'

'But I'm hanging here. Let me down, please.'

'If you insist, but my men will stay nearby. If our conversation is not to my satisfaction, you know what will happen.'

'I do.' With that the rope that had been holding the frightened man was loosened, and Ralph collapsed onto the ground. Picking himself up, he sat down on a wooden chair that was to one side of him, the wetness in his trousers causing him discomfort and acute embarrassment.

'Now when will I see my money?'

'Next week, as I told you.'

'Your time is running out. And remember, the interest accumulates. Your wife is an attractive woman, so I've been told. It'd be a shame if she had an accident, wouldn't it?'

'Leave her alone. Your issue is with me.'

'That's where you're wrong, Ralph. Before, it was with you, but now you have a sister, a son, a lover. Any of them will do if you fail to pay me back. Today would be better, tomorrow at the latest. If you want another week, that's fine, just add another eighty thousand pounds to your pay-out.'

'I can't.'

'Can't or won't?'

'I can't get that sort of money. My sister won't help.'

'Then maybe we should talk to her first. I'm sure she will want to see you safe. Or what about her husband?

He's got himself a good business, lots of rich clients. How many children does she have? Two, isn't it?'

'You bastard. You would do anything to anybody for your benefit.'

'You would cheat poor gullible tourists out of their retirement funds. We are very much alike, you and me, Ralph. Neither of us has too many morals. The only difference is that I use violence as a tool.'

'And what if I don't pay?'

'You know what will happen. I'm giving you another week, interest-free.'

'Why?'

'Because I like you, or maybe you'll need that week to recover, let the others see what will happen. Maybe your wife can convince the old man in Antigua to help. Your sister, what will she do? Help you out?'

'Give me a week, and you'll have your money,' Ralph said, his body shaking from cold and fear. A rat scurried by. Over to one side, lying on the floor, his jacket and shirt.

'Boys, you know what to do,' Frost said.

The first that anybody else knew was when Homicide received a phone call from the hospital.

'It's Ralph Lawrence,' Bridget Halloran said as she walked into Isaac's office. 'He's in casualty. He's been severely beaten.'

Chapter 20

Jill Dundas smiled when she heard about Ralph Lawrence and his accident, falling off a roof and onto a concrete floor. At least that was what Ralph had said it was, his own silly damn fault for not looking where he was going.

The team at Homicide were under no illusion, even if the man in the hospital bed said otherwise. He had received a severe beating. Sure, as the doctor had said, he had a dislocated shoulder, but there was no way that the bruising on his body had been caused by anything other than a man's fists.

'It's the truth,' Ralph said, his son on one side of his bed, his sister on the other, a nurse hovering nearby checking his temperature, ensuring that he was comfortable.

'Why lie to us, Mr Lawrence?' Isaac said, even though he understood why. It wasn't the first time that a man had lain in a hospital bed, too frightened to tell the truth.

'Why protect those who did this to you? You could have been killed.'

'I wasn't, that's all. I've no more to say. Can't you accept that?'

'Leave my father alone,' Michael said. 'Can't you see he's in agony?'

'You're playing this wrong,' Larry said. He had seen the flowers arranged around the room, noticed one bunch from Jill Dundas, another from Yolanda, now on a plane back from the Caribbean, her credit card revalidated. Another bunch from a mysterious sender, just a blank card, the only words 'Get well soon' printed in bold letters on one side in red. That one needed checking out.

'Whoever did this, they'll be back,' Isaac said. 'These people are professionals. Your only protection is with us.'

Ralph stirred in his bed, attempted to sit up, grimaced in pain, and lay down again. 'It was an accident. My fault for being on that roof. It wasn't that high, maybe fifteen feet, and I thought I'd be fine.'

Caroline Dickson came close to her brother and whispered in his ear.

'What did you just say, Mrs Dickson?' Isaac said, having noticed the sister leaning in near the brother, but not able to hear what was said.

'I just gave him my love. He's my brother, I care.'

'Mrs Dickson, let me remind you. If you and your brother, even Michael here, are concealing the truth, for whatever reason, it could have serious repercussions.'

'We've broken no law,' Michael said.

'The law you can deal with. Whoever did this is not held back by rules or regulations or the law. They believe they're invincible, and they'll be back. Maybe not today or next week, not even for a few months, but mark my words – these are dangerous men who could have killed Mr Lawrence but chose not to for a reason. And we all know why, don't we?'

'Do we?' Caroline said.

'They want something. This is a warning, and none of you here is capable of standing up to whoever it is. If they can't get it through Ralph, they'll get it another way.'

***

The inevitable presence of Chief Superintendent Richard Goddard in Isaac's office, not that anyone could blame him, certainly not in Homicide. The savage beating of Gilbert Lawrence's son was a development, the first for some time.

'Are you sure he was meant to live?' Goddard asked. He was sitting across from Isaac. In one corner, a potted plant that Bridget and Wendy had given Isaac some time ago after another of his failed romances. On the wall, a picture of Isaac when he had graduated from university, his face beaming, proudly holding his certificate.

'We don't know who it was,' Isaac said. 'But we're sure he didn't fall off that roof. Why would someone risk bringing attention to themselves? It's not as if Ralph Lawrence received any money from his father. He's currently renting a two-bedroom flat, nothing special, and his son's there as well.'

'His sister did, and what about his ex-wife? Plenty of money there.'

'We're investigating all scenarios. Nothing's certain, but we believe Ralph's owing money to someone, and he's having trouble paying.'

'Evidence?'

'None, just a hunch. We've seen it before. There's no point killing the borrower. A few days in the hospital, a few broken bones, and the borrower's more compliant, may even commit a crime to pay it back.'

'Loan shark?'

'Gangsters, loan sharks, even one of the man's dubious friends. It wouldn't be the first time Ralph Lawrence has found himself in hot water. He may have meted out similar treatment to others when he had been flush with money.'

'Whatever, whoever, don't take long on this one. Questions are being asked.'

'They always are,' Isaac said. As much as Isaac respected his senior, it was as if the man was playing the same old record. There was always a budgetary issue, the key performance indicators were down, he needed the current murder solving, or there was pressure from above.

Although the pressure, as both of the men knew, was through the office of Commissioner Alwyn Davies, the head of the London Metropolitan Police, a man who did not rule by consensus and professional leadership but by adroit political manoeuvring and intimidation. Goddard and Isaac were very much in the man's line of sight, having crossed swords with Davies on more than one occasion, and the commissioner wasn't a man to forget. To both of the men, how Davies survived was of concern, but as Goddard had said before, get on and do your job, I'll deal with the commissioner.

With the superintendent out of the office, Isaac called in the team. It was still early in the morning, the best time Isaac always thought to formulate the actions for the day.

Wendy Gladstone was first in, closely followed by Bridget Halloran, the office supremo, and then Larry Hill, Isaac's detective inspector.

'Find out who gave Ralph Lawrence a good beating, is that it?' Larry said.

'Critical, but his sister knows something. We need to talk to her first.'

'Before we plan the day's activities, let's recap on yesterday. Bridget, what do you have?'

'More details from Spain as to what Lawrence was up to. The man's associate was released from prison two weeks after Ralph Lawrence returned to England. He cleared out any bank accounts and disappeared, left a string of debts behind him.'

'Debts someone wants to be paid?'

'The company had leased a couple of vehicles through a local company, and the premises they operated from were owned by a local businessman. Apart from that, and the tradesmen who fixed up the office, there doesn't appear to be anyone with any criminal connections.'

'It depends on whether Lawrence's colleague borrowed from loan sharks,' Isaac said.

'There's no way to find out, and besides, that's a Spanish problem. If Lawrence is beaten up here, and there were signs that his wrists had been bound and he was missing one shoe when found, then he almost certainly borrowed in England. Any idea how much?'

'Not yet. It's not a loan that would have been registered.'

'Any luck with bank accounts?'

'We know that the scam in Spain had almost two million pounds in a local bank. The Spanish police have supplied us some information, not all.'

'Why?'

'They're investigating a crime in their country. We're not the most important, although they've been helpful up to a point.'

'What do you mean?'

'A murder in England is not their priority. The current government is attempting to cut down on corporate crime, scamming of tourists. The normal thing that gets the country a bad reputation, keeps the tourists away, as well as the genuine investors. The police, no doubt, are feeling the heat. The only person I've been in contact with is a junior officer, good English, and she's tried her best.'

'Should we ask Chief Superintendent Goddard to speak to his counterpart in Spain?' Wendy said.

''It won't help,' Bridget said. 'You soon hit bureaucracy, and the wheels will grind slowly.'

'Bridget's right,' Isaac said. 'Any indication as to how much Ralph might have borrowed?'

'There was a cash injection into one bank account of four hundred thousand pounds. It may not be money that Lawrence borrowed, but it seems possible. The money had been transmitted by an offshore bank, and the bank's not telling whose account, but I've been on to Fraud, and they reckon it's probably an English account holder.'

'Okay, enough said. We need to find whoever gave our man Ralph a few days in the hospital. Bridget, keep checking, Wendy, you can come with me to see Caroline Dickson.'

'I'll get down on the street. Start checking out who's lending big,' Larry said.

'We're dealing with someone who's not averse to violence, and a police officer may not scare him. Easy enough to take him out, never to be found again,' Isaac said.

'I'll find out a few names first, and then we'll discuss it. After that, we can figure out what to do.'

***

Caroline Dickson agreed to an interview at her house.

'Mrs Dickson, I need to caution you,' Isaac said. 'There is vital information that you are withholding from us, we know that now.'

'I've been totally honest with you, so has my husband,' Caroline said.

'Your brother is in trouble, and you know it. He told you something in the hospital.'

'He's borrowed money he can't pay back.'

'Are you going to help?'

'I don't know. It's a lot of money, and these people can't be trusted.'

'If they can do that to him,' Isaac said, 'they are capable of more, even murder.'

'Ralph's frightened, and he told me not to tell you. It complicates matters.'

'Not for us, it doesn't. Your father's murder, could it be related?'

So far nobody in the Lawrence family knew of Molly Dempster's remarkable confession. The revelation that Ralph was her son may well have provoked an interesting reaction from Caroline, but now was not the time and place. Ralph was in the hospital not because of who his mother was, but because of his father. Isaac could see Gilbert's death as related, but it was a long shot.

'My father's death, why?' Caroline said. 'He was old, not in good health, and he would not have lived forever.'

'Five, ten years, long enough for someone to have become nervous, become desperate. Now we know your brother didn't kill him, proof from the Spanish police on that one, and we've ruled out Molly Dempster.'

'Molly's a saint, always has been. She brought us up as if we were her own children,' Caroline said, showing more affection for the woman than she did for her brother.

Wendy looked over at Isaac, saw an imperceptible shake of his head. Both the police officers knew that the woman had said something closer to the truth than she would ever know. It was clear that at some stage Ralph would have to be told. He was illegitimate, the bastard son of a wealthy man and the family housekeeper. Further scandal for a family that had had its fair share. And how would Caroline take the news? Would she distance herself from her half-brother? Neither shared an unbreakable bond; maybe when they were younger, but they had spent many years apart, and Caroline led a decent life with a man she loved, whereas Ralph had become disreputable, a disgrace to his father and to her. Caroline's children were upstanding members of society, Ralph's son was struggling to find his way, full of the weaknesses that had blighted his biological father.

'Molly had lived above the garage, and then spent the remainder of her time looking after your father, only once venturing into the main house. Doesn't that sound strange to you?' Isaac said.

'That was Molly. She was just a good person. You'll never find either Ralph or myself say a bad word against her. And as for killing our father, not possible. Even if she suspected what was upstairs, it would not have changed her. She was devoted to my parents, even loved them.'

'Explain love,' Wendy said.

'A deep friendship. Once, my mother, I was in my teens by then, told me that if something happened to her, I was to ensure that Molly was looked after.'

'What did you take that to mean?'

175

'I was in my teens, the silly teens, too much alcohol, too many late nights, and no doubt too many unsuitable men. She was trying to tell me something, but I wasn't listening that closely, trying to get out of the house. Molly came in, and that was the end of the conversation.'

'You're older now. What do you think she meant?'

'The love that Molly felt for my mother was sisterly. For my father it was romantic. We always knew, Ralph and me. Sometimes we'd tease her, not that she said or did anything, only smile. Our mother wanted Molly to be with our father if she was not there.'

'Did your mother sense an early death?'

'Sometimes she would have these episodes where she would need to be confined to the house. No doubt she would have been suicidal, into self-harming.'

'Any proof?'

'Not really. We were away a lot of the time, although Molly would have seen it. My mother was clear that she didn't want our father to be on his own, and if it wasn't her, it was to be Molly. To Ralph and me, she was a second mother, but she never interfered in the family. She'd just be there, always in the background, always trustworthy.'

'In the end, Molly wasn't with your father, was she?'

'After our mother disappeared, although we didn't know that she was dead and upstairs, our father became reclusive. He became what you know of him. The loss of our mother must have affected him greatly.'

'And Molly?'

'She was distraught, but she continued regardless. Always stoic, always a meal on the table. I never saw her cry.'

176

'Some people don't,' Isaac said. 'Sometimes they just bottle it up, keep busy, although when they're on their own, they let go. Molly could have been one of those people.'

'Probably, but she was the rock when our father went to pieces with grief.'

'And you?'

'I was at the house every day after our mother disappeared, out on searches for her. We dredged the canal, the ditches, looked in manholes, checked the train station, local buses, taxis, but nothing. The police were involved. You must have records.'

'We do, but what about Ralph?'

'He wasn't there. By then, he had gone overseas, and it was two years before he made contact again. He was in Thailand, or maybe it was Cambodia. It appears he had met someone and he was planning to stay. When I told him about his mother, he came back, not that there was any point. Our mother was gone, we even held a memorial service for her at the local church, and our father was already in seclusion. He only started going to the off-licence in the last ten years. Before that, Molly would deal with everything. A list of requisites in the kitchen of a morning and she would buy what was needed, prepare his meals, change his bed, the one that had been placed in the room off the kitchen.'

'Why did she do that for all those years?'

'That was Molly.'

'Coming back to Ralph,' Isaac said. 'What are we going to do to help him?'

'He needs to tell you the truth. The money can be dealt with, but do the people who put him in the hospital take what's given and leave well alone?'

'They probably will, but it's a different circumstance here. Your father was incredibly wealthy. A temptation to most people, not only the criminal.'

'We've had enough begging letters and emails. My family of long-lost relatives is over two hundred now. You wouldn't believe that I have family on all continents.'

'We've seen it before; lottery winners are the more susceptible. Some have even squandered their wealth on the more deserving cases,' Wendy said.

'Were they?'

'Who knows. It's not criminal to beg, not criminal to give. It wasn't a police matter, only if it was a scam.'

'We've got a big bin, that's where they all go,' Caroline said.

'It doesn't stop them knocking on your door, jumping out in front of your car, feigning an injury.'

'It's happened. Desmond's considering hiring a guard for outside the house, but for how long? Has Molly been pestered?'

'We don't think so, but we'll check. There are some questions for her.'

'Don't trouble her too much. She's just an innocent. All this is beyond her,' Caroline said.

Chapter 21

Larry worked his contacts, attempted to find out who was lending big, who was likely to use violence if anyone defaulted.

Harry Eckersley, a low-life that Larry had heard of before, operated out of a shop in Hammersmith, no more than a couple of miles from Challis Street. The shop was rundown, full of second-hand phones, laptops, and computers, assorted bric-a-brac and more than enough family mementoes, deposited there for sale or return to the owner if they came up with the ready cash. It was not the sort of place that Larry liked, and he knew that some of the merchandise wasn't legally acquired. He didn't expect a friendly welcome.

'Detective Inspector Larry Hill, Homicide, Challis Street. Are you the owner?' Larry said as he showed his warrant card, his photo and name displayed.

'No one's died in here, copper,' Eckersley replied. 'No need to kill anyone for what they leave here in exchange for some of my hard-earned.'

Insults from the general public weren't unexpected. Larry had heard it before, even in the pub he visited on a Friday night for a quiet drink of beer. The rough element that sometimes got in there knew that the police were powerless to respond to verbal threats, and after a few drinks, some had attempted to bait Larry and other police officers more than they should, usually being egged on by their drunken mates.

Larry had experienced one a couple of weeks previously. It was close to closing time, and the man who had been hurling names had come out of the pub feeling pleased with himself. He didn't see the man standing to one side out on the street, not until it was too late. He fell to the ground after one blow in the face from a clenched fist. 'Next time, it'll be your groin,' Larry said.

'That's police brutality. I could report you.'

'No witnesses,' Larry said. He knew he had been wrong to hit him, but sometimes enough was enough. The next time Larry encountered the man, he had walked over, patted him on the back and bought him a pint of beer.

'Sorry about the other week. Too much beer, not enough brains,' he said.

'Forget it. You're not the first, you won't be the last.'

'I pity the poor guy who you hit in the balls. You packed a punch.'

'Just make sure it's not you, or any of your smart friends.'

'It won't be. You've got our respect.'

Larry looked Eckersley square in the eye. 'I'm here about murder, not whether half the stuff in here is stolen. Unless you want this place turned over by the uniforms looking for stolen merchandise, I suggest you stop your insults and give me some answers.'

The miserly little man reflected on what to do. 'Okay, Inspector, what do you want?'

'It may be better if you close your door, or we can talk out the back.'

'Here's fine. It's a mess back there.' Which to Larry meant that the evidence of stolen goods hadn't been dealt with yet.

With the door at the front closed the two men sat down on a couple of chairs produced from behind the counter. 'We'd better make ourselves comfortable,' Eckersley said.

'We're looking for big lenders. I'm told that you're one.'

'I lend if the risk is acceptable. But I have a limit.'

'What is it?'

'One hundred thousand, but I'm reluctant. If they don't pay me back, I'm out of pocket, not much I can do about it either.'

'You can threaten them, give them a taste of what will happen if they don't pay you back with interest.'

'Even if I did, that doesn't mean I'll get it back, does it? And besides, that's not how I operate.' Larry knew when he had been told a lie. Eckersley was just the sort of man to send in his men if someone was giving trouble, late on his repayments, had given some dumb tale about next week and paying in full.

'Don't feed me nonsense,' Larry said. 'I'm not here for you. I'm here for someone who lent four hundred thousand, someone who's not averse to giving someone a serious beating, someone who would probably kill if the debt couldn't be recovered.'

'No profit in that, only a lot of hassle.'

'Let's assume this person can afford to carry the debt if there's no other option.'

'There are one or two, but if they find out that I've spoken to you…'

'They won't. And don't give any of that "I'm just an honest man trying to make an honest quid" nonsense. It's an insult to my intelligence.'

'You're a tough bastard, Detective Inspector Hill,' Eckersley said.

'I'm a good friend if you help me. Help me, I help you. Deal?'

'It's a deal.'

'Good. Who do you have?'

'There's one not far from here. Goes by the name of Dennis Bartholomew. Some call him Dennis the Menace, after the cartoon character in the boy's magazines back in the fifties, or maybe it was the sixties, not sure which now. Find an original, and they can be worth money.'

'Why the nickname?'

'He's not into the rough stuff. With him, you sign a contract, sign over your car, jewellery, whatever you've got of value. He'll charge high interest, not as high as some, and with him, it's a regular beating every few days until you settle. Anyway, that's when he becomes a menace.'

'It's violence, it's criminal, but our man is much more violent. Break bones, put you in the hospital violent.'

'There's one I've heard of. Low profile, rarely seen out on the street. I've heard him referred to as the lender of last resort.'

'Nowhere else, that's where you go?'

'Tough bastard. I heard of one mug who borrowed heavily from him. He took the money he had made and skipped the country, failed to pay back the loan,' Eckersley said.

'What happened?'

'Rumours, may not be true, maybe that this lender put it about to make sure anyone else who borrowed from him paid up.'

'Assume they're true. We believe this individual to be dangerous. He's already put someone in the hospital.'

'It could be him. Anyway, the story is that this fool, he came from around here, has got this great idea for an illegal gambling club, high-rollers, no limits. These clubs appear from time to time, make their money and close. The bribes are too high, the security's a nightmare, and then there are the extortion merchants. Illegal gambling doesn't always attract the best clientele. The club opens, the guy is pulling in serious money, dealing with those trying to rip him off, breaking a few arms if anyone's caught cheating. Very soon, he's got himself two million in cash sitting in a safe in his office, another one and a half shipped out of the country. The lender staked him a quarter of a million, and he wants it back along with the ten per cent per week interest.'

'Ten per cent per week?'

'That's what I said. And he's not slow to show you what will happen if you borrow, normally some hapless fool on the floor or strung up who hasn't kept up the payments.'

'How do you know this?'

'Someone who came in here, nasty divorce, cleaned him out. He wants to get back into business, the banks are not biting, telling him to go take a running jump. You know what they're like?'

Larry did, having renegotiated his mortgage to accommodate his wife's plan to buy another house. The manager had sat there, telling him what a privilege it was to be able to help one of our fine police officers, before slapping the offer down on the table. Larry had looked at the proposal, looked at his wife, looked at the bank manager. He knew that he could just about make the payments, although his wife's reaction to the disappointment if he had not signed, meted out for the next few weeks, he couldn't. Larry even managed to thank

183

the sanctimonious parasite who had just suckered him into more debt.

'I know,' Larry said.

'This man I'm telling you about. He'd been over to see this person we're talking about. He's on the other side of the Thames. The conditions were laid out. A volunteer, not that he had any choice, was on display to show what happens if you don't pay. They shot out the man's kneecap, then dumped him fifty miles away.'

'He could have told them who had shot him.'

'Not him. It's either keep quiet, or it's the other kneecap or the concrete boots. Anyway, this guy with the gambling club. He's skipped the country, not paid his staff or the lease on the premises he'd been using, not that they can do much about it. But our lender, he's got connections, and he finds out where the man's gone. Supposedly, he's swanning around Dubai, a couple of Russian tarts in the back seat of the Mercedes with him. They come up to an intersection, outside of the city, in the desert, so I've been told. A couple of motorcycles pull up alongside, passengers on the pillion seats. They level a couple of Kalashnikovs into the car, killing the man, the two whores, and the driver. After that, the man's hotel room is broken into, the safe is opened, and out pops the best part of seven hundred thousand in fresh notes, some in Euros, some in American dollars.'

'Tough justice.'

'Not to this man whose name you want. You sure you want to get mixed up with him? He'll not have any issues with a nosy policeman.'

'Your friend, the one with the divorce?'

'The deal with the lender is, if you don't take the loan, then no issues, just never tell anyone what you've witnessed. At least the man's fair. Anyway, the man with

184

the divorce comes back here. I lent him fifty thousand, not what he wanted. He's got a small shop down the far end of Portobello Road. He's making a living, and his kneecaps are safe, even found himself another woman. And he paid me back.'

'The name of the lender?'

'Gary Frost. He's got a penthouse down in Greenwich. Ask around, you'll find him. Don't blame me if you get yourself shot.'

'I won't.'

'And for the record, the merchandise in here is not stolen, not by me. It all belongs to those who are desperate. I give them money for it. It's then on sale, and either someone else buys it, or they repurchase it.'

'I'll trust you,' Larry said, not that he believed Eckersley, but the man had helped.

Chapter 22

Homicide had the name of someone with a dubious history, although with no criminal record. Of the two men who were always close to Gary Frost, one had served time for grievous bodily harm, the other was known to the local police in Greenwich as a man with a foul temper and likely to drink more than he should on a Saturday night, and then to take to brawling. The last time, according to a police sergeant that Larry had spoken to, it had taken three police officers to subdue the man. The next day, sober and in the cells at the station, he had been contrite and exceedingly agreeable. The sergeant reckoned he was the more dangerous of the two.

Gary Frost remained an enigma. He kept a low profile and was rarely seen out in public, and if he was, it was invariably in the back seat of a top of the range Mercedes.

Everyone in Homicide was focussed on the man who gave out money and violence in equal measure. The man with the busted kneecap that Eckersley had mentioned had been found. He had been doing it tough since his release from the hospital, and he limped badly, a crutch under one arm, but he was alive. Attempts to find out if others had not fared so well were proving unsuccessful. The gambling club owner who had made it out to Dubai, found himself a couple of Russian women, as well as a surfeit of bullets as he and the women had been gunned down, appeared to be just one of the colourful tales on the street, although Isaac and Larry weren't so sure it was just a story. It may not have been Dubai but somewhere less desirable, and the Russian women, attractive and readily available in the city in the desert built on money and oil and not much else, could instead have been a couple of local slappers of no great beauty and not that young either.

The limping man with the destroyed kneecap wasn't talking, nor was Ralph Lawrence, who kept to his story that he was inspecting a property he was interested in purchasing and he had slipped. Isaac and Larry had pressured the man, could see that he was nervous, wanted to speak, but wouldn't.

Outside of the building where Frost's penthouse was located, Larry stood, unsure of what to do next. It wasn't the best of days, and the wind was biting. He wasn't sure what he was trying to achieve, knowing full well that knocking on the door would not get him far, may even get him into trouble: police intimidation, upstanding citizen, no criminal convictions. That was the problem, Larry knew. The most accomplished criminals, those with the mental acumen, always ensured that someone else did the dirty work, leaving them clean.

'I need you back at the station,' Isaac said on the phone to Larry. 'Leave Frost for the moment, we've got something to deal with.'

Larry made the trip back over the Thames to Challis Street, parked his car, noticing that the weather was better there than it had been over in Greenwich where it was more exposed.

In the office, all the key people were there. 'What is it?' Larry said as he sat down.

'Ralph Lawrence is out of the hospital and back at his flat. If Frost was responsible for having the man beaten, then he's not going to give up because of us. And

Helmsley's in Michael's ear. We're expecting fireworks. In fact, we should consider creating them. We need Ralph to talk, then we can pressure Frost. He's a definite suspect, not sure how and why, but he's the sort of man that kills.'

'Molly Dempster knew more than anyone,' Wendy said. 'Does Ralph know about her?'

'Not yet. It may be time for him to find out his background. We can judge his reaction, see if it makes any difference.'

'How do you want to do this?'

'Caroline Dickson's house, make sure all the key people are there. Make it for tonight, six in the evening. Bridget, make a few phone calls, make sure Caroline and her husband are there, also Ralph and the reluctant Molly.'

'She'll not like it,' Wendy said.

'You can go and see her, tell her it's necessary if we're to solve who killed Gilbert. And besides, she said that she wanted to hug her son once and for him to recognise her as his mother. Tonight might be the night, although the reactions may be hostile.'

'What's the point of upsetting an old woman?' Bridget said.

'I can understand your sentiments, but this is a murder enquiry. We have Ralph who won't tell us who put him in the hospital, Molly who knows more than she's telling us, and Caroline who's playing a strategic game with Jill Dundas. Everyone's hiding something. We don't know what yet, but we need to move the investigation forward.'

'I'll look after Molly,' Wendy said. 'I don't like this. She's a nice woman who just wants a quiet life.'

'No doubt you're right, but she could have killed Gilbert for retribution. Even though she loved him, at least when he was younger, he had kept Dorothy, a person Molly loved as a sister, dead and in her bed for all those years. And can you imagine the kind of horrors that the man must have perpetrated on his dead wife, burying her in the cellar, stripping her flesh, feeding her to those beetles? If it were a movie, we'd all be out of our seats or out of the cinema. Larry, you and me, we've got a door to knock on.'

'Gary Frost?'

'Who else? We'll need a police car outside just in case our visit is not welcome. Is the man at home?'

'He is. I've got the local station updating me as to his movements. If we let on that we know he's lent money to Ralph, it could get nasty.'

'That's what I'm hoping for. And the kneecapped man, where is he?'

'Not far, but he'll not talk,' Larry said.

'If he doesn't, we'll let him know that we're talking to Frost, may let it slip that we've told his lender that he's been very helpful.'

'Not strictly by the book.'

'I know it, but we're only implying. We need the man to tell us the truth. Frost could be Gilbert's killer. The man's smart. He could have realised that he'd lent money to the wayward son of a real estate mogul. He may not have known it when the money was lent, but he finds out and takes a calculated risk that the death of one would lead to another gaining the wealth. We need to frighten everyone, raise the emotions, look for the reactions. Bridget, any more from Spain?'

'Nothing. The police are too busy with their own problems down there to worry about us.'

'There goes the trip to Spain to meet up with our Spanish colleagues, the chance to get a suntan,' Isaac said.

'No problems for you, sir,' Wendy said.

'I could still do with some warm weather.'

'We all could, but it's not likely to happen soon, is it?'

***

Isaac had to admit to being impressed with where Frost lived. He and Larry had called in at the local police station, met with Inspector Emily Matson.

'Frost is loan sharking,' Isaac said.

'We're aware of the man's reputation, but we've had no reason to bring him in, and besides, there's been no complaints, nothing criminal,' Matson said. Isaac judged her to be mid-thirties, maybe closer to forty, attractive in an efficient way, with her hair pulled back tight, minimal make-up, blue eyes. She was dressed in a blue suit, not regulation, but civilian. 'I'm giving evidence at 11 a.m. Fraud caught a man using false credit cards, not uncommon around here. I was the arresting officer, so I can't come with you to Frost's.'

'That's fine. We can deal with him on our own.'

'Just watch out for his men. One of them spends time here occasionally. He goes by the name of Ainsley Caxton. Tough individual. He put one of our guys in the hospital for a night after three of ours tried to take him down outside a pub one night. Apparently, a couple of drunks inside had started making fun of his name, putting on funny walks, telling him it was a little girl's name. Mind you, they weren't smiling the next day. One of them ended up concussed after Caxton rammed his head into the pub wall. The other copped a boot right where it hurts, brought tears to his eyes. From what I heard, he sings soprano now. The other tough that Frost keeps nearby is Hector O'Grady. He's not been in trouble with us, but he's a big man, bigger than Caxton.'

'We'll be careful. We were just letting you know that we're following up on a homicide in our part of the world.'

'Frost responsible?'

'Nothing's proven, not yet.'

Isaac and Larry left the police station and drove the short distance to where Frost lived. Outside, a police car, two patrol officers inside. 'We'll call if we need you,' Isaac said. He had brought them two coffees, which was appreciated.

'We'll be here. Be careful with Caxton. He put me in the hospital once,' one of the uniforms said.

'Inspector Matson told us. And the guy singing soprano?'

'He always had a squeaky voice, but it's a good story.'

Isaac rang the bell at the security door to the block of flats. A gruff voice answered. 'What do you want?'

'DCI Cook, DI Hill, Challis Street Police Station, Homicide.'

'You've got a warrant?'

'We can get one, haul your sorry arse down to the police station. Tell Mr Frost we want a few words with him, or we'll come back later with a piece of paper, make it official.'

'Very well. I'll press the button. Enter the lift and enter 756 into the keypad.'

Outside Frost's penthouse, the two men stood, Caxton and O'Grady. One was squat and menacing, the other taller, fitter, and altogether a better-looking man, although that was subjective, and neither would have been regarded as handsome. Caxton had a scar above his left eye, O'Grady had broken his nose on more than one occasion, and the bridge was skewed to one side.

'Mr Frost doesn't like uninvited guests,' Caxton said.

'Then maybe he shouldn't go roughing up people, lending them money they can't afford to pay back,' Isaac said. Larry thought Isaac was playing a dangerous game, baiting the heavies even before they had met Frost. It wasn't the first time Isaac had gone on the offensive, and most times it worked, produced the appropriate reaction, but they were on the seventh floor of the building. It was a long way down, and the security door at the front of the building would be strong enough to hold any help at bay for long enough.

'Mr Frost isn't going to like you coming in here accusing him.'

'Tell him we're here. We don't have all day.'

'Go easy,' Larry said. 'We're in Frost's territory here.'

'We need a reaction. A black eye won't do you any harm, and if they do hurt us, we'll have the measure of them, know that Frost is our man.'

Inside, sitting on a brown leather chair, was the man himself. The penthouse was too warm for Larry, just right for Isaac. 'What can I do for you?' Frost said as he got up from the chair. Even though he was at home, he was dressed in a suit, white shirt, and a tie.

'We understand that you lend money?'

'Nothing wrong in that. I'm even registered, an office in the city. More of a broker really, put those who want the money in touch with the lending institutions, take the commission.'

'You don't work from there?'

'What for? Employ people, that's the secret. Ideal for me, ideal for them.'

'Okay, that's the legitimate side of the business,' Isaac said. 'What about the other side, the high-risk clients, those who can't get money from the banks?'

'I can't do much for them. If they've got themselves in trouble, destroyed their credit rating, that's their problem, not mine.'

'Why the two men outside? If you're legit, you've no need of protection.'

'Not all those that get loans can pay them back. The bank forecloses, divorces occur, and then the man is on his own, looking to blame someone. He can't take on the bank, but he can take on my company and me. Caxton and O'Grady can deal with anyone who comes near me, plus drive the car, run errands.'

'Mangle kneecaps part of their job description?' Isaac added.

'Chief Inspector, you've been reading too many gangster books, watching too many films. That's not how it works in real life.'

'It does. We've seen it before, and you're involved. What about the man you had kneecapped, walking with a permanent limp?'

Frost appeared agitated, started walking around the room. Larry could see Isaac getting under his skin.

'I've let you in here in good faith. I thought I was helping with your enquiries, not aware that you intended to insult me, accuse me of being a criminal.'

'Mr Frost, we know all about you, not that we can prove it, not yet. No one's speaking. It appears that they're more frightened of you than they are of the police. Why is that?'

'I've done nothing wrong. If people want to borrow money, that's up to them. If they can't pay it back, I can be sympathetic, but I'm not a charity.'

'Ralph Lawrence, you lent him money?'

'I'll not say I've never heard of the man, as I read the newspapers, surf the net, the same as everyone else. He's the son of Gilbert Lawrence, the madman with all the money and his dead wife upstairs in her bed.'

'And you've never met him?'

'What for?'

'The man's borrowed money, a lot of it. We know he came to the lender of last hope, he came to you.'

'I suggest you leave. I would call the police, but you're here already. I'll be making a complaint.'

'Do what you want, Mr Frost. We'll be watching you, and the next time you put someone in the hospital, we'll be there. And remember, neither Ralph Lawrence nor the kneecapped man has spoken to us. They keep telling us it was an accident, although how you can shoot yourself in the knee is a mystery to us.'

Isaac and Larry got up to leave. Larry turned around and looked at Frost, already on his phone making a call. 'Where was it? We were told it was Dubai where you had Steve Samuels killed.'

'Samuels?' Frost said.

'The gambling club owner who borrowed a lot of money from you, skipped the country, a couple of Russian whores in the car. You had him killed.'

'Inspector, I'm not a man without influence, my name counts for something, at least it does in this city.'

'Any action against Lawrence and the other man and we'll be back. And if we see Caxton and O'Grady anywhere near them or us, we'll take them in for questioning. No doubt we'll find something to charge them with,' Isaac said.

'A fertile imagination, Inspector Cook. I hope the Met treats you well when you're back in uniform.'

Chapter 23

Jill Dundas, now without the guiding hand of her father, realised the responsibility and burden on her shoulders. Not only was there Gilbert Lawrence's substantial real estate holdings to concern herself with, but there was also Caroline, Gilbert's daughter, close by, attempting to find out more, and now Ralph. As far as she was concerned, he was a man of little worth, a man who had justifiably been derided by his own father. What worried her was that there were people out there who used violence as a weapon, and she was the most likely target. Even a modicum of information from her, a password, an account number, could be worth millions. And some people knew how to hack computers, even though her father had been fastidious about ensuring that no one other than the two of them knew the full extent of Gilbert's wealth, and the office computers, the internet connection, had the best protection that money could buy.

Jill knew of the account squirrelled away in the Cayman Islands, one of the places in the world that didn't enquire too closely into where the funds came from. That was her father's special account, unknown to anyone in the office, and even she didn't know the passwords, but she knew where to find them. There was also a house there, set back from the beach, no more than two miles from the centre of Georgetown, the capital. Idyllic when the tourists weren't there, annoying when they were. All in all she believed that with her father's tutorage she was well placed to deal with all financial matters, but violence frightened her. Even as a child, a fight in the school playground would upset her for days, but that was other people, and if whoever had confronted Ralph hauled her off to some dingy room and threatened her, even hit her, she knew she would weaken.

And now Caroline was adamant that Ralph would come along to the meetings at the office as her special adviser. It was a weakening of her position, Jill knew. Ralph may be many things, most of them negative, but he wasn't naïve about how to conceal money in foreign bank accounts, how to set up companies and trusts to hide assets. Jill was aware that he would be asking pertinent questions, questions that she couldn't divert with legalese and financial jargon. The man was a threat, and if she knew who it was that had beaten him, she would have asked them why they hadn't finished the job.

Jill Dundas made a phone call. 'Caroline, we need to meet.' She hadn't wanted to make it, she knew she had to.

The two women did not meet at the office of Dundas and daughter, nor did they meet at Caroline's house. The conversation was important, and they met at the Savoy hotel in the centre of London, in Westminster, on the Strand.

'Caroline, we have a problem,' Jill said. There had been a brief embrace when first meeting, more a courtesy than a show of affection. Caroline was under no illusion, and she had not brought Ralph with her, at Jill's request, 'to each other's mutual benefit' had been the words that the solicitor had used. Ralph was still convalescing, drinking too much, and complaining at not being fully mobile, and Michael bringing his girlfriend over every other night, their bed banging on the shared bedroom wall, was making him crankier by the day. Caroline knew that with his current temperament he wasn't much use to her anyway.

Ralph's temper, justified at the reading of their father's last will and testament, was not needed now. Now, it was time for reasoned argument, a breaking down of the barriers that Leonard Dundas, and now his daughter, had put up.

'It's just you now. What are you going to do?' Caroline said. She was not in a mood to be conciliatory.

'Ralph is in trouble, isn't he?'

'That's Ralph, but what's it to you? You're not the bleeding-heart type, and I doubt if you care what happens to him, to us. To you, Ralph and I are like something the cat dragged into the house.'

'Honest words, Caroline,' Jill said. 'Neither of you deserve any of your father's money. The man was a genius, my father's friend. What are you and Ralph, the spawn of a great man? Your only skill was to be born his child. I worked hard for what I've got, so did my father, so did yours.'

At least the woman is honest, Caroline thought. 'You've opened up, but why and now?'

'Ralph's just a pawn, a charming nonsensical pawn. It's me that's the target. I'm the one with all the information, and I'm willing to admit that I'm afraid, more so than ever before.'

They were sitting in the Thames Foyer. Jill ordered afternoon tea, a favoured pastime of the hotel's guests and tourists to the city of London. She helped herself to a cake, Caroline chose a homemade scone with clotted cream and jam.

'What are you suggesting? That we make some kind of a deal?'

'We need to protect ourselves, and at this time, you'd quite happily see me go to the devil,' Jill said.

'You and your father have stolen our legacy. I don't know how, maybe I never will, but your father had managed to control my father and to take his money.'

'Your father was eccentric, maybe even slightly crazy with your mother upstairs, but he still knew what he was doing. Your father had amassed a fortune, and he put in safeguards to ensure it was not squandered. And yes, my father helped himself to plenty, but he wasn't going to throw it away, and nor am I. Work with me, Caroline, to protect ourselves, and I'll make it worth your while.'

'Pretty words, purely because you're frightened, but what do they mean? The police are out looking for who put Ralph in the hospital. What happens when they catch them? Will you renege on what we decide here today? And what about Ralph? He may be all that you say, but he's still my own flesh and blood. I can't cast him off just because of something you say.'

'They could come for you as well, you know that,' Jill said.

'I know. What do you suggest?'

'Ralph's owing money?'

'He is, and I know how much.'

'We pay his debt, make a deal with him, and then get him out of the country.'

'And leave me high and dry? How can I deal with you? Jill, you may sit there with your mouth full of cake, a cup of tea in your hand, looking pretty, but you're still a devious woman. You're no better than those who dealt with Ralph. I'd be putty in your hands.'

'Not if I pay you out, as well.'

'How much?'

'Fifty million pounds.'

'How much is my father worth, and the truth?'

'Six hundred and twenty-five million, but you can't realise on it all, only a fraction.'

'Why?'

'It's tied up in real estate, bonds, investments. It would take years to liquidate.'

'Fifty million, when?'

'As soon as Ralph is dealt with.'

'You're still exposed.'

'I need protection, but I need to know, are you interested? It's a generous offer, and I'll make sure that I keep you informed, ensure another two million a year for the next ten.'

'We can deal,' Caroline said. She had no interest in attending meetings, pretending to understand finance when she didn't, and Ralph was always going to be unreliable; it was in his DNA.

***

Yolanda was back in town and attempting to nurse Ralph back to health. With Michael and his girlfriend, an attractive tattooed young woman, monopolising the flat, Ralph had moved in with Yolanda for a few days, not that either was committed to the other. Even on the drive over in a taxi, the two of them had argued. Yolanda was concerned that the man she was transferring her affections to wasn't worth the effort, and he'd never have the money to look after her as well as her man in Antigua, who was keen and exceedingly generous, did. Ralph didn't want a nursemaid, and Yolanda was high-maintenance, and if he scored big time with his father's money, then he'd get himself into shape and play the field. A man with a fortune could have as many young and willing partners as he wanted; no need to be with a woman who complained and was starting to show her age, even if she was the mother of his son. Not that he could profess to any strong emotion for him, and now a bottle of alcohol had snuck its way into the flat. Michael, he knew, was on the downward spiral, aided and abetted by the girlfriend, vacuous and well-meaning, who was not helping at all. As the doctor at the rehabilitation centre had warned, a lot don't make it.

Yolanda had raised objections when Ralph had insisted that the 6 p.m. get-together at his sister's house was necessary and she wasn't invited. The police were to be there, and there was to be an update on his father's murderer. If his father was proven to be insane, then the man's will could be challenged, and if Leonard Dundas had been involved in the murder, it would be another plus for his and Caroline's case.

Chapter 24

At Caroline's, the front door was open. Inside, the assembled cast. On one chair, Molly Dempster sat. Wendy had brought her along and was seated nearby. Isaac could see that Wendy was the mother duck and she wasn't going to let anyone upset her duckling. Isaac preferred raw emotions to be the order of the night, and his sergeant close to one of those assembled could be a problem.

Caroline sat with her husband, Desmond. On the table in the centre of the room, a bottle of red wine, sandwiches, sausage rolls. Larry was hungry. He had had a busy day with Inspector Matson out at Greenwich, going through the case against Gary Frost, checking CCTV to see if Ralph had been in the area, also the man with only one functional kneecap, but it was like looking for a needle in a haystack. Too many people in the area, too many cars, and no clear idea of dates and times. Emily Matson had been interested when told about the gambling club owner, and she was making enquiries overseas. Larry had been more interested in recent cases pertaining to Ralph Lawrence, possibly Gilbert, but drawing blanks.

Ralph sat on another chair. Isaac could see that his condition had improved. Apart from slight bruising on his face, and the fact that he was squirming to get comfortable, he looked almost back to normal.

'Thanks for coming tonight,' Isaac said.

'It wasn't far for us,' Desmond said.

'It was either here or at Challis Street,' Isaac reminded him.

Isaac felt trepidation about what he was doing, realising that the emotions of those in the room would be challenged, but it was a murder enquiry, and those closest to the dead man had skeletons, and skeletons cause conflict, subterfuge, concealment. Someone in the room may know something hitherto unrevealed. He needed the raised and raw emotions, he needed people to open up.

'This is what we have,' Isaac said. 'Ralph is involved with a villain by the name of Gary Frost. Neither will admit to it, but it was Frost who put Ralph in hospital. He would have used two thugs named Ainsley Caxton and Hector O'Grady. We've been to see Frost, and we and the local police where Frost lives are following up on a few cases of violence meted out to those who get on the man's wrong side. We've found no connection between Frost and Gilbert Lawrence's death, and we don't think we will. Lawrence was killed with a degree of finesse. Frost's thugs are slash and burn, and none too subtle. Ralph has got off lightly, just a savage beating, although the marks on his wrist indicated that he was bound, and we don't believe his story that he fell off a roof.' Ralph sat quietly and said nothing, not even making eye contact with Isaac.

***

Molly Dempster sat in her chair; she was not looking up, not drinking from the cup of tea placed in front of her. Wendy could only imagine what was going through her mind, the reality of what she was about to tell the people in the room. Isaac and Wendy knew, had checked DNA with Forensics. What Molly had said was true, she was

Ralph's mother, and now her son was sitting on one side of the room, she on the other. The young boy that she had raised with Dorothy, spent more time with than the woman who had disappeared all those years ago – tonight the grown man would find out the truth.

'Caroline is in contact with Jill Dundas, a woman she doesn't trust, neither do we totally,' Isaac said. 'Now, we're not accusing her of murder, but the bequeathment by Gilbert is not usual. Whatever Jill Dundas and her father came up with, they've certainly done best out of the man's death. It may be what Gilbert wanted, it may not, but neither Caroline nor Ralph has the full picture. We've had people checking, and it's not that easy to know exactly what Gilbert Lawrence's wealth is, only that it is appreciable. We've also called on our overseas colleagues to do some checking. Caroline's received five million, her two children a million each. Not bad for most people, but Caroline and Ralph were expecting hundreds of millions. Am I correct?' Ralph and Caroline nodded in the affirmative.

'I'd have stayed in Spain if I'd known that I was going to be cheated,' Ralph said, the first words of any consequence he had uttered since entering his sister's house.

'Not likely,' Isaac said. 'You were deported, lucky that we were in contact with the authorities down there.'

'I would have come to an arrangement. A few pesetas here and there, problems disappear quickly.'

'It's euros now,' Isaac said. Wendy was keeping quiet, so was Larry. Their DCI was on a roll, he wouldn't appreciate their chipping in with a few comments, not that they had any. Wendy felt sorry for Molly, knowing that Ralph, her son, was a man of little worth, but then the old woman had admitted that Ralph's behaviour was only like her father and her grandfather, decent men but dreamers, always taking a chance when the odds were against them.

'Euros, pesetas, I'd still be back there.'

'You would still have had Frost to deal with.'

'I could have paid him off.'

'You've heard about Samuels and Dubai, the two Russian women?'

'Who hasn't? It's folklore out on the street. And besides, it was Belgium, a couple of streetwalkers, and it wasn't a Mercedes, it was an old Peugeot. Doesn't sound so romantic, though, that's why Frost embellished the truth, made him sound more important, more dangerous.'

'Are you admitting to your involvement with Frost?'

'Okay, I borrowed some money, but it was a roof that I fell off. With my father's money, I was hoping to buy somewhere in England, settle down with Yolanda, even find a place for Michael.'

Isaac had an admission that Ralph had borrowed money from Frost, the first time the man had spoken the truth. 'We'll bring Frost in at some stage. We'll not linger on your denials for now. Caroline, you met with Jill Dundas in the West End, correct?'

'There's no harm in that,' Caroline, on the defensive, said.

'Unusual, considering that you've been disparaging of her in the past.'

'You've not heard me say anything, have you?'

'We keep our ears to the ground. Jill Dundas controls all of your fortunes. She's one woman, what if anything happens to her?'

'We're lost. We need her alive, even if we don't trust her. Nobody in her office knows where everything is.'

'You've tried bribing some of them?'

'No. One of them came to us, offered to help for a cost.'

'And what did you do?'

'Nothing at this time, and besides, what would a junior know? Leonard Dundas was a smart man, the same as our father. He'd not leave loose pieces of paper around. Even if this junior could help, it would be limited. Jill Dundas is the key. That's why I was at the Savoy, afternoon tea, very expensive, but she was paying.'

'What was said?'

'She's frightened, interested in making a deal.'

'Frightened?'

'You'd better talk to her.'

'We're here talking to you. What's she frightened of?'

'What do you think? Ralph's half-killed, and he only owes a million and a bit. Jill's controlling hundreds of millions, and she can lay her hands on twenty, maybe thirty without any difficulty, and she's not a brave woman. She admitted to me that she's scared, and I don't blame her. If Ralph weren't such a fool, we'd all feel a lot safer, even Desmond and I.'

'You're right to be scared,' Isaac said.

'Can't you arrest them?' Desmond said.

'No proof. No one's talking, not even Ralph, not even the man they kneecapped. Caroline, you've fared well enough with your father's death. Could you have killed your father?'

'Not me. I still loved him, even though we hadn't spoken for many years, and I didn't need the money.'

'But what if you had known about your mother?'

'I don't think I would have done anything, other to have taken down that door that was always bolted with a sledgehammer, and to make my father tell me the truth. Did he kill her? It could have been one of her episodes. She could have slipped, fallen down the stairs. He could have been frightened of what would be said, confidence could have fallen in his empire, his line of credit could have dried up. Even if it was an accident, mud sticks, you must know that.'

Isaac knew, but he wasn't about to elaborate on his involvement with a Swedish au pair when he was younger who turned out to be a serial killer, or how, when DCI Caddick had temporarily occupied Isaac's seat in Homicide, the man had laid all the department's ills on the previous incumbent. It took the best part of a year after the man had left for Isaac to overcome the negativity and the aspersions made by Caddick. Even now there were still some who believed that Caddick was a competent police officer, and Isaac was just smoke and mirrors, a good-looking charmer with a mild Jamaican lilt in his voice.

'Let's recap,' Isaac said. 'Ralph was beaten half to death by Caxton and O'Grady on Frost's orders, a warning to pay up, deal us in on your father's fortune, or else. Caroline's talking to Jill Dundas, finds her more willing, probably willing to deal Ralph out. And that's because she's scared that those who beat Ralph may come for her, string her up, apply lighted cigarettes to her, and God knows what else until she opens the safe, hands over the account numbers, gives the passwords. Frost would only need a laptop and an internet connection, and he could bleed her for millions, maybe even arrange an accident in the River Thames afterwards, swimming lessons with weights. Caroline, Desmond, he could even go for you. If I were you two, and Jill Dundas, I'd be working on Ralph, get him to talk. He's scared enough, and if we go near Frost, bring him into the station and charge him, we can't make it stick, and he'll grab Ralph wherever he is. Quite frankly, I don't have much hope for him. He's a weak specimen of manhood, and I can't blame his father for being critical.'

'You can't talk to me like that,' Ralph said.

'Why not? You've not got long to live. How are you with swimming? Or maybe they'll string you up, take your manhood with a sharp knife. Not a pretty sight, and we've seen it before. What will Yolanda say, how about Michael? I'm not sure your sister will care much.'

Wendy could see that Isaac was pushing, probably harder than he should. The line between police questioning and harassment was clouded in grey, and Isaac was feeding the man, wanting him to agree, rather than let him volunteer it.

'Stop,' Molly said. The first word that she had said all evening. 'I need to tell the truth.'

Caroline looked over at Molly, expecting her to say that she had killed her father, not wanting to believe it was possible. After all, this was Molly, the one constant in her and her brother's lives, the one person they could always turn to, never to receive an admonishment, only a willing ear and sound advice. It had been Molly she had gone to when her first boyfriend had dumped her, on her birthday even, and the first person she had told when she had met Desmond, and how they had made love on their first date, and now the woman was on her feet and wanting to confess. Caroline couldn't believe it, didn't want to.

'Are you sure, Miss Dempster? I could do it for you,' Isaac said.

'It's my responsibility. It's been a secret for too long, but with Gilbert's death and Ralph's condition, I must speak now. It is not something I want to take to the grave. I want to go with a clear conscience and to be judged with respect, not derision. Caroline,' Molly said, looking over at the woman, 'I have loved you as if you were my daughter, you must know that.'

'I do, and we have always loved you,' Caroline replied, not sure what was coming next.

'When you were young, your father and mother were desperate for a son. Of course, you were too young to realise this. Your mother had had a difficult birth with you. She couldn't have any more children.'

'But she had Ralph.'

'She did not. Her name is on his birth certificate, as is his father's, but Dorothy, your mother, did not carry him for nine months and give birth to him in a private hospital in the north of England. Your mother was there, she was the first to see him.'

'What are you saying?' Ralph said. He was no longer looking down, attempting to sit comfortably and not exacerbate the pain he still felt in his chest. 'Caroline is not my sister, I'm not a Lawrence?'

'Ralph, dear Ralph, you can't remember suckling at my breast, can you? You are a Lawrence, Gilbert was your father.'

'That's proven,' Isaac said.

Molly shifted on her feet, her knees buckling as she spoke. Wendy stood up and put an arm around her, only to have it pushed away. 'Sorry, I must do this now, and on my own.'

'Who is the mother?' Caroline said. She was not sure what to think. Ralph, troublesome as a child, disreputable as an adult, had always been there. They had a bond, a bond that couldn't be broken, and now Molly was on her feet and telling them that she and Ralph were not related.

Molly calmed herself, took hold of the arm of the chair where she had been sitting. 'I loved your parents, both equally. Dorothy was like a sister to me, and Gilbert was the kindest, most gentle man that anyone could imagine. They were so much in love, and I was happy for them. They were my life, as you and Ralph were. I would do anything for them, even bear the son that they so desperately wanted. It was my gift, my honour.'

'It can't be,' Ralph said. He looked over at Caroline, could see the horror on her face, the bewilderment, as if it were a movie, not real life.

'I loved Gilbert as much as I loved Dorothy. Dorothy told me if she wasn't around, that I was to be with Gilbert, but we never had an affair, although Ralph thought we might have had when he was younger. But then he was young and pubescent. His mind was not in his head but somewhere else. Ralph, do you remember me looking the other way when you brought a young girl home with you, telling you to be careful?'

'But how? If you're my mother, can it be proven?'

'It has been,' Isaac said. 'We've taken a blood sample from you, saliva from Miss Dempster, and we already had Gilbert Lawrence's DNA. There is no doubt that you are the son of Gilbert Lawrence and Molly Dempster.'

'Don't you see? I did it out of love.'

'But how?' Caroline said.

'It was a natural conception. I only slept with your father to become pregnant. Apart from that, we never slept together before or after. If Dorothy hadn't been there, then maybe, but my act of love, our lovemaking, was for the purest intent. Surely you must understand. You and Ralph are brother and sister, and Gilbert is the father of both of you. It was Dorothy who was Ralph's mother.'

Caroline went over and placed her arms around Molly, tears streaming down her face. 'Thank you,' she said.

Ralph did not move. 'It makes sense now, doesn't it? I always sensed something, I never knew what.' He then raised himself from his chair and went and hugged his mother. Wendy was in tears, Isaac wasn't sure what to feel, Larry was mute, and Desmond Dickson sat in his chair, shaking his head.

'I'm sorry,' Isaac said when everyone had calmed down. 'To solve the murder of Gilbert Lawrence, we need openness. The secret you've just heard had to be told, either now or later. Emotions are frayed, and no doubt you will need to discuss what has been said here tonight. It still doesn't bring us any closer to solving the crime, though.'

'I'm not sure what to think,' Ralph said. 'On the one hand, I'm pleased to know the truth, on the other I'm confused. Molly, or should it be Mother, has always been special to all of us, but what she has said brings in another dimension.'

'Your mother's a target if this gets out,' Caroline said.

'Very well, I will give DCI Cook a full and open statement as to who and what Gary Frost is. The police, in turn, must ensure the safety of my mother and Caroline and her family, also Michael and Yolanda.'

'We will,' Isaac said, although he knew they were dealing with a man who gave little credence to the police and the law.

Chapter 25

Bridget Halloran, an inveterate computer junkie, was pleased with herself. She loved nothing better than surfing the internet, both in her spare time, although there wasn't much of that at present, and at work in Homicide, diving deep into police databases, or scouring for information about places and people and procedures. Now she had hit the jackpot.

'It's your show,' Isaac said in his office. It was late afternoon. Larry had been hoping for an early night; there was a school play, his eldest had two lines to say, and his wife was adamant that he had to be there to show support for the family.

'I've passed on the information to Larry's contact out at Greenwich,' Bridget said. It was not usual for her to be so excited.

'Belgium?' Larry said, the primary area of interest for Inspector Emily Matson at the police station in Greenwich, as well as his. If Frost could be linked to an actual crime, something that could be proved with a chance of a conviction, then so much the better.

Ralph Lawrence had given a full account of Gary Frost, his two henchmen, and how he had been trussed up like a Christmas turkey while Caxton and O'Grady had worked him over. Also, how the money was sent to his account overseas, the interest payments, what would happen if payment was not received on time or if he tried to cheat. He had recounted how Frost had bragged that the police were irritants, no more annoying than a mosquito of a summer's night, and how he had contacts in the right places.

Emily Matson had taken exception to Frost's assertions, seeing that her station was the closest to where the man lived, and any official police enquiry would focus on Greenwich Police Station, and then fan out from there. Two years previously, an inspector by the name of Fredericks had been charged after he had been exposed for taking backhanders from a local drug dealer. He had been Inspector Matson's boss at the time; she had been a sergeant on the rapid promotion ladder: young, female, university degree. She was seen as indicative of the future of a modern, educated, and professional police service, and association by default had impacted on her.

She had suspected him at the time, although she had failed to report it: no proof. Larry understood where she was coming from when she told him the story. It was one thing to inform on a dishonest police officer, it was another to prove it, and for several months she would have been ostracised by some of the others in the station. A word in the ear of the offender, a talk with his colleagues was seen as better, but even that had its risks. Another policeman in the station had taken that course of action. A trio of thugs on his way home, and two weeks in the hospital for him, and then he had left the service, taken a job as a security guard; better pay, though.

The promotion to Inspector for Matson had come about one month previously, a reward for good work, and a new superintendent in the station who recognised good people and ensured they received the recognition they deserved. And now an email in her inbox from one of DI Hill's colleagues outlining in detail what she had been trying to find. Little did she know that Bridget was not a two finger typist with limited computer

214

skills, but a whizz who could type a hundred words a minute, and could access the overseas databases of a myriad of police stations, strictly legal, look for the keywords, and then run any document through an online translation service.

At Challis Street, Bridget told the team what she had already sent to Emily Matson, copied to Larry, who hadn't had a chance to read it yet. 'Nineteen months ago, a Peugeot car was sprayed with bullets in Belgium,' Bridget said.

'Confirmed?' Isaac said.

'I've a copy of the police report at the time, as well as an English translation. The occupants of the vehicle included the driver, Alain Courtois, 38, a Frenchman living in Brussels, the capital. He ran a private taxi service, cheap and reliable according to his website. Also, in the backseat, three passengers: two females, one male. The females were subsequently identified as Freya Brepoels, 29, prostitute, and Sonia Colen, 26, prostitute. Both of the women were Belgian nationals.'

'The man?' Wendy said.

'English, false passport. I've run his photo against that of the dead man. It's Samuels.'

'I thought he had taken off with a fortune,' Larry said.

'Maybe he had,' Isaac said, 'but if he thought Frost could find him, then a low profile would have been more appropriate, or maybe he liked Peugeots and local tarts.'

'How do we tie him into Frost?'

'We can't,' Bridget said. 'They were shot near a small village outside of Brussels, a wooded area. No witnesses and the vehicle had been pushed off the road into a ditch. Someone in the vehicle that rammed them had got out and sprayed Samuels' vehicle with one hundred bullets from a semi-automatic rifle. Apart from that, nothing.'

'No link back to Frost?'

'The Belgian police never made the connection between the dead man and Samuels. If there's a connection, it's up to us to make it.'

'No joy from the kneecapped man?' Wendy said.

'No. He's still frightened, so is Ralph Lawrence, but he's still carrying on. Not sure if we can protect him and the others,' Isaac said. He could see a lot of possibilities, no proof, and the primary case, the murder of Gilbert Lawrence, was going nowhere.

'If Samuels was killed in an assassination, that means someone paid, and plenty. And why? Frost would have wanted his money back, and a dead man isn't going to give him any.'

'Maybe he did have the money or some of it. We know that Frost is devious. Samuels was making plenty at his club, but was everyone losing? And Samuels would have had to ship the money out of the country. He's hardly likely to have been carrying it on him.'

'Bank records?'

'I'm looking,' Bridget said. 'So far no luck. But he could have opened an account anywhere in a false name. All he'd need after that is the account number, the password, and a debit card.'

'Not much of a life for someone who supposedly stole millions,' Larry said.

'He was meant to be in Dubai: Mercedes, Russian women out of the Cyclone Club, not in Belgium, a Peugeot, and a couple of locals.'

'Made up to suit tough man Frost's image?'

'It's possible,' Isaac said. 'Larry, phone up Inspector Matson. Tell her that tomorrow she's on a trip to Belgium with you. Bridget, you make the bookings, and I'll phone Matson's boss to okay it. Check out the area where Samuels was staying, the murder scene. There must be witnesses somewhere. No reflection on the Belgian police, but they may have just put it down to an English gangster getting his comeuppance, a drug deal gone wrong. They've got their hands full over there with all the migrants trying to get across the channel.'

***

Yolanda was dismayed at Ralph's pathetic attempts to gain some of his father's fortune, only to get himself put in hospital, and her son was no better, succumbing to his old habits. The last time she had seen Michael, a few days previously, he had been drunk, and it had been clear that he had been smoking something other than cigarettes.

A pragmatist, Yolanda knew that father and son were weak individuals, more suited to each other than to her. In Antigua, there was a house and a good life with people such as herself: expats away from the cold and the bleakness, lapping up the sun, playing golf or bridge, or lying next to a swimming pool drinking cocktails. Ralph knocked on her hotel door, looking for a bolthole away from Michael and his girlfriend who had moved in on a permanent basis at the flat in Bayswater. That was when he found out that she had checked out, the hotel taking her to the airport.

Ralph knew the situation was tenuous. He was no longer Dorothy's son but Molly's, not that it concerned him as much as it should. And so it was that at three in the afternoon the only son of Molly Dempster and Gilbert Lawrence presented himself at his mother's door.

'Mother, I've come to stay for a few days, if that's alright.'

Molly looked at the man, not the best specimen with his two-day stubble, his breath smelling of beer, his clothes creased. She knew that if it had been anyone else she would have said no, but it was her son: the babe in arms, the young boy who had come to her for sympathy after falling out of a tree, the pubescent youth who had struggled with growing up. She had looked after him through those years, and even though he was in his fifties, he still needed caring for.

'Come in,' she said, overjoyed to be able to spend time with him, good or bad. It had come full circle from the child to the father and back to the child. For her, regardless of what others may say, Ralph was her son, and she was proud of him. 'I'll make up the spare room for you.' Molly knew that she was happy.

Michael meanwhile languished in his bed, his woman by his side. On one of the bedside tables, a syringe. He was back in heaven or purgatory, he did not care which. His girlfriend, a woman whom he loved when he was drugged, unsure about when he wasn't, was in euphoria.

A knock on the door. Michael stirred from the bed and opened it. 'What have you done to yourself?' Helmsley said. Dressed in a checked jacket, a pair of blue jeans, a large scarf around his neck, he looked every part the eccentric professor that he was, not that the young Lawrence could see him, his eyes blurred. He only wanted to go back to his bed and make love to his girlfriend, knowing she would not refuse him. After all, hadn't it been him who had used the money from Jill Dundas to feed her habit, and if she refused, then there were others. He was flush with money, sufficient for his life. A flat belonging to another, a woman, a drug dealer who sold only the best and at a reasonable price. The only blight on his life was the man standing at the door, disapproving, the same as his mother. He had spent a lifetime on his own, neglected by his parents, and he did not care for either or where they were.

'The cause needs you clean,' Helmsley said as he pushed through the door and into the flat. The girlfriend came out of the bedroom, took one look around. 'Who's he?' she said. She was stark naked, as was Michael. Helmsley looked at them both: the seductive young woman with the tattoos and the needle marks and Michael, young, masculine, with bulging muscles. He knew which he preferred, but now was not the time to put the young woman back in her room and to attempt the seduction of a young man who probably would not resist, probably would not remember. Instead, Helmsley put on the kettle. 'Strong coffee and plenty of it,' he said. 'And get rid of that woman.'

Chapter 26

At St Pancras Station, Larry carried a small bag, Emily Matson arrived pulling a suitcase.

'It's only overnight,' he said.

'Better to be prepared, just in case,' Emily said. It was seven thirty in the morning, the Eurostar direct to Brussels was due out in one hour, and then a trip of just under two hours. Larry reflected that he had got up, showered, driven to the airport, parked his car, and waited for the train, in total nearly three hours, almost long enough to travel under the channel and to return to London. And if he and Emily had travelled out to the airport, it would have taken even longer.

'A coffee?' Emily said. Larry could see that she had purchased new clothes for the occasion, crisp and still showing the mark on the blouse where it had hung on a hanger. She wore a red skirt, high boots, and around her shoulders was draped a shawl. 'I've got a coat in the case if the weather turns.'

'Not snowshoes, I hope,' Larry joked. He had to admit she was agreeable, competent, and most of all, enthusiastic.

'Married?' Larry asked as the two sat down at a table in the coffee shop, keeping their eyes peeled for an update on their train. It was Larry's first time on Eurostar, Emily's second.

'Not yet. I've got a live-in boyfriend. We've been together for a few years, but he's a bit slow on the uptake. I've given him enough hints to get down on his knee.'

'Necessary these days?'

'The wedding ring, down on the knee? Not really, but it's romantic. I'd like him to do it, just the once.'

'And then marriage?'

'If he's for me, we'll stick together. No need for a piece of paper.'

At 8.31 a.m. the train pulled out of the station; two hours later it pulled in to Brussels Midi Station. Inspecteur Jules Hougardy, a distinguished looking man in his fifties, met Larry and Emily as they left the station.

'Pleased to meet you,' he said. 'I was involved with the original investigation.' His English was excellent, which was as well as Larry's French was rudimentary, and Emily's good enough to order a meal, find a hotel, ask for directions, but certainly not up to the standard required for a murder investigation.

'I've prepared a full day,' Hougardy said, 'but first, lunch. It'll give you both a chance to update me, me to update you. We've been working on the case ever since you contacted us.'

Emily hoped for something traditional for lunch, not the fish and chips that the Inspecteur chose.

'We'll drive out to the murder scene. We've been around the local village with the photos you sent over, with some success.'

'The Peugeot?'

'It's an old case. We can have a look at it, but you'll not gain much from it. You're both booked into a hotel in the centre of town, adjoining rooms.' Emily didn't like the look in the Belgian's eyes. She had heard that the French were incurable romantics, always looking for a dalliance. She didn't know that it applied to the Belgians as well. And besides, the man may dream, but

221

the reality was a solid day of policing and an early night, alone and without interruption.

The trip out to the murder scene took twenty-five minutes. They passed through a small village before coming to an isolated area. To one side there was a ditch, large enough for the front end of a car.

'A four-wheel drive rammed the Peugeot near here,' Hougardy said as he slowed down.

'Did you find the vehicle?'

'Never. Although if it had bars at the front, it might not have sustained a lot of damage, and if it had been used off the road, as many are of course, then it would not have been distinguishable, not around here anyway.'

'Make, model?' Larry asked.

'We believe it to be a Toyota, but that's supposition. We found a trace of paint on the Peugeot. Forensics ran it through a spectrometer, conducted solvent tests, came up with a Toyota green. Unless someone had resprayed the vehicle, we believe it to be a Toyota Land Cruiser, 1985 to 1992. There are a few around here and the borders are open.'

'The photos?'

'We've one witness to someone buying food in a supermarket not far from here. The man was English, no French, and not very pleasant. He became agitated that the person behind the counter didn't understand what he was saying.'

'Sounds like the English they get down in Spain,' Emily said, having been embarrassed by her fellow English on holiday there, getting drunk, making fools of themselves. In her teens she had been there with a few friends, but they hadn't enjoyed themselves, what with the local lotharios fancying their chances, and the English

222

louts assuming that every English woman was there for their benefit.

'Not the person we've got here. Big, muscled, not the sort of man to sit on a beach.'

'We've got two people of interest. Any chance of meeting this person who was abused?'

'Next stop.'

In the town square of Herzele, an attractive village not far from the murder scene, the three police officers entered the shop. Jules Hougardy spoke French most days of the week, but the shop owner, a woman in her sixties, small and neat, shook the hands of the two English police officers, especially Emily's, and spoke in a language that neither Larry nor Emily could understand.

'It's Flemish,' Hougardy said. 'Most people speak both. In Brussels you'll find the majority of conversations are in French, but outside of the big city, some prefer French, others Dutch, and some converse in Flemish. It pays to be trilingual if you want to be a police officer in Belgium.'

'And you are?' Emily said, noticing that Hougardy had no trouble talking to the woman.

'I was brought up in a Flemish-speaking family, but regardless, at the station, we can speak in all the languages of our country. Not like the British, am I correct?' Hougardy smiled.

'Only English, and not even the Queen's,' Larry said, responding to the gibe.

Emily held two photos for the woman to look at. She studied them for a few minutes, putting on her glasses, before pointing at one of them, pulling a face to indicate non-verbally what she thought of him. She even gripped the tip of her nose and pulled at it. The definition of a stinker translated across countries and languages.

'You know this man?' Hougardy said.

'We do. Please thank the lady for us,' Larry said. 'Would she be willing to testify that he came into her shop?'

'She would. I've already asked her. We have another witness. Our people found him this morning. He nearly had an accident with the Toyota.'

'Let's go and see him,' Emily said, as she shook the hand of the old lady, who in typical Belgian fashion grabbed hold of her and kissed her on both cheeks.

'She likes you,' Hougardy said. 'She thinks you're attractive and that you should find yourself a good Belgian man to settle down with, her son, for instance.'

'Thank her for the offer, but I'm taken.'

Outside the small shop, where Emily was still feeling a little embarrassed by the woman's exuberance, a man stood. He was a robust individual, ruddy complexion, extended belly. Larry liked the look of him. He was farming stock, his clothing indicative of that, as well as the tractor that stood not far away.

'This is Monsieur Mathy. He is quite happy to converse in French.'

Emily tried out her French. Surprisingly, it wasn't as bad as she had imagined, and Mathy grabbed both of Emily's hands in his and shook them vigorously.

'You're a hit here,' Larry said. 'Maybe you should come back and marry the son.'

'Maybe I will if there's any more cheek.'

Emily showed Mathy the photo. He responded in French, Emily understanding what he said.

'It's confirmed. What else do we have today?' Larry said to Hougardy.

'A meal tonight with my team, a copy of our case files, in French originally, but we've translated most of them for you. And tomorrow I'll drop you off at the station.'

Larry took the opportunity to phone Isaac on the way back into Brussels. No action would be taken until he and Emily were back in London. Two witnesses of the one person was not sufficient proof in itself. They still needed to find additional evidence, and they didn't want the man to disappear.

Jules Hougardy drove past the police holding area where the Peugeot was stored on the way back. As he had said, the Peugeot did not reveal much in itself. It was severely dented at the front, the bodywork was peppered with holes where the bullets had pierced the metal, the windows were all broken apart from one side window, and inside there were still bloodstains.

'The women?' Emily said.

'Locals, off the street. Both were addicts, neither was attractive. Sorry about the lack of detail, but there's not much more to say about them. They had been picked up an hour earlier, heading out for the night to a house in the country. Samuels, now we know his name, made the booking in the name of Smith, Airbnb. It was just their bad luck, the same as the driver.'

***

Giles Helmsley had control of the grandson of Gilbert Lawrence, a useless lump of a drug-addicted attempt at manhood, whose only delight was to screw the bitch who had just left, no doubt intending to come back as soon as he had gone. Helmsley wasn't sure what to do. He wanted to stamp out of the flat, find another willing recruit and to bleed him and his family for what he could, but no one else had the wealth of the Lawrence family. He plied Michael with coffee, put him into a warm bath, only to see him almost collapse, his head slowly sinking below the surface of the water. It was a hopeless situation, he knew that.

All that money at the rehabilitation centre, and one woman, one syringe, and the man was as bad as he had ever been. He needed him clean, he needed help. He made a phone call. Forty minutes later, the two men that had dossed with Michael were at the door. Fully dressed – Helmsley had had to dress him – the grandson of the wealthy man was soon downstairs and in the back of Helmsley's vehicle, a late-model Jaguar. *No use in driving around in an old bomb*, Helmsley thought as he pulled away from the kerb, hoping that Michael Lawrence wouldn't throw up or urinate in the back seat, hoping the other two wouldn't either.

'I want my girl back,' Michael mumbled, the others in the car attempting to get him to shut up. Back at the dosshouse, the man was roughly thrown back on the mattress where he had come from. Helmsley administered the heroin into his vein, not sure what he was doing, only knowing that he needed Michael quiet for now while he planned his next move. He knew that heroin was the last thing that Michael needed, but he needed him to stay and to sleep. Tomorrow, the man would detox the hard way: cold turkey.

At the back of the dosshouse was an old washroom, a solid lock on the door. When he entered the austere room, Michael Lawrence would have gone from the five-star luxury of the Waverley House Rehabilitation Centre for the rich and feeble to a flat in Bayswater, then back to his old doss house mattress, and then to a washroom with concrete walls and a concrete floor. Five days in there, maybe six, and then he would be let out, cleaned up, and sent off to get more money, to the same place he had obtained money before.

And to hell with the revolution, Helmsley thought, not that he didn't believe in it, but what was the point. Those he collected to his side were only the disenfranchised, the lunatic fringe, the people that he despised.

If only the London School of Economics hadn't been so rigid, he could still be there, formulating the manifesto to take the next step forward in his quest for justice for the people of England: equality and prosperity in equal measure. Not once did he consider that he, Giles Helmsley, could be mad; that was the arrogance of the man.

Chapter 27

Emily Matson did the rounds at Challis Street, Larry doing the introductions. She liked the freshness of the police station, the camaraderie that existed. She had confided to Larry on the Eurostar coming back to London that the environment at Greenwich Police Station was toxic, the after-effects of her previous inspector who had been found guilty of taking bribes.

And now everyone in the station was careful to be on their best behaviour, excessively documenting everything, looking for flaws in others. Even she had been reported for not informing the Admin Department that she would be out of the country for a few days, although the station superintendent had been notified in a phone call from Isaac. Regardless, there'd be some on her return to the station who would make disparaging remarks about her getting ahead of herself, becoming involved in Homicide when she should be focussed on theft and the cat burglar who had been making his way around the area.

'There's one DCI who was hostile that I became involved with Challis Street. He thought that his seniority should have ensured that I handed the investigation into Frost over to him.'

'And?' Larry said.

'He complained to our superintendent when the Belgium trip came up, said it was his right to go, not a junior.'

'Which meant?'

'Not a woman. He's a chauvinistic misogynist. The super told him to button his lip, and to get back to work. The superintendent's a good man.'

'This DCI, what did he hope to gain in Belgium? And besides, we would have scuttled him.'

'Nothing to do with the case. For him, it would have been Belgian chocolates, Belgian beer, a sampling of the local talent.'

'Fancies himself?'

'He's the only one that does. The superintendent's been trying to get him out, but the man sticks like glue. He gave evidence against the other DCI, gained a few more brownie points, a friend of the commissioner.'

'Alwyn Davies?'

'You've met him?'

'We've had our problems. He had DCI Cook and Chief Superintendent Goddard out of their seats for a while. The man's odious, but he plays it smart.'

Isaac's office was too small with Emily in the department. Down the hall, a conference room was secured.

'Emily, Larry, an update,' Isaac said.

'There's no doubt that Hector O'Grady was seen in the village of Herzele. We've two independent corroborations, one the owner of a small shop, the other a farmer who states that O'Grady's vehicle nearly caused an accident.'

'O'Grady driving?'

'Nobody recognised a photo of Ainsley Caxton,' Larry said, 'although the murder of Samuels would have required some time. It's logical to assume that one person did the shooting, another the driving.'

'Is there any way to find out if Caxton and O'Grady were in Belgium at the time?' Wendy said. She was anxious to be out of the office and following the two heavies would have suited her fine.

'It was nineteen months ago,' Emily said.

'Still, there must be CCTV here and in Belgium. Two men travelling in a green Toyota Land Cruiser must have been seen.'

'Without a doubt, but that's a lot of work, going through all the videos, and would they still be available?' Bridget said. She had previously been the CCTV viewing officer, a skill she had been trained for. She would find proof if anybody could, she knew that.

'Two people identifying O'Grady won't hold up in court. It's supposition, not proof. Emily, Larry, good work, but we need to follow it up,' Isaac said. 'What's the current status of the two thugs?'

'They're still in Greenwich. O'Grady's been out and about, Caxton was seen three days ago, but nothing since then. We believe he's in the area, though,' Emily said.

'You're maintaining surveillance?'

'Low-key. We don't want to let on that we're closing in.'

'We need something we can pressure them with. And then we can go after Frost, make the man sweat. His arrest may lead us to whoever killed Gilbert Lawrence. Wendy, work with Emily and her people. Find out the movements of Caxton and O'Grady, see if they're predictable, see if they're committing any crimes. Emily and her people are obviously doing a good job, so liaise, no need for you to be pounding the pavement any more than necessary.'

Wendy could see her DCI aiming to protect her, to keep her increasing immobility concealed for as long as possible. She had to thank him for his consideration, regretted that it was necessary. Regular exercise, massaging, and medication were helping, but the decline was continuing. And besides, Greenwich suited her fine for a few days. She had wanted to get up to the Greenwich Observatory for some time, a chance to see the Prime Meridian, zero degrees longitude, and the Cutty Sark, an old clipper ship, its restoration complete after a devastating fire. She had been there with her husband in their courting days. It would be good to go back, nostalgia for her, a remembrance of what a good man he had been, even if he had been difficult sometimes. She had to admit that she still missed him.

'I've been checking names with Eurostar, the ferries, the airlines,' Bridget said. 'So far, no Caxton or O'Grady, although the checks are not that rigorous. Easy enough to forge documents, and no one is keeping a record of the photos on them,' Bridget said.

The team were excited. For once, some decisive action. Emily was pleased to be in an office where negativity did not abound. She thought she could enjoy being in Challis Street on a more permanent basis, but her boyfriend was over the other side of the River Thames, and she did not see him that often as it was. Homicide involved much longer hours than she had worked before. It was the conflict between being a professional police officer and a person in a relationship. She knew she was not willing to make the ultimate decision of one at the expense of the other. She had seen too many relationships fall apart, she was not about to allow hers to become one of those as well.

'The vehicle seen in Belgium, left- or right-hand drive?' Isaac said.

'No one's sure,' Larry said. 'The lady in the shop did not see the vehicle, the farmer swerved to avoid it. It's important to know, but there's no way we can tell.'

'Bridget, any luck?'

'Nothing registered to Frost and his associates. I've been checking with records, stolen vehicles. There are two possibilities for UK registered vehicles. A Toyota Land Cruiser, 1990, stolen to the south of London, found abandoned in Brighton. Another vehicle, 1991, reported missing in Earls Court. The dates tally, and of the two, only one has been recovered.'

'Is anyone checking?'

'Forensics have the vehicle. Inconclusive at this time. The vehicle had been returned to the owner, and he subsequently tidied it up and sold it on.'

'Dented, condition indicative of an accident?'

'The owner was a keen member of an off-roaders club. The vehicle was not in good condition when it was stolen, no better or worse when it was returned. According to him, it was a good workhorse, had given him lots of fun, and he had been sorry to see it go.'

'Why did he sell it?'

'Child on the way. No doubt his wife had something to do with the decision.' Larry understood. Before he had married, and before his wife had become pregnant with their first, he had been driving around in a two-seater, an MGB. A lot of fun, but not very practical. He had been sad when he sold it, even sadder when he drove out of the dealer's with a four-door Ford Mondeo. He had mourned the change, a sign of passing from youth to adulthood and married responsibility.

Isaac phoned Forensics, received an update on the Land Cruiser. After two minutes, he put his phone down and spoke to the team. 'It's probably the vehicle in

Belgium. Damage at the front is consistent with hitting another car, and they found paint from what looks to be the Peugeot. They've been in contact with Belgium, received a detailed analysis of the Peugeot's paint. Bridget, you've a registration number, run it through the system, see what you can find.'

'Will do, also I'll access the databases in Belgium, talk to Inspecteur Hougardy.'

'Get yourself on Eurostar and sit with their CCTV viewing officer. If we have a vehicle, we have a driver and a passenger. No problems over there, and they've probably kept records. It's the most lit up area on the planet, lights on all the motorways, so no trouble with visibility.'

'I can access our records from over there. I suggest that I continue here for the next two hours, and then take the train. We need to know if Caxton and O'Grady are in the vehicle in the UK, but we need to place them near to the scene of the crime.'

'Sorry, Wendy,' Isaac said. 'You'll need to stay in London, no souvenirs for you, no late-night drinking with Bridget.'

'That's understood,' Wendy said.

Bridget leant over, touched her on the arm. 'Don't worry, I'll bring you back a big box of chocolates, as well as a bottle of beer.'

'I'd rather the farmer that took a fancy to Emily,' Wendy said, Larry having recounted the story earlier.

'If he fits in my bag, I may just do that,' Bridget said.

***

Giles Helmsley may have been credited with a high intellect, a PhD from Oxford University, but he was not the man to administer drugs, especially the narcotic kind. It was five in the morning when one of the two men who had helped Helmsley with Lawrence knocked on the door of his flat.

'It's Michael,' the man said. His visit was not appreciated in the building where the radical academic lived, a door opening on the floor below, a curious person looking out, telling whoever it was to keep the noise down.

'Mind your own business,' Coyote said, with a few expletives. It was not the addict's name but the moniker taken from a cartoon that he answered to. He thought it made him sound cool; it did not. It only made him appear to be more stupid than he actually was. A typical anarchist follower, Helmsley would have admitted if pressed.

'What's up with him? Has he left?'

'He's not moving. I've tried shaking him, even threw water on him, but nothing.'

Helmsley pulled Coyote inside the flat. 'Shut up and sit quietly while I get dressed.'

Coyote wrestled with the concept of quiet, and he moved around the flat, looking at this and that, staring out of the window. He was shaking and sweaty, and in need of a fix, and the professor had taken his drugs and given them to Michael the night before.

Helmsley came out from his bedroom, put on a coat that was hanging from a hook on the back of the door to the flat. He then grabbed the addict, not willing to call him by his silly name, and dragged him out. On the landing outside, Coyote said, 'It's Michael, he's dead.'

'For Christ's sake, be quiet,' Helmsley said, increasingly annoyed that the man knew his address.

234

As they walked down the stairs, Coyote was still complaining, grabbing hold of the bannisters, brushing up against a couple of the doors. One of the disturbed residents opened his door and made a comment; Coyote tried to get free and to smash him one. 'That's all they understand,' he said.

Giles Helmsley had kept his anarchist beliefs separate from where he lived. He had a cause to follow, a cause that required sacrifices, but not his. To his neighbours, he was a quiet, studious man, and now that was unravelling as Coyote continued to cause trouble. Outside, on the street, he gave the addict a smack across the face with an open palm – it had some effect. In the Jaguar, cold at first, but soon warmer with the heater, the two men drove to the dosshouse.

Inside on the floor, lay Michael Lawrence. 'He's not dead,' Helmsley said. 'He's still breathing.'

'He's OD'd,' Coyote said. The other occupant of the room, another addict who preferred being called 'Stud' to Gerald, continued to sleep, his snoring raucous. Helmsley opened a window, the cold air taking some of the smell in the room. He phoned Emergency Services.

Chapter 28

When Bridget arrived at the railway station in Brussels, Jules Hougardy was waiting outside for her. She was as impressed with the man as Emily and Larry had been. It was late afternoon by the time she arrived, and although she had spent the morning checking through the databases, attempting to access CCTV footage of the cross-channel tunnel and the ferries, it hadn't been entirely successful. Forensic analysis of the Land Cruiser had not come up with anything more. The vehicle, returned to the owner after its now known sojourn on the continent, had been patched up, driven along rough tracks, had its underside bashed, its bodywork scratched, before being subjected to an amateurish three-month restoration by the owner. It had then been sold on to another off-road enthusiast. Any evidence of Belgium, Caxton, and O'Grady was long gone, apart from a sample of the Peugeot's paint. The only piece of good news was the confirmation that the vehicle had crossed into mainland Europe three days before Samuels died, and had returned two days after. No doubt the delay in the return had been to check that the vehicle wasn't wanted by the police: the usual practice being to park it somewhere prominent, somewhere legal, somewhere the police would have been checking. If it was still there after a couple of days, then it was safe to drive.

'I've booked you into the same hotel as Inspectors Matson and Hill,' Hougardy said, 'but first, we must have dinner. I've arranged a local place, somewhere the tourists avoid. All they want is fish and chips, but for you, the works.' Bridget remembered Emily's comments about the Belgian police officer's love of fish and chips, but that was not what she ate. For her, it was Carbonnade Flamande, a beef casserole cooked in wine. For dessert, waffles and ice cream. The meal was delicious, the company excellent, and she made sure to phone Wendy on her return to her hotel.

'Perfect gentleman,' Bridget said.

'The evening wasn't a total success then,' Wendy said.

'It was. Tomorrow I'm meeting with his team and spending time with the CCTV viewing officer. Not all of it's available. Hopefully, it'll be enough. They've got cameras everywhere.'

'Nowhere has more than London but focus on the farmer's village.'

'I'll go and see the farmer for you, see if he's your type.'

'He will be. Hurry back soon. The office is not the same without you, and I've got another report to file. I could do with your help.'

The next day, Bridget tucked into a good breakfast. The hotel offered either continental or English. She chose the English, realising that she was falling into the trap of the reluctant tourist, wanting to see the exotic as long as it was accompanied by a cup of tea and bacon and eggs.

At the central police station in Brussels on Rue du Marché au Charbon, Bridget met her counterpart, a moustached man who smelt vaguely of mothballs. She imagined Hercule Poirot, but this man was not short or rotund, and his moustache was neatly trimmed, not curled up at the ends. He was also talkative and did not use his little grey cells to the same extent as Agatha Christie's most famous creation.

'Bridget Halloran, I am pleased to meet you,' Hendrik Brun said, his Belgian accent strong, his English understandable. He also took her hand and kissed it. Bridget blushed. She could never imagine her DCI or her DI kissing her, hand or cheek.

'We've got a lot of work to do,' Bridget said. The office was better than Challis Street, more modern, more open. To her, it lacked the charm that Challis Street offered, the homely touches she had brought to it. She took out her laptop, logged on using the police station's Wi-Fi, the password supplied by Brun.

'We've obtained records from the cameras out at Herzele,' Brun said. 'One of the cameras was faulty. Also, the videos from another have been deleted. We do have two others. With your permission, we'll concentrate on them. For our purposes, I suggest we divide the videos, you taking the time after the murders, and I'll take before.'

Bridget could see that the man was no-nonsense, straight down to work, and as competent on a computer as she was. They first checked the videos at the ferry port where the vehicle had entered the country. The date and the time were now known. It was not difficult to spot the Toyota coming off the ferry and driving up the ramp and onto the dock. The road markings took the cars from driving on the left to the right, and numerous signs reminded the drivers that this was Belgium, and all vehicles were left-hand drive, and great care was to be exercised.

'The windows are darkened,' Brun said. 'We can't see the driver or the passenger.' Bridget could see that he was right. The vehicle that had been recently checked in England had clear windows. Someone had applied a film,

238

probably purchased at an automotive store. Whoever had done it had complicated their work. None of the CCTVs in Brussels were of any use, as the department responsible prided itself on erasing all footage after six months.

Herzele was a different situation. The records were kept in Ghent, a city not far from Brussels, and the deletion of video files was not so rigorous. Bridget sat on one side of Brun's desk, he sat on the other. In front of them, a large monitor each. Brun slowly scanned back from the closest time to the shooting, Bridget scanned forward. The video from one of the two cameras was clear, the other was blurred and out of focus.

It took two hours before Brun saw the vehicle in the village. He and Bridget then focussed forward from that time. It was another twenty minutes before he had traced it as far as he could, which was still two kilometres from the murder scene. With times established, he used enhanced imaging technology to look for additional detail. 'The tinting is only on the windscreen and the front windows, the rear tailgate has none,' he said.

Bridget wondered why they had not picked up the Toyota at the time of the murders. But then, as Brun explained, English tourists driving around were not that uncommon, and the registration number wasn't easy to read. In fact, it was almost impossible, the first and last letters covered in mud or rust or both, the numbers scratched and unreadable. It was either done on purpose or the result of bashing over muddy tracks or logs with the off-roaders.

After nine hours solid looking at the monitor screens, neither of the two officers was able to focus any more. Bridget phoned Wendy who brought in Isaac on speaker. The time in Brussels had been successful in that

239

the vehicle had been identified. It would need another day, when she and Hendrik Brun would focus in detail on the time that one of the men had entered the shop in Herzele. The almost accident with the farmer had been outside of the village, in an area where there were no cameras. Nothing would be gained by trying to look for further verification from the farmer or any other drivers on the road. It had been a overcast day when the murder occurred and the road had been mainly deserted, the reason that the farmer had pulled his tractor out into the centre of the road without due care and attention.

***

In Belgium, the prosecution case was firming against Ainsley Caxton and Hector O'Grady. In London, there were other developments, in particular, the hospitalisation of Michael Lawrence.

The first Homicide heard of him being there was when the hospital administration had phoned, his name being on a database of concerned persons, a possible drug overdose. The second was when Molly Dempster called to tell Isaac that Ralph was on his way to see his son.

In intensive care at St Mary's Hospital, where Alexander Fleming had discovered penicillin, and not far from Paddington Station, two doctors stood by Michael's bed, three nurses hovered close by. The man was Gilbert Lawrence's grandson, and as Jill Dundas had said, money was not an issue. She wasn't sure why she had said it when she had arrived at the hospital ten minutes after Ralph, five minutes after Isaac and Wendy. Larry had taken over following up on Caxton and O'Grady, attempting to find more evidence against Gary Frost, anything that could stick.

An intravenous drip was to one side of the bed, the patient lying flat on his back. Only Ralph had been allowed in initially, Isaac after he had shown his warrant card and insisted that it was vital to see the patient.

Michael's face was covered by a mask supplying oxygen, an ECG machine standing by. 'It's not good,' one of the doctors said. 'The man had three times the normal amount from what we can see.'

It was known that Giles Helmsley had made the phone call for the ambulance, but he was not at the hospital. Isaac made a phone call to Larry. 'Pick up Helmsley, make sure he's at Challis Street within the hour.'

On the bed, Michael moved, not conscious of his actions. Ralph was present, although Isaac had left and was talking to Jill Dundas and Molly Dempster.

'Waste of time getting him detoxed,' Jill Dundas said. Isaac could see the hardness in her face. She had professed sadness at Gilbert's death, at the death of her father, but had it been feigned? Isaac couldn't be sure.

'Too long without treatment. We could have helped him earlier, but now? There's possible brain damage as well,' one of the doctors said as he came out and spoke to Isaac. 'Not much of a life, not much of a death either, although he'll not know much about it.'

Michael Lawrence died at 11.08 a.m. on a Thursday morning. Ralph was heartbroken, so was Molly. Jill Dundas stood nearby in the reception area, mouthing the words the others wanted to hear. She did not shed a tear, neither did Ralph, although Wendy and Molly did.

Larry phoned; Helmsley was at the police station. After another twenty minutes at the hospital, Isaac left, leaving Wendy with Molly. She would look after the woman who had aged in that short time at the hospital. She had gained a son, a grandson, and now one of them was dead, and the other was not the healthiest, and his future looked bleak.

At the station, Helmsley sat quietly. He was holding a cup of tea: Earl Grey, at his request. He looked into vacant space, saying nothing, seeing nothing.

'I found him at the dosshouse,' Larry said, 'lying down on that filthy mattress that Lawrence used. He looks as if he can't take it all in. Bizarre when you think about it. A brilliant man they said down at LSE, and yet he's out there leading the good fight, believing that people are waiting for the revolution.'

'Genius level intelligence comes with its own problems,' Isaac said. 'Better to be like us, smart enough to know what's good for us, smart enough to leave the rest well alone.'

Larry led Helmsley into the interview room. He had committed no crime as far as was known, and legal representation was offered but declined.

'Mr Helmsley, you phoned Emergency Services,' Isaac said.

'One of Michael's friends woke me up, told me that he was in trouble. I went over there, found him on the floor. That's when I made the call.'

'The other man could have,' Larry said.

'Coyote, that's the name he likes to use, was the same as Michael, an addict.'

'But Michael was with Ralph. What happened?'

'Michael was weak. I was at his place. He had a woman with him, doped up as well. The two were on heroin, and Michael needed help.'

'The woman?'

'I've no idea. I kicked her out. Michael could have served the cause, but what does he do? He finds himself a drugged-out female. The two of them, naked in that bed, a syringe to one side. I took Michael, thrust him into the shower, plied him with coffee and brought him back to where the woman couldn't find him, neither could his father.'

'Even if we accept what you've told us, it doesn't explain why he had OD'd, does it?'

'One of the others must have injected him,' Helmsley said. Larry noticed the twitch in his face when he spoke.

'You're lying, aren't you, Mr Helmsley? A drug addict is not going to waste perfectly good heroin on someone else. You injected him for your own purposes.'

'I was going to put him in a room at the back of the house, make him go cold turkey. A fancy rehabilitation centre in the country with its five-star accommodation and runs around the lawns couldn't fix him, no doubt charged thousands as well. But that's the capitalist system: screw the poor, bleed the rich.'

'Mr Helmsley, we don't need a political party broadcast. Did you inject Michael Lawrence on that mattress?'

'I did it for him. My intentions were honourable.'

'Your intentions have killed him, and they were not honourable, they were for your own distorted purpose. You're a hypocrite, you wanted his family's money. You will be charged with involuntary manslaughter. Further charges may be laid against you. I suggest you find yourself a good lawyer.'

Chapter 29

Bridget had to admit she enjoyed being in Brussels. Hendrik Brun was proving himself to be a man after her own heart, a computer aficionado. He had admitted the previous night that he enjoyed surfing the net, learning from the computer, and his typing was even faster than hers.

Bridget was confident the following morning that the day would wrap up her time in the Belgian capital, so much so that she checked out of the hotel, booked herself on Eurostar for six o'clock that evening, and arranged for Wendy to pick her up on her arrival at St Pancras Station.

In the office at the police station in Brussels, there was no need for Bridget to set up her laptop, having done it the previous day. The two of them, she and Brun, went straight into reviewing the CCTV from outside the shop in Herzele, the one monitor between the two of them. Scrolling back, the vehicle could be seen entering the town square, and then parking.

'See there,' Brun said. 'You can see Caxton getting out of the passenger's side.' Bridget looked closer, could see another person in the driver's seat, a large man, even larger than Caxton. Bridget was sure who it was, but it wasn't conclusive.

The pair moved to another monitor with higher definition. Zooming in helped but blurred the man. An overlay of O'Grady was imposed on the monitor, an attempt to align features: the nose, the mouth, the chin.

The identity was required first, the proof later. Both admitted defeat. Scrolling forward from where the vehicle had parked, it stopped just before driving out of range of the camera. Two men got out of the car. This time their features were unmistakable; it was Ainsley Caxton and Hector O'Grady. O'Grady could be seen picking up the phone: a time, as well as a location.

'Traceable,' Brun said. He sent an email, Bridget could not understand what was written as it was in Dutch. 'A colleague. He'll give us the number phoned.'

'You don't have O'Grady's number.'

'We must assume he dialled an English number. My colleague is very thorough. He will not let us down.'

Inside the Land Cruiser, with a brief side view in through the passenger's door, they could see a weapon, its barrel visible.

'There's proof,' Brun said.

'Proof that they committed the crime. Wherever the weapon is now, it's long gone. They could have brought it over from England, tied it to the chassis underneath, or they could have purchased it locally.'

'Only on the black market. The laws are strict here: residency, proof of address, police check.'

'The same as in England,' Bridget said, not sure of her facts.

'They would have brought it from England. Coming into Belgium, the checks are not that strict. Unfortunately, the trade in illegals, contraband, drugs, is one way, not two. The checks will be more vigorous going back to England. They would have dumped it; the river is the most likely. No chance of finding it now.'

'The deaths of Samuels and the others are murder,' Bridget said. 'It will be difficult for the Belgian authorities to prove a case.'

'Almost impossible. Circumstantially, yes, but the defence lawyers are smart. It'll never be proved. I'm afraid it's up to you in England to bring these two men to justice.'

***

Ralph Lawrence, no longer evicted from his flat, moved back. His mother was holding up, tearful at first, then stoic. For a reason he could not explain, he was sad. It wasn't as if Michael had amounted to much, but he was his son. He reflected on a cheerful baby, a playful young boy. Even Yolanda had eventually found some affection for him.

He had once caught her singing a lullaby as her son gurgled in his cot, only to pull away and make some excuse about trying to get him to sleep. She had a busy day the next day: socialising, a meeting at the magazine where she submitted the occasional article. He knew that she cared, but the woman was driven to better herself, and wasted emotions were not needed.

Two years later, she was away more than she was at home. He had followed her once, found out that the articles and the magazine were no longer needed. She had found herself a fancy man, a banker in the city. Ralph remembered the confrontation that night, where she defended her position, the child crying in the other room. After that, they never slept together, until she had finally left when Michael was six, old enough to be boarded out for five days a week at school, and then at seven years of age for the full week, long weekends and holidays excepted.

Yolanda had gone, he had an empty house, and he needed money. It was a friend from school who had told him about the rich pickings in the South of France and the Costa Brava. An Englishman, well-educated and speaking with a plum in the mouth, could get anything, be anything, he had told Ralph.

Two weeks later he had been in St Tropez, only visiting, checking if his friend was right, when a woman approached him. 'You must be a lord,' she said. Ralph knew that he had dressed well, something he always prided himself on. Instinctively he had replied. 'Lord Lawrence, the second son of the Earl of …' somewhere he couldn't remember now.

'My husband and I, we love the Royal Family.'

'Oh, yes. I get to spend time with them, went to school with one of them.'

Ralph unintentionally had struck the mother lode. His friend who had said it was easy pickings stood back in amazement as Ralph was whisked off to dinner, and then invited to stay at the mansion the woman and her husband had rented for the season. Over two weeks, he continued to spin them tale after tale: how the castle was in need of repairs; if only they could come over sometime, but it wasn't suitable for them; how he could introduce them into society, maybe even be able to get them to meet a prince.

It had been so easy, only interrupted because Michael was coming home for two weeks. As he left the mansion, the wife thrust a cheque for fifty thousand pounds into his hand. He had done nothing, hurt nobody, not even committed a crime. All he had done was entertain them, give them a thrill. The money to them was nothing, to him it was a godsend.

Michael, on his father's return, had found him to be generous and attentive, but he was still only young. It was the last time that they had spent any time together until the flat in Bayswater, and now he was dead, the victim of drugs, the victim of callous and shallow parents, the victim of Helmsley. The man had annoyed him at school, and now he had taken his only child from him.

Ralph Lawrence took a handkerchief from his trouser pocket and blew his nose, as well as dabbing his eyes. He then picked up his phone and dialled Antigua.

***

Bridget had debriefed Homicide on her return to Challis Street, also giving Wendy the largest box of Belgian chocolates that she could buy.

The team watched the edited video replays from Herzele, crystal clear images of Caxton and O'Grady, the rifle inside the vehicle. 'It's them,' Isaac said. 'The only problem is that it's not proof, just more evidence if we manage to secure enough evidence against them for a trial.'

'The weapon?' Bridget said.

'Without it, Forensics can't do bullet analysis. Regardless, we do have a case against the men. We can pull them in, make them sweat. We've got Ralph Lawrence's evidence as well. Anyone else?'

'Not yet,' Larry said. 'Give me twelve hours while I go and talk to the man who put me onto Frost. He knows more, I'm sure of it.'

'He's not going to allow himself to be compromised,' Wendy said.

'Who knows how these people think. If Frost is out of the way, then there are more suckers for them to bleed. My man's no saint, even if he pretends he is. I'll push, see what I can get. Maybe best if you phone up

Emily Matson, tell her to keep a close watch on Frost and his henchmen, and to be prepared to pull Caxton and O'Grady in at short notice. Not Frost, though. We need him to sweat some more. Without them around, who knows? Easy to be tough when you're protected, not so good when you're on your own.'

Emily Matson intensified the surveillance on Caxton and O'Grady. The DI whose nose was out of joint was once again complaining to the station's superintendent about being sidelined while his junior was getting all the glory. He had been quick on the phone after leaving the super's office, Emily overhearing the gist of what was being said, certain he was speaking to Alwyn Davies.

Larry told Emily to stay focussed and to ignore the office politics. She had the full support of Challis Street Homicide and Chief Superintendent Goddard. He only hoped her superintendent was up to the task. If he wasn't then Isaac and Goddard would make a personal representation at Greenwich, endeavour to bolster the superintendent, a man with just over one year to go for his full pension and retirement, and who did not crave the ignominy of a reduction in his rank and his pension.

Caxton was out and about, buying McDonald's one day, a pizza the next. O'Grady was not so visible, although he had been seen in a local gym pushing weights. Both men were feared in the area, both as likely to grab someone by the collar than wish them a good day.

If they were to be brought in, Emily knew, it would have to be one at a time. Indications were that they would not come voluntarily. Neither had committed any offence in England, not in recent years, although Caxton had picked up more parking fines than most, but that wasn't an arrestable offence as he had paid them all on time. O'Grady had nothing against him.

The hotel in Brussels where Caxton and O'Grady stayed had been found, the bill paid, no trouble from either man, although they had drunk too much in the bar. Isaac knew the case was weak, and he could bring them in, but a smart lawyer would have them out within a couple of hours. Ralph Lawrence would testify, but only if Frost had murdered his father and was locked up, otherwise he wasn't going to confront the lender of no hope and his henchman purely on the say-so of the police that they would protect him. They had not managed to protect Michael, and he had seen the police protection already offered to him and his family: minimal at best, useless if the truth were known. No doubt subject to budgetary constraints or some other jargon that everyone seemed to use.

'The kneecapped man, what about him?' Isaac said to Larry. They were out of the office, walking around Gilbert Lawrence's mansion, trying to go over what they had so far. Arresting Frost looked possible, especially if they could get Caxton or O'Grady to break. But Frost had no apparent connection to Gilbert's death, no prior knowledge that Ralph and Gilbert had been related.

Inside the previously bolted off main section of the building, the two police officers could see that the CSIs had been careful, no fingerprints, no footprints, but they had walked through with their equipment, and the floor, previously covered in dust, had been disturbed. Larry and Isaac had ensured to put on gloves and overshoes and to let Gordon Windsor know that they were in the house, a matter of courtesy rather than a procedural requirement. They climbed the sweeping staircase, the steps creaking as they moved. It was not a pleasant place to be, still smelling of decay and death, although the death was more imagined than real.

At the top of the stairs, a cold breeze. Larry froze, not sure what to do. He had read his children a bedtime story the previous night, a fairy tale about a princess in a draughty castle. It was recommended for ages five to seven, although it had a touch of the melodrama about it, not that it concerned them at the time, or even him. But now he and his senior were in that castle, even though it was smaller, and the princess, a dead body, had been in the second room along the landing. Isaac opened the door, saw that the bed remained, although the body was long gone. He phoned Picket in Pathology. 'Any reason why you can't release Dorothy Lawrence for burial?'

'I'll write the death certificate.'

Isaac phoned Caroline Dickson to tell her; she was relieved.

Outside the mansion, decaying after such a long time of neglect, the two officers stood to one side of where Molly Dempster had found Gilbert lying on the ground. The area was still marked off, but the grass had since grown.

'It could still be Ralph, even though he was with the Spanish police,' Isaac said.

'He could have arranged someone else. Not Caxton and O'Grady, bulls in a china shop, those two.'

Chapter 30

Jill Dundas made contingency plans. There had just been too much interest in Gilbert's death, too much sentimentalising about Michael's death, too much morbid interest in Dorothy. Her father had been a brilliant man, a man to be revered, but he was not mentioned, while a drug addict and a skeleton were given preference.

The popular press continued to write on the subject. Michael's death, and the subsequent arrest of a known agitator for involuntary manslaughter, raised speculation in the scurrilous newspapers and on social media about the possibility of demonic practices in the case of Dorothy, the sacrificial death of Gilbert, the just reward from God for Michael's death.

Jill knew that none of it was true, but it was not possible to give a truthful account of all that had transpired. Gilbert had indeed been senile but showing moments of lucidity. His business mind had remained detached from his social behaviour: the death of his wife Dorothy unhinging him for many years. It was only her father who had been able to get near to the man, and he had known, he must have, of the horror that was on the second floor of the mansion. But not once did her father reveal what had been committed, not until the last few months when she came to know that her father's time was up, the doctor picking up an ongoing degradation in his health, a fluctuation in his heart.

'Jill, you must know the truth,' he had said. It was late at night, and he had been sitting in his favourite chair, a glass of port in his hand. As she sat there, he recounted the saga of Gilbert Lawrence, Dorothy's death, the irrational and unsound mind of his friend as if he was having a brainstorm, the pressure too much for the most lucid of men. It had been her father's decision to ensure Gilbert Lawrence's legacy. It had required the signature of the great man, gladly given as he suffered, unsure whether he was alive or dead. After that, her father had told her, Gilbert vacillated between sanity and utter madness, not willing to leave the prison he had created. The trips to the off-licence, even though they had commenced years previously, were the man's attempts to reconnect.

Her father had convinced her that it was better to let sleeping dogs lie, and not to resurrect the past, to never let on what had happened in that house to that man, that woman. Dorothy had been an ill woman for a long time, her father said. A woman who had hurled herself off the top step of the staircase, dying at the bottom, not from a broken neck, but from despair complicated by grief over her son, anger with her daughter for marrying Desmond and moving away, from internal bleeding.

'Don't you understand,' Leonard said that night to Jill, 'Gilbert blamed them all. Dorothy for dying, Ralph for what he had become, Caroline for upsetting her mother. It was only me that he would see, not Molly. She raised other emotions in him, not that I always understood why, but he cared for her. He never mentioned an affair, but…'

And now Jill knew about Ralph, and Molly being his mother. Legally it did not impact on Gilbert's last will and testament, although it may give her leverage, a means to delay what would become certain in time: that Gilbert had been mad, but he was becoming saner, and even at his advanced age he had decided to ease out of seclusion and to take control of his empire, to make his peace with his family.

***

The man didn't phone often, but Frost knew he was worth the monthly retainer that he paid, a package left under a bench at the entrance to Greenwich Observatory on the first Thursday of every month at eight thirty-three in the evening, the man arriving at the spot two minutes later. The news was disturbing. Caxton and O'Grady were liable to be picked up at any time. Frost trusted Caxton, not so much O'Grady. The evidence was flimsy, and the police technique would be to arrest the men, pressure them heavily and hope that one would crack. He knew one of them would; he could not take a chance.

Frost knew that it was all due to Ralph Lawrence, a malignant sore of no worth. Lawrence had brought the police to his doorstep, and they were putting two and two together, coming up with three, but soon it would be four. And then it would be him at the police station, the connections made with Lawrence, with Belgium. A private man, Frost knew that if he wanted to stay where he was, free and not in prison, he would need to break the links joining him to the crimes that had been committed.

Inside his penthouse, he summoned one of his men. 'How do you like fishing?' he said.

'We go out occasionally, rent a boat not far from here.'

'Good. Take your partner out today. Make sure he doesn't come back.'

'Can I ask why?'

'It is better that you don't know. And make sure that he rents the boat and picks you up somewhere else, somewhere you will not be seen.'

'Are there more?'

'The first must be today. The others, if there are to be any, we will discuss after you return.'

Frost, a man who did not procrastinate, felt calmer, confident that he was making the right decision. Two previous decisions were proving troublesome, he knew that. First, the murder of Samuels, motivated more by the man's intransigence about paying the interest, although he had repaid the principal, done as a warning, and then lending money to the weak and insignificant son of Gilbert Lawrence.

Another phone call from his informer. 'Tomorrow afternoon.' Two words only, but it was enough for Frost. The police were getting closer, and he could not hold them at bay indefinitely. Whatever he did, he needed to ensure his survival, Caxton's if he could, but if he couldn't, then he would have tried. Frost logged onto his laptop, checked his bank accounts. He started transferring money out of the country: somewhere warmer, somewhere that not too many questions were asked, somewhere he did not want to go, but freedom was better than the alternatives.

By the time he had finished two hours had passed. He had seen the boat go by on the Thames. It was not a large boat but sufficient for two. In the small cabin, dressed in wet weather gear, was Hector O'Grady. Further down the river, close to where Caxton had parked his car, O'Grady would pull in before the two men headed out into deeper water, a fishing spot that both knew. Fishing was a passion of O'Grady's, and Caxton had been out with him on a few occasions, invariably bagging more fish.

'Unusual for the boss to let us off for a few hours,' O'Grady said.

Caxton looked over at the man he regarded as a friend. The water was choppy, the beer was cold, and both men had to admit to enjoying themselves. A container ship went past, its wake rocking the small boat. O'Grady's rod started to move, a fish testing the bait, and then the rod bent further, the fish hooked.

'I've got one,' O'Grady said. He started reeling in the line, the fish fighting him, Caxton to one side leaning over the stern of the boat, a net in his hand ready to scoop up what had been caught.

'Keep the net there,' O'Grady shouted.

Caxton took two steps back and drew a small gun from his pocket. 'Sorry,' he said. 'The boss wants you out.' He pulled the trigger and shot twice, one in the back and another in the man's neck, his aim deflected by the rocking of the boat.

Lying prostrate on the boat's decking, his fishing rod discarded, O'Grady gasped, 'Why?'

'It's nothing personal,' Caxton said. He retook aim and shot O'Grady through the brain. He then pulled up the anchor, secured it firmly to the body of his former partner and then threw him over the side. With the man sinking to the bottom of the river, Caxton started the engine on the boat and headed for shore. Once he was within ten yards of it, he turned the boat around and pointed its bow out into deeper water. He then took his gun and shot two holes in the wooden hull, before enlarging them with a safety axe that had been secured to a bulkhead. He set the throttle to maximum, the engine revving, the boat gaining momentum. He then jumped over the side of the boat and swam to shore, although he almost didn't make it as the cold water sapped his strength. Ashore, he made for his car, felt on top of the front offside tyre, and retrieved a key. He started the engine and turned on the heater. On the back seat, dry clothes and a towel.

Chapter 31

The number that O'Grady had phoned from the village of Herzele in Belgium had been traced back to Gary Frost. Even more evidence for the case against him. The content of the conversation that had lasted for less than one minute was not known.

A sorry-looking man was brought into Greenwich Police Station at two in the afternoon. He had not resisted when Emily Matson took him into custody on suspicion of murder, as well as the grievous bodily harm of Ralph Lawrence. The kneecapped man was still not willing to talk. The evidence in both cases was dependent on Caxton admitting that he was guilty, and Larry had been with her when the arrest was made. There was no sign of Hector O'Grady, and the low-key surveillance of the two men had missed his disappearance.

Technically the murder of Steve Samuels was the responsibility of the Belgian police force, and Inspecteur Hougardy was on his way to England, although he wouldn't be present in Greenwich for the first interview with the man who had been detained. The proof was flimsy, purely a chain of events leading to an inevitable conclusion, and although Caxton and O'Grady had been identified by two people in Herzele, another in the hotel in Brussels where they had checked in under false names, there were no fingerprints, no forensic evidence. Emily would be conducting the interview, her first of a murderer. Larry would also be in the interview room, and Isaac would be outside, chafing at the bit, knowing that he would go in harder than the other two, although he hoped that Larry had learnt enough by now to get Caxton flustered and to make the man contradict himself.

Alongside Caxton sat the offensive figure of Edward Sharman, which surprised Isaac, not sure how the man, a singularly ill-mannered and belligerent person, had managed to find his way across the river. Sharman was competent, Isaac knew that, good at getting the guilty off on a technicality. Isaac knew that DIs Matson and Hill had drawn the short straw. They were going to be hard pushed to break through, and Sharman would be doing the majority of the talking for his client.

Outside in the reception area of the police station, Gary Frost was conspicuous by his absence.

A full team of uniforms had been mobilised, even bringing in more manpower from Challis Street, to look for Hector O'Grady. The last that had been known of him was that he had gone out fishing, not unusual in itself, the man at the boat shed said. 'Hector, he's keen, even when the weather's not good. No doubt he takes some liquid refreshments to keep him warm. Always brings the boat back in good condition, even cleans it for me. And yes, he took it out yesterday, not a good day, but the fish should have been biting, not that I'd eat them myself, too small mainly, but Hector, he would have. Tough guy from what I've been told, but when the boat never came back, that's when I started worrying.'

The evidence about the boat was still coming through; another fisherman had seen it sink into the water. The detective inspector who resented Emily Matson usurping him, especially with the trip to Brussels, had been assigned to look for O'Grady. It had been a direct order from his superintendent, a directive he accepted graciously, although he had been seething behind his clenched teeth. 'Don't you worry, Superintendent. Always pleased to help a fellow officer.'

On the river, the local coastguard, the Thames River Police, and a couple of men who worked at the boat shed where the boat had come from trawled up and down in the vicinity of the area identified as O'Grady's most likely destination. Each boat used GPS to keep to their path as they crisscrossed an area of five square miles. The tide was on the turn as they moved up and down, ideal for finding something, but another two hours and a stiff breeze from the east would come up, and if anything was floating, then the chances were that it would be lost.

In the station, Emily Matson followed the correct procedure, informed Ainsley Caxton of his rights, asked everyone to state their name, and in the case of the two police officers their rank. An immediate rebuff came from Sharman, stating on the record that his client was not guilty of any crime. Isaac had briefed Emily beforehand to take the blustering, the rhetoric, in her stride and to keep focussed. She heeded the advice, but she still felt unnerved by a man in a three-piece Savile Row suit, a man who had practised law for as long as she had been alive, a man who knew all the tricks, and a man who was very expensive, more expensive than Caxton could afford, but Frost could.

Isaac knew that Frost was not protecting Caxton for Caxton's benefit. He could see that the heat needed to be raised on Frost, and soon. The surveillance of the man was tighter now, and it was known that he was in Greenwich. Isaac and Wendy left the police station and drove the short distance to the man's penthouse, the man himself answering the intercom on the door this time.

'Detective Chief Inspector Isaac Cook, Detective Sergeant Wendy Gladstone, Challis Street, Homicide. We have a few questions for you.'

'I'm not talking to the police without my lawyer being present.'

'An innocent man would let us in, but maybe you're not. Sharman's going to be busy for some time with Caxton, no doubt he'll weasel him out of there, but how about you, Mr Frost?'

The latch on the door released. 'Come up, I've nothing to hide.'

Isaac turned to Wendy. 'He's feeling vulnerable. O'Grady's not here, and Caxton's under pressure. We can break this case yet.'

'Gilbert Lawrence?'

'The pieces are falling into place. Deal with this, then we raise the heat on the others. Ralph's still not in the clear, neither is his sister. And as for Jill Dundas, a nasty piece of work behind that façade, she will still need further questioning. Once we start solving one case, everyone's nerves will become ragged.'

'Of course, I'm supporting Caxton. He's been with me for years,' Frost said. He was standing at the window of the penthouse, staring out at the river. The weather was looking increasingly wild.

'Hector O'Grady, what can you tell us about him?'

'He's been with me for three years. A good man, and his not being here is out of character.'

'How did you manage when they were in Belgium?' Isaac said.

'And when was that, Inspector?' Frost said. He moved to the other side of the room, sat down on a sofa, beckoned the two police officers to make themselves comfortable. Wendy thought him to be an attractive man, not that it didn't make him guilty.

'When they killed Samuels. We've got the dates, the time that O'Grady phoned you. An error using your number. Arrogance on your part, I suppose, believing that you could thumb your nose at the Belgian police.'

'I receive a lot of phone calls. No doubt some of them are from overseas. It doesn't, however, prove that Caxton and O'Grady were in Belgium. I knew Samuels, I'll not deny that. From what I was told, he had skipped the country, owing me and others money.'

'You didn't pursue him?'

'I tried to find him, but with no success.'

'And if you had?'

'The man knew the conditions of the loan.'

'Violence?'

'Not me. That's not how I operate.'

'It is, so don't give me your nonsense. You use violence as one of the conditions of default. Kneecapping, trussing a man up and beating him senseless, following another overseas and murdering him, and then letting it be known it's what happens to defaulters. What do you think we are, fools? And how do you keep one step ahead of us? Do you have corrupt cops feeding you information? Where are they? Who are they? Mr Frost, you will be next at the police station, and I intend to make sure you can't wriggle out of this one. The case will be so watertight that even Sharman won't be able to help you.'

Frost sat back on his chair, a grin on his face. 'DCI Cook, you have got it all wrong. I am an innocent man. Successful, I'll grant you, and tough with those I deal with, but I am an honest and peaceful man, the sort of person who feels sorry for an animal in distress. I even donate to several charities in the area. Ask around, you'll find that people don't always like me, but there is respect.'

***

Ainsley Caxton, a man who had learnt the art of saying little in a police interview, knew nothing about boats, especially the type that showed up on echo sounders. One of the boats from the boatyard, equipped with one to show fish shoals, the depth of the water, picked up the unusual shape.

The initial detection was relayed by the river police to Greenwich Police Station and then on to DCI Isaac Cook, the highest-ranking officer attached to the investigation, even though he was operating outside of his area.

It would be two hours before the police divers could be on station at the location. The boat, almost certainly the one of interest, was resting on the river bottom at a depth of twenty feet. The visibility was virtually zero, although one of the two police boats carried a submersible camera. Lowering it over the side, and taking into account the slow-moving tide, the boat moved up and down over the area. On the third run, with the camera at a depth of fifteen feet, an image could be seen on the monitor in the cabin. It was not clear, but it was recent, and it could only be O'Grady's boat.

The interview with Caxton was halted for six hours, long enough to allow a full investigation of the sunken boat in the River Thames. Caxton had been brought in for murder, so the twenty-four-hour deadline before charging or release did not apply. He could be held for thirty-six hours, subject to the inevitable paperwork being dealt with, long enough for the boat to be brought up from the river bottom and for Gordon Windsor and his team of crime scene investigators to check it out, and to bring in Forensics if needed.

At the penthouse, Gary Frost was being kept up to date on developments. At St Pancras Station, Inspecteur Jules Hougardy was climbing into the back seat of a taxi, and at Greenwich Police Station, Ainsley Caxton sat in a cell calmly eating a pizza, confident that his boss would get him out.

The Lawrence family, especially Ralph, were also being updated, a ploy by Isaac to relax their stance, to make them believe that Frost was more than likely the murderer of Gilbert, or the man behind the murder, and that he had engineered it to allow him to close in on Ralph. Not that Isaac believed it, but he wanted the guilty to feel as though they had got away with the crime. Caxton and O'Grady were known villains, men who had made a career of violence, but they had not killed Gilbert. Frost was not a murderer, just a smart man who used those capable of such crimes to his advantage.

Larry sat with Emily at Greenwich Police Station, anxiously waiting for updates. The inspector who had taken umbrage at her usurping him hovered in the background, coming in close sometimes, attempting to draw Larry away. It did not work. Larry had spent time with Inspector Emily Matson, knew that her lack of experience was offset by her dedication to the job and that she was honest. From what Larry had heard of the other inspector, he did not trust him. The superintendent had come down, introduced himself to Larry, told him that he and Chief Superintendent Goddard were friends from a long time back.

Out on the water, the two river police boats waited. A barge was on its way from upstream, as was a floating crane with straps suitable for lifting the sunken boat. It wasn't a big boat, no more than twenty-two feet, but it was important that no evidence was destroyed unnecessarily. Typically, a sunken boat would be brought up if it was a hazard to navigation, or if there were extenuating reasons: insurance, valuables on board, a dead body. The first of the divers had been inside the cabin, found no corpse. The second diver had scoured around the immediate vicinity. Both divers were tethered to the surface by lines, another diver on standby up above just in case one of those down below got into trouble, but he was not needed.

Seven hours and twenty-five minutes after the boat had first been located it broke the surface of the River Thames. Even after such a short time, it was covered in mud and a few crabs, some crayfish, as well. It was eased onto the barge and secured. The nearest land where it could be tied up was close to the boatshed it had first set out from.

Isaac was at the dock as the barge tied off. Frost watched from his penthouse, disturbed by what he could see. The instruction to Caxton had been explicit enough, but then the man wasn't the smartest. He should have known the river that close into Greenwich was not that deep. A more intelligent man would have taken the boat further downstream and into deeper water, but Frost realised that nothing could be done now.

On the boat, now starting to dry out, Gordon Windsor was standing. He had donned his coveralls, his overshoes, his gloves, and he wore a mask, not so much to prevent contamination but to minimise the smell of the river and the drying mud.

Inside the small cabin, Windsor picked up a jacket, inside it the name of Ainsley Caxton. He held it up for Isaac and his team to see.

'It wasn't there when the boat went out,' said Joe Garibaldi, second-generation English with Italian grandparents. 'I always check when the boats go out that they're clean and no one's left anything in them. Sometimes they leave a phone when they come back, or a wallet. You'd be amazed at how careless some people are.'

Isaac wasn't.

'Isaac, kit yourself up. Inspector Matson, Larry, you as well,' Windsor shouted.

The three moved closer to the boat after following instructions. 'No need to come onboard,' Windsor said. 'Just look underneath.' The three could see the holes. 'What does it mean?' Isaac said.

'The boat has been scuttled. There are signs of a bullet being fired through the hull, not that it would have been a big enough hole to have sunk it that quickly. Someone's gone at it with something bigger, an axe probably. No sign of the gun or the axe, though.'

'Anything else missing?' Emily asked.

'The anchor. If your man has killed someone out on the river, he's probably been thrown over the side with the anchor tied to him.'

'Any chance of finding the body?' Larry asked.

'Don't raise your hopes too high. A few weeks and a body will be down to bones and a few bits of flesh: natural putrefaction, plus the fish and the crabs. After that, the bones could go out with the tide, the current can get strong out there. We're checking for fingerprints, but don't hold out for us finding anything conclusive.'

Bridget phoned, Larry answered. 'That's great. I'll be there within the hour.'

Larry turned to the others. 'Keith Waters, the kneecapped man, he's heard about Caxton being taken into custody, also that O'Grady's missing, presumed dead. He's willing to give a statement.'

'That means we can bring in Frost, and make it stick,' Isaac said.

'For grievous bodily harm, not for murder.'

'Okay, leave Frost to stew for the time being. Larry, you and Wendy take the man's statement. Emily, it's your show,' Isaac said. It was her jurisdiction, and he recognised the need to bow to her authority and input.

'A few more hours won't do any harm. I'll make sure that Caxton knows what's going on. Let him sweat a bit longer.'

Chapter 32

Yolanda had been sad when Ralph Lawrence phoned to tell her about the death of her son. He had wanted to see her again, to make her come back to him, but he knew she would not. 'He's gone, Ralph,' she said. In the background, Ralph could hear the sound of people laughing. In the Caribbean, she had a life and money and friends. All he could offer was a two-bedroom flat in Bayswater, and possibly years of legal wrangling while he, and hopefully his sister, took on Jill Dundas.

'I understand,' Ralph had said. 'Will you come back for his funeral?'

'Not now. I will mourn in my own way. One day I will return and visit his grave, place a few flowers, shed a tear. I loved you, Ralph, you know that, but we will never meet again.' And then she was gone, back to her life in the sun. It suited Ralph to think that she would sit down in her quiet moments and reflect on her son, on him, the love that all three had once had, but he knew she probably wouldn't. She had been a selfish woman back then, she still was, but he would miss her.

***

Keith Waters gave his statement, Larry and Wendy witnessing it. Out at Greenwich, Inspecteur Jules Hougardy looked out at the River Thames from Zizzi's restaurant on Greenwich Promenade. On the other side of the table, Isaac and Emily. It was Italian, and all three were eating pasta.

'We have an old-fashioned fish and chip shop in the town,' Emily said. 'We'll take you there before you go back, as long as you don't mind it soggy with vinegar.'

'A pint of warm beer afterwards,' Hougardy replied. 'But, for now, what do we have?'

'If we can prove that Caxton murdered O'Grady, then he's subject to English law. Whatever happens, he can be sentenced for grievous bodily harm.'

'The case against him in Belgium is still circumstantial. We know he's guilty, but our defence lawyers are as good as yours. Are you searching the river for O'Grady's body?'

'We are, but it's like looking for a needle in a haystack. Unless it catches on something, the chances of recovery are slim. Larry and Wendy will be back within the hour. Then Emily and Larry can go to work on Caxton again.'

***

Caxton was led into the interview room at Greenwich. He had now been formally charged with the murder of Hector O'Grady, a fingerprint having been retrieved from the sunken boat, as well as the lesser charge of grievous bodily harm inflicted on the persons of Keith Waters and Ralph Lawrence. The recovered boat continued to dry at the wharf, no more than two hundred yards from the police station.

Emily was taking the lead role, Larry backing her up. In another room sat Jules Hougardy, Isaac and Wendy.

'My client wishes to make a statement,' Edward Sharman said. Procedurally, they were remiss in not

269

advising him of one late development, but Emily, as well as the rest of the team, wanted the final blow to come as a surprise.

'I, Ainsley Gregory Caxton, of 15, India Street, Greenwich, wish to state that I was not involved in the disappearance of Hector O'Grady, a colleague as well as a friend. The boat he had rented and which has subsequently been found indicates the worst. I had been out with him before, and I can only hope that he is recovered alive and well. The statements by Ralph Lawrence and Keith Waters are lies. They are both weak men who had failed to keep their finances under control. They are using fraudulent untruths as leverage against my employer, a man who lent them money in good faith.'

'Is that it?' Larry said after Caxton had finished.

'The evidence is circumstantial,' Sharman said. 'I am insisting that my client is released immediately.'

'It's not so easy, Mr Sharman,' Emily said. She remembered Isaac's advice: 'Start gently, slowly raise the tempo, keep your final arguments for last. Fluster, confuse, get them to make mistakes, not you.' She knew that at the first interview she had not followed the advice given and that Sharman had bettered her. She was not willing to let it happen a second time.

'Why?'

'Mr Caxton and Hector O'Grady were in Belgium when Steve Samuels was murdered along with a taxi driver and two prostitutes. We have impounded the Toyota Land Cruiser they took to Belgium; CCTV footage and facial recognition technology have confirmed it to be them. They were travelling on false documents. We also have two witnesses who saw them there. If Mr Caxton is released from this station, an extradition order is in place for him to be rearrested, pending extradition to

Brussels. Whatever happens here today, your client is in for a lengthy prison term. Bail will be refused here and in Belgium. Mr Caxton's track record is not good; no judge will allow him freedom while he waits to be tried.'

'I've done nothing wrong,' Caxton said. He looked over at Sharman who took no notice.

'A bullet has been recovered from the boat,' Emily said.

'Is that proof?' Sharman said.

'The bullet is with Forensics.'

'And what do you intend to do with it? It's a bullet, not a gun. There are no fingerprints on a bullet.'

'But there is on the boat, and we do have Mr Caxton's jacket.'

'I lent it to him. It was a cold day, and his jacket wasn't as warm as mine,' Caxton said.

'Even if it was, and you're telling the truth, it still doesn't explain the fingerprint.'

'I'd been out on the boat before. Maybe it's old.'

'We've checked with the owner of the boat. You had never been on that boat. There are three boats for hire. One was out of the water for maintenance. The other one was already rented out. We have full records and the testimony of the owner. You had been on that boat once, and that was when Hector O'Grady was shot and thrown over the side. Mr Caxton, you are guilty of murder. Now is the time to own up,' Emily said.

'It was an accident, I swear it. Hector was in a funny mood, someone had taken his girlfriend. We went out with a few beers, a can of worms and a couple of fishing lines. He was my friend. I wanted to help him.'

Sharman looked at his client, shook his head. The first rule of defence, never admit to anything, no matter how inconsequential.

'Why kill him?'

'It was an accident. He's out there, he's argumentative, and the beer is getting to him. He was never a big drinker, and now he's into his fifth. I tried to stop him, attempted to take the gun off him. He's going wild, shooting into the water just because the fish aren't biting. I grab the gun, it goes off.'

'He's dead?'

'Dead, yes, he was. I'm panicking. You would never believe it was an accident. What was I to do? I couldn't come in here, throw myself on your mercy.'

'O'Grady's body?'

'He fell off the side when the gun went off. I tried to grab hold, but I'm not good with boats. Hector knew all about them, I didn't. I always wore a life jacket out there. Hector said they were only for young girls and weaklings. He could sometimes be insulting, not that I took much notice most times, but out there he was dangerous. I'm telling you the truth.'

'And the axe through the bottom of the boat, the bullets as well?'

'I was panicking. I've told you this. What more do you want to say?'

'How did you get to shore? You've told us you wore a life jacket, but we found both of them on board the boat.'

'I swam.'

'You scuttled the boat first. And why didn't you get on at the boatshed, the same place as O'Grady? Was this part of the plan?'

'My client needs time to consider,' Sharman said. Emily continued with her questioning.

'Mr Caxton, you've lied about being in Brussels, you've lied about Ralph Lawrence, about Keith Waters. Why should we believe you now?'

'Because it's the truth. I didn't mean to kill him.'

'Mr Caxton, you will be held pending a trial. You will also be charged with the murder of Steve Samuels in Brussels. Also, the charges of grievous bodily harm will stand. Whatever happens, you, Mr Caxton, will be spending many years in prison.'

***

'Five years for grievous bodily harm,' Isaac said. 'That's the maximum for what Caxton did to Lawrence and Waters, concurrent sentences. The judge may decide on consecutive, but it's unlikely.'

The team, including Jules Hougardy, were sitting in the Prince of Greenwich pub. Everyone had a pint of beer, including the Belgian police inspector. Caxton was locked up, Frost was still sweating it out in his penthouse, and a search of the River Thames downstream from where O'Grady had disappeared, presumed dead, had found nothing. The sunken boat had provided no more clues, and the case against Caxton for the murder of O'Grady was based on the man's confession, although he was holding to his story that it was an accident.

'No chance of a conviction in Belgium, either,' Hougardy said. He had to admit to enjoying himself away from his office in Brussels. Even Bridget had made the trip across the Thames, one of the few occasions that her routine varied from Challis Street to home and back. Both she and Wendy were making a night of it: a few too many drinks, a couple of sore heads in the morning.

'We'll bring in Frost in the morning, lay it on heavy. He'll have the indomitable Edward Sharman with him,' Emily said, jubilant about how she had handled herself during the interview with Caxton. Outside the pub a river mist was closing in, a clear sign that the search for O'Grady would be called off.

Gordon Windsor and his team had concluded their work on the boat and were now back on their side of the river. The bullet recovered was with Forensics, although it would only reveal the calibre, not the make of the gun and who had fired the shot. Even so, breaking Caxton had been a good result. The car taken to Brussels had yielded nothing more of interest, only that off-roaders were a breed unto themselves in that they could take perfectly good machinery and subject it to so much abuse.

In the pub, Hougardy talked, his accent endearing him to the police officers and the other patrons in the pub. He was a hit, and he appreciated the warm welcome afforded him.

It was eleven in the evening, and the team were on their last drinks. Downstream from Greenwich, an elderly couple were walking their dog along the shore. They spotted a dead dolphin, not seen often in the lower reaches of the Thames, but with the cleaner water of the last few years, not unknown. The man, more agile than his wife, who was relegated to using a walking stick, followed his dog down to the rotting carcass. It was covered in seaweed and slime, and it was neither pleasant to look at nor to smell. Albert Gravelly, a retired bus driver, forty-two years with the same company and never an accident, took the stick that the dog always carried in its mouth. Looking at the carcass again, the moonlight reflecting off it, Gravelly prodded it with the stick. It was not what a man with a weak constitution needed. He shouted to his wife who was sitting on a bench ten yards away. 'You had better phone the police,' he said.

Albert Gravelly, a man who had seen many things over the years, especially on the late-night shift, had never seen what his dog had wanted to sniff. He took the stick and threw it for the dog as he walked back to his wife.

Chapter 33

'You'd never make a sailor out of Caxton,' Hougardy said. The full team from the pub were present at the site where O'Grady had washed up, all except Bridget who had left, not to go home, but to update her records in Challis Street. A former lover had accused her of being a workaholic, but she knew she wasn't. She was just a person who enjoyed her job, and if the others in Homicide were out and dealing with an unexpected development, she would have felt guilty just going home.

The crime scene investigators were on the scene, floodlights had been installed, and a generator was up on the path above. The Gravellys, both in their eighties, had been taken back to their small cottage, the dog barking in the back seat of the police car. Larry and Wendy were taking their statements. They had found the body or, more correctly, the dog had, and apart from that, there wasn't much more they could say.

Gordon Windsor and his team attempted to place a crime scene tent around the body, although a wind was blowing, and it was very exposed. In the end, a decision was made to move the body to a more sheltered position. A thorough check was completed in the immediate vicinity first.

Five uniforms had come over from Challis Street, another four from Greenwich Police Station. They were moving up and down from the crime scene looking for further evidence, although that was deemed unlikely, as the body recovered was fully clothed.

'Not much of a sailor?' Emily reminded Hougardy of his earlier comment.

'If he had wanted the body to remain undiscovered, he'd have made sure to weigh him down, tie him off to prevent him floating to the surface. There's still a piece of rope attached to the body, a sloppy knot.'

'Are you into sailing?'

'When I was younger. The man had tied a granny knot, not a reef. Not that either is ideal if he wanted to body to stay submerged. Are we assuming the man had been tied to the anchor?'

'We are.'

'Then why had he not been secured properly? Under the water, there are currents that ebb and flow, some colder than others. And knots are subjected to that movement, and they and the rope are buffeted. Some will loosen, some will stay in place, even tighten, and others will eventually unravel. That is what has happened here.'

'He's right,' Windsor said. 'The condition of the body indicates that it has been submerged, and not just floating on the surface. Also, the man had been shot three times, one of them in the head, area of the brain. There are signs that crabs have been on the body, but not many, as the body has not started serious decomposition yet.'

'Murder?' Emily said.

'Three bullets, one in the head, it seems likely,' Windsor said. 'We're not staying here any longer. The body will be taken back to Pathology. Isaac, you can go and annoy them later on this morning.'

***

Gary Frost, updated by his source, could only see the noose tightening. If it hadn't been for Ralph Lawrence, none of this would have happened. He felt intense anger towards the man, a need to strike out. Used to making decisions, he wasn't sure what to do. He was dithering, he needed out of the penthouse, out of Greenwich.

Downstairs, in the garage beneath the building, a car. He took the keys, left his penthouse and found the Mercedes. He did not drive often, but this time he would. As he came out from the garage, a police car opposite saw him and reported it to Greenwich Police Station, to the inspector charged with keeping a watch on Frost.

'Let him go,' had been the instruction. 'We'll keep a watch from here.'

The two police officers who had kept watch overnight complied with the instruction. After all, the man was their senior.

One of those in the vehicle, a smart young man, ambitious as well, phoned Emily.

'What did he say?' Emily reacted with alarm. It was still early, and she had just fallen asleep. She had set the alarm for two hours, not fifteen minutes, but the information was startling.

'Inspector Camberwell told us to let Frost go. It made no sense to us, but we followed instructions.'

'Any idea where Frost is now?'

'None. He took off, heading west.'

Emily phoned Isaac to update him, then her superintendent. He was straight out of bed and on the phone. 'Camberwell, fifteen minutes, my office.'

Bridget, also woken up, was at the office at Challis Street within twenty-five minutes, and logging into the CCTV cameras in Greenwich. The registration number of the Mercedes that Frost was driving was known, and the police cars in London were equipped with automatic number plate recognition.

Meanwhile, Frost had parked across from Ralph's flat in Bayswater. He was in a side street, concealed from view.

An arrest warrant had been issued, with instructions for Frost to be detained and taken to Greenwich Police Station, suspected of being an accomplice to murder. He was not considered dangerous, but officers were advised to approach him with caution.

At Greenwich, Jules Hougardy was back in the police station. He had stayed the night in a hotel no more than five minutes' walk away. Isaac and Larry were finding their own way back across the Thames. Wendy was with Bridget, helping if she could, lending moral support if she couldn't. Both women were feeling the effects of a heavy night, although now was not the time to complain.

Edward Sharman arrived at Greenwich Police Station at ten minutes after nine in the morning. He was not in a good mood. Emily was pleased, so were the other members of the team. He had been updated as to the situation, a full report of the current status at his disposal. Ainsley Caxton, on being advised that Gary Frost had left his penthouse and was nowhere to be found, realised that he was vulnerable. He had admitted to the charge of assault, minor to him, as he had committed far worse crimes in the past. Sharman had chastised him for his outburst in the interview room. 'You bloody fool,' he had said. 'All you had to do was to keep your mouth shut, and I would have got you out, but where are you now? Five years, if those fools testify.'

'You can fix it,' Caxton had said in reply.

But now, the situation had changed. Gary Frost was no longer around, a warrant was out for his arrest. He would be defending himself, not one of his employees, and where was the man, what was he doing?

Was he running, or was he planning something more serious?

Sharman and Caxton sat together to discuss the situation. Sharman reflected on his fee for services rendered, realised that he was committed to continuing for the time being, but unless Frost transferred money to his account, then he and Caxton could find someone else.

'O'Grady's been found,' Sharman said. As usual, he was wearing the three-piece suit, his hair immaculately parted down the middle. 'Three bullets, one in the brain.'

'It was an accident. He was out of control.'

'They'll not go for it. How do you want to plead?'

'What will happen if I admit to it?'

'Sixteen years minimum.'

'And the GBH?'

'Five each, although we should be able to get all sentences served concurrently.'

'You can't get me off?'

'Not on this one, and now Frost has done a runner. They'll take what you've admitted to, the statements from Lawrence and Waters, the proof of you and O'Grady being in Brussels, no more than one mile from where Samuels and three others were killed. I can cause confusion in the jury, raise an element of doubt, but you'll be convicted of the murder of O'Grady, and if you're not, the Belgian police will have you extradited. No chance of their proving their case, but Frost has made fools of the police. They'll not forget.'

In the interview room, Emily and Larry sat. On the other side of the table, Ainsley Caxton and Edward Sharman.

Outside, listening in, Isaac, Jules, and Wendy. In another part of the building, Inspector Camberwell was clearing out his desk, with another inspector checking that what he took wasn't police related, only personal. He had been suspended on full pay while a disciplinary hearing was convened, a chance for him to explain why he had called off the surveillance of Gary Frost. His badge was with the superintendent, as was his phone. He knew that if they checked the numbers dialled, they would find the calls to Frost. He knew that he should have used another phone to call the man, but in the last few days, with the frenetic pace, the information that needed passing on, he had not had a chance to add credit to the phone that he kept hidden underneath the dashboard in his car. There was nothing that the police force disliked more than a bent policeman, and if he were in prison, there would be some that would remember who had put them there. Commissioner Alwyn Davies had brought him into London, put him out at Greenwich, and he was not answering his phone.

Camberwell snuck out of the office and headed to the nearest pub. He needed a stiff drink, and he needed it now.

Chapter 34

Ralph Lawrence turned in his bed. It had been a late night, what with Yolanda on the phone, yet again not wanting to return to London. In the end, he had drunk a full bottle of whisky before collapsing. He blearily opened his eyes, realised that it was daylight outside and that someone was knocking on the front door to his flat.

Without checking, he turned the latch on the door and opened it. On the other side, Gary Frost. 'You bastard,' he said as he pushed his way in. 'You're going to testify against me.'

Ralph struggled with the situation. He was larger than Frost, the man was alone, but why was he here, what did he want? He slapped some water on his face from a tap in the kitchen, before looking at Frost again. The man was standing firm: his face red, his hands raised in anger.

'Frost, what do you want? We had an arrangement, but you wouldn't wait.'

'You've given the police a statement saying that I had you beaten.'

'What else would you want me to say? That you're a good fellow, a good mate? Get real. You're in trouble, and you're lashing out. When I came to you, what did I get? Sympathy, a shoulder to cry on? Not from you. I got Caxton and O'Grady beating me up, showing what would happen if I didn't give you what you wanted, and now O'Grady's dead.'

'How do you know?'

'It's on the news. And Caxton's singing like a bird.'

'He won't.'

'Without you to hold his hand, he'll be putty to the police.'

'I need to get out of the country,' Frost said.

'Why look at me? My father left me high and dry. Look how I live. Nowhere as fancy as you, although you can't go back, is that it?'

'I'm desperate,' Frost pleaded.

'Not such the big man now, are you? It's easy to be tough when you're on top, but down below, where I've been, you're frightened. Now, if you haven't got anything to add to our conversation, I suggest you leave while I call the police.'

Ralph picked up his phone, speed-dialled Detective Chief Inspector Isaac Cook. 'I've got a Mr Frost in my flat if you're interested.'

Frost rushed out of the door. 'You bastard, I'll get you for this.'

Ralph knew he would not.

***

Edward Sharman knew that the situation was hopeless as he sat in the interview room. On one side of the table, the two police officers were sitting up straight, full of pride because they had brought an investigation to a successful conclusion. On his side, Ainsley Caxton had shrunk in his seat. Before O'Grady's body had been found, and before he had discovered that Gary Frost had run out on him, Caxton had been full of himself, almost cheeky with the police constable who had brought him his breakfast, but now, it was over.

The confession had surprised even Isaac. Caxton had not spoken since entering the interview room and would not until he had left, except to give his name and to read his statement.

'I, Ainsley Gregory Caxton, do admit to the killing of Hector O'Grady. I was acting on the instructions of Gary Frost. He has been responsible for other murders, none of which were committed by me. I am guilty of the maltreatment of Ralph Lawrence and Keith Waters. O'Grady was proving to be unreliable. Frost demanded that I dispose of the man. I followed orders as a soldier would if given a command by an officer.'

Larry could see Sharman's clever wording. An attempt to convince a jury that his client Caxton, a man who did have a good army service record, was a man who did what he was told, a humble man who deserved leniency. It was a clever ploy, but Larry, like Emily, knew full well that with the litany of crimes against Caxton it would not lessen the sentence. He was going down for sixteen years at the very least.

'Frost's business empire was under threat. He needed to reduce his liabilities. O'Grady was a man likely to talk. He was physically strong, mentally and morally bankrupt,' Caxton continued. 'I joined the boat two miles from the boatyard. We had pulled in there before, and both of us were familiar with the place. Sometimes we'd make a small fire, cook the fish and then have a few drinks. I shot him, not because I wanted to, but because I had to. In Belgium, it had been O'Grady who killed Samuels. I was merely the bystander, but Frost intended, if there was no hope, to lay the blame on me. If I did not agree to kill O'Grady, he would implicate me in Samuels' death. It was known that he had received a phone call from Belgium, and the evidence was mounting against him. I had regarded Frost as a friend, but when he told me to kill O'Grady, I knew he was not. That is the end of my statement.'

Caxton was formally charged with the murder of Hector O'Grady and taken back to his cell. 'Where's Frost?' Sharman said.

'We're still waiting for him,' Emily said.

'Give me a call when he gets here. I'll be representing him.' Sharman stood up and walked out, not shaking the officers' hands, not saying goodbye.

***

Frost did not return to his car. He cut a sorry figure as he walked, keeping to the side streets as much as possible. He met Ted Samson, the small man who had kept a watch on Ralph Lawrence on his ignominious return to England.

Samson was pleased to see Frost in the coffee shop, knowing that their meeting would come with four fifty-pound notes being slipped across the table.

'Mr Frost, what do you want?' Samson asked. He had ordered a café latte, the man opposite to pay. 'I told you what I saw at Gilbert Lawrence's house.'

'You were looking for Ralph Lawrence, but he was in Spain.'

'That's right. You never paid me.'

'How much?'

'Another five hundred. In cash and now.'

Any other time, Samson would have been hanging upside down from a beam for his impertinence, but now the man who saw all, said nothing unless paid, was in control. Frost reached into his wallet and withdrew ten fifty-pound notes. He passed them across the table, the little man hurriedly putting them into a pocket.

'You're a little bastard,' Frost said.

'Little, I'll agree with, but not a bastard. You're in trouble, and the police are looking for you. The word is that Caxton's pleaded guilty, put the blame on you. The police have your photo on a list of the most wanted. You'll be lucky to stay free for more than a few hours.'

'How much?'

'Another ten of what you just gave me. A disguise, is that it?'

'I need to get out of the country. Can you arrange it?'

'A good passport costs money. I can't help you there.'

'Okay, a disguise. What do you have that you haven't told me?'

'I kept a watch on Gilbert Lawrence's house. I saw people going in, people going out.'

'Which people?'

'The housekeeper, the postman, the old recluse.'

'Anyone else?'

'Another five hundred.'

Frost was running short of cash, but he managed to give the man what he wanted.

On a piece of paper, Samson wrote down the name of one more person. 'That's who'll get you a passport.' He also handed over a timed and dated photo from his iPhone.

'I could have bled this person for a fortune,' Frost said.

'You still can. I've no need of a fortune,' Samson said. 'Just a quiet life, enough for my needs, a couple of pints of an evening.' And with that, he left. Fifteen minutes later he returned and placed a bag on the table. 'That'll cost you two hundred,' before he disappeared once again, this time not to return. For the first time that day, Gary Frost smiled.

***

Jill Dundas sat in her office, the door was closed. At the reception, a man stood. 'Tell Jill I'm here about an unpaid debt. Tell her it's personal.'

The lady on reception made the phone call. Jill Dundas came out of her office. 'Yes, what do you want?' she asked as she looked across at a man with a mop of black hair.

'Look at this,' Gary Frost said, as he opened his wallet to reveal a time-stamped photo.'

'Come into my office, please.' The woman maintained her cool.

Inside the office, Frost removed his wig. It had itched, and it had made him look stupid. It had, however, allowed him to walk past two police cars. 'My name's Gary Frost. I'm about to be charged with murder, and you, Miss Dundas, are going to get me out of the country.'

'Why, how?'

'You saw the photo. It is you, isn't it?'

'But what does it mean?'

'Let me tell you a little story,' Frost said. 'I had lent a lot of money to Ralph Lawrence. I did not know of his family connection. And why should I? But then Ralph's a naughty boy, and he's not answering his phone.'

'Get to the point.'

'I don't know what to do. I need time to consider, and I get one of my men to watch out for him, but he keeps the information to himself, bleeds me for more money.'

'Is there a point to this?'

'My man finds the father's house, realises it probably the one place that Ralph will come to. He sees the housekeeper, the postman, old man Lawrence. He's a devious man that I employ. He's like a ferret, here and there, scurrying around, taking me for money, taking it from whoever else. Maybe he took some from you, but it's not important now. Anyway, my life's taken a turn for the worse, and I met with the ferret. He tells me that he knows something, something that I've not paid for. He may be right, or maybe he's been paid off. He gave me a photo, the one I just showed you. I've taken a copy, emailed it to the police, a twenty-four-hour delay before it's sent. I could cancel it, but that's up to you.'

'I'll deny it all, the best lawyers.'

'If he's as good as mine, you'll be arrested for murder.'

'What do you want?'

'Not money. I want to get out of this country, a false passport.'

'That can be arranged, but it takes time.'

'How long?'

'Eight hours.'

'Where?'

'To the north of London.'

'You've done this before,' Frost said. He had to admit he admired the woman: cool as a cucumber, a heart of pure ice.

'I've not admitted to anything.'

'Nor should you. Get me out of the country, a false identity, and your secret is safe with me.'

'Can I trust you?' Jill said.

'What do you think?'

'I think that you will honour the agreement. You will have your passport.'

Frost could see no reaction in the woman: no sweating, no nervous twitches, no sign of panic.

Outside, in the reception area, the noise of people entering. Frost stood up. 'You've called the police.'

'I haven't. They must have followed you. Our agreement stands. Get yourself out on bail, and I'll get you out of the country.'

'It's a deal.'

***

Gary Frost sat in the interview room at Greenwich Police Station. On his right-hand side, Edward Sharman. Across from them, Emily Matson and Larry Hill.

'We received a tip-off,' Emily said. 'What were you doing at the offices of Jill Dundas?'

'My client has no comment,' Sharman said. 'He has given you a statement stating his innocence. He is a wealthy man who is being accused by others in an attempt to discredit him.'

'Mr Frost will be charged with conspiracy to murder. We have sufficient proof to secure a conviction for that charge. Mr Sharman, you have seen the evidence against your client, as well as the testimony of three other persons. It would be advisable to prepare his defence.'

'I know what I need to do,' Sharman said.

Outside of the interview room, Sharman shook the hand of Emily. 'Not so good for my client, but you did a good job.' With that he left the police station.

'Who tipped us off about Frost being with Jill Dundas?' Isaac asked.

'We don't know,' Larry said. 'A squeaky voice said something about Frost having cheated him out of a hundred pounds. Unlisted number, so no point in tracing it.'

Emily arrived at Inspector Camberwell's home at eight in the evening. The man was still asleep after a twenty-four-hour bender at home and in the pub. A security camera had picked up Caxton placing the package under the bench near the Greenwich Observatory, Camberwell picking it up a few minutes later, even checking that the full amount had been paid. It had been another piece of information that Caxton had put forward in an attempt to deny his guilt and to portray himself as a weak man. It was not going to work, but it did allow Camberwell to be arrested: the most heinous of crimes, a police officer guilty of taking bribes. He would be detained in the cell next to Frost.

Nineteen hours after Frost had been remanded, almost twenty-four from when he had sat in Jill Dundas's office, an email arrived in Isaac's inbox. He opened it and forwarded it to the team. Bridget printed out a high-definition jpeg and pinned it to the evidence board in Homicide.

Jill Dundas was arrested later that day. She protested that the photo was a fake, an attempt at extortion, and that was why Frost had been in her office. She was charged with murder; the date matched the time of death, the blood stains visible on the hem of the dress as she had left Gilbert Lawrence's mansion. At her house, the dress was retrieved. The woman may have been financially smart, but she did not understand forensics. There had been an attempt at cleaning the dress, but the marks remained inside the fold of the hem. Forensics were confident that they would be able to extract enough to match Gilbert Lawrence's DNA.

'I had to. All that work of my father's, and Gilbert wanted to come out of seclusion, to make contact with his family. For them to forgive him, for him to forgive them. I couldn't allow it. I had to kill him.'

Ralph Lawrence and Caroline Dickson were stunned at the revelation. The full extent of their father's assets, or whatever could be recovered, would be theirs.

Yolanda phoned from Antigua on hearing the news. She intended to be on the next plane to London. Ralph told her not to bother.

The End

ALSO BY THE AUTHOR

Death by a Dead Man's Hand – A DI Tremayne Thriller

A flawed heist of forty gold bars from a security van late at night. One of the perpetrators is killed by his brother as they argue over what they have stolen.

Eighteen years later, the murderer, released after serving his sentence for his brother's murder, waits in a church for a man purporting to be the brother he killed.

The threads stretch back a long way, and now more people are dying in the search for the missing gold bars.

Detective Inspector Tremayne, his health causing him concerns, and Sergeant Clare Yarwood, still seeking romance, are pushed to the limit solving the current murder, attempting to prevent any more.

Death at Coombe Farm – A DI Tremayne Thriller

A warring family. A disputed inheritance. A recipe for death.

If it hadn't been for the circumstances, Detective Inspector Keith Tremayne would have said the view was outstanding. Up high, overlooking the farmhouse in the valley below, the panoramic vista of Salisbury Plain stretching out beyond.

The only problem was that near where he stood with his sergeant, Clare Yarwood, there was a body, and it wasn't a pleasant sight.

Death and the Lucky Man – A DI Tremayne Thriller

Sixty-eight million pounds and dead.

Hardly the outcome expected for the luckiest man in England the day his lottery ticket was drawn out of the barrel.

But then, Alan Winters' rags-to-riches story had never been conventional, and there were those who had benefited, but others who hadn't.

Death and the Assassin's Blade – A DI Tremayne Thriller

It was meant to be high drama, not murder, but someone's switched the daggers. The man's death took place in plain view of two serving police officers.

He was not meant to die; the daggers were only theatrical props, plastic and harmless. A summer's night, a production of Julius Caesar amongst the ruins of an Anglo-Saxon fort. Detective Inspector Tremayne is there with his sergeant, Clare Yarwood. In the assassination scene, Caesar collapses to the ground. Brutus defends his actions; Mark Antony rebukes him.

They're a disparate group, the amateur actors. One's an estate agent, another an accountant. And then there is the teenage school student, the gay man, the funeral director. And what about the women? They could be involved.

They've each got a secret, but which of those on the stage wanted Gordon Mason, the actor who had portrayed Caesar, dead?

Murder is the Only Option – A DCI Cook Thriller

A man, thought to be long dead, returns to exact revenge against those who had blighted his life. His only concern is to protect his wife and daughter. He will stop at nothing to achieve his aim.

'Big Greg, I never expected to see you around here at this time of night.'

'I've told you enough times.'

'I've no idea what you're talking about,' Robertson replied. He looked up at the man, only to see a metal pole coming down at him. Robertson fell down, cracking his head against a concrete kerb.

The two vagrants, no more than twenty feet away, did not stir and did not even look in the direction of the noise. If they had, they would have seen a dead body, another man walking away.

Death Unholy – A DI Tremayne Thriller

All that remained were the man's two legs and a chair full of greasy and fetid ash. Little did DI Keith Tremayne know that it was the beginning of a journey into the murky world of paganism and its ancient rituals. And it was going to get very dangerous.

'Do you believe in spontaneous human combustion?' Detective Inspector Keith Tremayne asked.

'Not me. I've read about it. Who hasn't?' Sergeant Clare Yarwood answered.

I haven't,' Tremayne replied, which did not surprise his young sergeant. In the months they had been working together, she had come to realise that he was a man who had little interest in the world. When he had a cigarette in his mouth, a beer in his hand, and a murder to solve he was about the happiest she ever saw him. He could hardly be regarded as one of life's sociable people. And as for reading? The most he managed was an occasional police report or an early morning newspaper, turning first to the back pages for the racing results.

Murder in Room 346 – A DCI Cook Thriller

'Coitus interruptus, that's what it is,' Detective Chief Inspector Isaac Cook said. On the bed, in a downmarket hotel in Bayswater, lay the naked bodies of a man and a woman.

'Bullet in the head's not the way to go,' Larry Hill, Isaac Cook's detective inspector, said. He had not expected such a flippant comment from his senior, not when they were standing near to two people who had, apparently in the final throes of passion, succumbed to what appeared to be a professional assassination.

Gordon Windsor, the crime scene examiner, came over. 'Apart from you two talking while I'm trying to focus, I'll give you what I've found so far.'

'You know this will be all over the media within the hour,' Isaac said.

'James Holden, moral crusader, a proponent of the sanctity of the marital bed, man and wife. It's bound to be.'

Murder in Notting Hill – A DCI Cook Thriller

One murderer, two bodies, two locations, and the murders have been committed within an hour of each other.

They're separated by a couple of miles, and neither woman has anything in common with the other. One is young and wealthy, the daughter of a famous man; the other is poor, hardworking and unknown.

Isaac Cook and his team at Challis Street Police Station are baffled about why they've been killed. There must be a connection, but what is it?

Murder is the Only Option – A DCI Cook Thriller

A man, thought to be long dead, returns to exact revenge against those who had blighted his life. His only concern is to protect his wife and daughter. He will stop at nothing to achieve his aim.

'Big Greg, I never expected to see you around here at this time of night.'

'I've told you enough times.'

'I've no idea what you're talking about,' Robertson replied. He looked up at the man, only to see a metal pole coming down at him. Robertson fell down, cracking his head against a concrete kerb.

Two vagrants, no more than twenty feet away, did not stir and did not even look in the direction of the noise. If they had, they would have seen a dead body, another man walking away.

Murder in Little Venice – A DCI Cook Thriller

A dismembered corpse floats in the canal in Little Venice, an upmarket tourist haven in London. Its identity is unknown, but what is its significance?

DCI Isaac Cook is baffled about why it's there. Is it gang-related, or is it something more?

Whatever the reason, it's clearly a warning, and Isaac and his team are sure it's not the last body that they'll have to deal with.

Murder is only a Number – A DCI Cook Thriller

Before she left she carved a number in blood on his chest. But why the number 2, if this was her first murder?

The woman prowls the streets of London. Her targets are men who have wronged her. Or have they? And why is she keeping count?

DCI Cook and his team finally know who she is, but not before she's murdered four men. The whole team are looking for her, but the woman keeps disappearing in plain sight. The pressure's on to stop her, but she's always one step ahead.

And this time, DCS Goddard can't protect his protégé, Isaac Cook, from the wrath of the new commissioner at the Met.

Murder House – A DCI Cook Thriller

A corpse in the fireplace of an old house. It's been there for thirty years, but who is it?

It's clearly murder, but who is the victim and what connection does the body have to the previous owners of the house. What is the motive? And why is the body in a fireplace? It was bound to be discovered eventually but was that what the murderer wanted? The main suspects are all old and dying, or already dead.

Isaac Cook and his team have their work cut out trying to put the pieces together. Those who know are not talking because of an old-fashioned belief that a family's dirty laundry should not be aired in public, and certainly not to a policeman – even if that means the murderer is never brought to justice!

Murder is a Tricky Business – A DCI Cook Thriller

A television actress is missing, and DCI Isaac Cook, the Senior Investigation Officer of the Murder Investigation Team at Challis Street Police Station in London, is searching for her.

Why has he been taken away from more important crimes to search for the woman? It's not the first time she's gone missing, so why does everyone assume she's been murdered?

There's a secret, that much is certain, but who knows it? The missing woman? The executive producer? His eavesdropping assistant? Or the actor who portrayed her fictional brother in the TV soap opera?

Murder Without Reason – A DCI Cook Thriller

DCI Cook faces his greatest challenge. The Islamic State is waging war in England, and they are winning.

Not only does Isaac Cook have to contend with finding the perpetrators, but he is also being forced to commit actions contrary to his mandate as a police officer.

And then there is Anne Argento, the prime minister's deputy. The prime minister has shown himself to be a pacifist and is not up to the task. She needs to take his job if the country is to fight back against the Islamists.

Vane and Martin have provided the solution. Will DCI Cook and Anne Argento be willing to follow it through? Are they able to act for the good of England, knowing that a criminal and murderous action is about to take place? Do they have any option?

The Haberman Virus

A remote and isolated village in the Hindu Kush mountain range in North Eastern Afghanistan is wiped out by a virus unlike any seen before.

A mysterious visitor clad in a space suit checks his handiwork, a female American doctor succumbs to the disease, and the woman sent to trap the person responsible falls in love with him – the man who would cause the deaths of millions.

Hostage of Islam

Three are to die at the Mission in Nigeria: the pastor and his wife in a blazing chapel; another gunned down while trying to defend them from the Islamist fighters.

Kate McDonald, an American, grieving over her boyfriend's death and Helen Campbell, whose life had been troubled by drugs and prostitution, are taken by the attackers.

Kate is sold to a slave trader who intends to sell her virginity to an Arab Prince. Helen, to ensure their survival, gives herself to the murderer of her friends.

Malika's Revenge

Malika, a drug-addicted prostitute, waits in a smugglers' village for the next Afghan tribesman or Tajik gangster to pay her price, a few scraps of heroin.

Yusup Baroyev, a drug lord, enjoys a lifestyle many would envy. An Afghan warlord sees the resurgence of the Taliban. A Russian white-collar criminal portrays himself as a good and honest citizen in Moscow.

All of them are linked in an audacious plan to increase the quantity of heroin shipped out of Afghanistan and into Russia and ultimately the West.

Some will succeed, some will die, some will be rescued from their plight and others will rue the day they became involved.

ABOUT THE AUTHOR

Phillip Strang was born in England in the late forties, during the post-war baby boom.

An avid reader of science fiction in his teenage years: Isaac Asimov, Frank Herbert, the masters of the genre. Still an avid reader, the author now mainly reads thrillers.

In his early twenties, the author, with a degree in electronics engineering and a desire to see the world, left England for Sydney, Australia. Now, forty years later, he still resides in Australia, although many intervening years were spent in a myriad of countries, some calm and safe, others no more than war zones.

Made in the USA
San Bernardino, CA
05 July 2018